CW00404874

BEHIND

THE

SCENES

Punam Farmah

BEHIND

THE

SCENES

www.horticulturalhobbit.com

www.twitter.com/horticulturalh

www.facebook.com/horticulturalObbit

Also by Punam Farmah:

Playing with Plant Pots: Tales from the allotment

Sow, Grow and Eat: From plot to kitchen

Fragments

Retreating to Peace: A Peace Series Novella

Kangana

Postcards from Peace: A Peace Series Collection

Peace Betrayed: A Peace Series Novella

Dedication:

To Ketan, Surrinder and Howard

Table of Contents

Behind the Scenes: A context

At the time of writing and publishing, I will have written seven books. Two of these are non-fiction and based upon my experiences as a gardener. The other five works span two fictional Universes and to the greater part, fall into the genres of contemporary romance and general fiction. The first of these Universes, is the Fragments Universe. This is the third book, to be in that realm. The other two, are Fragments and Kangana, respectively. The former, is a book based upon a model of grief. The latter is a romance.

The thread between these two books, the connective tissue, if you like, is one very specific character. His name is Gorbind Phalla. Gorbind originated as a minor character in Fragments. When I wrote that particular book, Gorbind was only meant to be round very briefly, for a matter of a couple of pages. He was, in my mind at least, a supporting artist to another character and their story. However, there was a compulsion to write more; to explore this rather interesting figment of my imagination. There as a spin-off; Gorbind helped me to make a foray into the world of writing Contemporary Romance.

A foray, that had actually started with a different fictional universe entirely. This other universe is the Peace Novella Series Universe. This is a series of romance novellas. The brainchild of fellow author S.H. Pratt, being part of the team saw me contribute to the life and times of a fictional town of Peace, Montana. My contributions centred on a would-be hooch baron, by the name of Devan Coultrie.

The stage is therein set. Two gardening books. One piece of general fiction. Four, bits of contemporary romance. All of which have paved the way for what you are currently holding in your hand and reading.

With this book, I explore something a bit different. I take a look, in the first half, at what those characters might be getting up to, when not being channelled through my fountain pens. What is it, that happens exactly, beyond being figments of my imagination?

As the title suggests, we are going Behind the Scenes.

We see, read and experience the characters out of character, as it were. What you read, is their life of camera and beyond the traditional audience that might watching. In this case, this is the readers of the books.

And the key, is the panorama that exists across the two universes. There are characters, who we know about in terms of their existence in Kangana, Fragments and the Peace Novella Series.

There are also others, that all being well, will take their place in the Fragments Universe.

You are going to me my rendition of Hades, Lord of the Underworld as well The Lady Aurelia and a chap called Pencil-Sketch. He does have a given, but whilst a larva in a chrysalis waiting to actualise his potential, that his how he will be addressed. Each of these, will in time, have a story of their own; each, has a notebook, waiting to be filled with my fountain pens.

Hades, I borrow from Greek Mythology. A fascinating figure, who with his relationship with Persephone, is ripe for exploration. I relish the prospect of re-telling his story, in a separate work. Fear not, the standard features of the myth will remain, and are by their nature, sacrosanct.

With this book the Hades that you read, is a shadow waiting in the wings. He is a Hades in waiting for the story that currently resides on my desk in a notebook. What we have here, is the pre-cursor to the Man, the Myth, the protagonist in a romance to be re-told.

Hades is also very experimental. This links very neatly to The Lady Aurelia.

Imagine. Vampires and in Birmingham.

As with Hades, Aurelia will be part of the Fragments Universe. She will form a very close alliance with another character-his name is Joel, you may want to go find. Him is Fragments, the book. As she waits in the wings, in her own notebook, I envisage a story that spans the centuries as she makes a home in the City of Birmingham. A city, that ebbs and flows, through the course of historical events such as World Wars and women's suffrage. She will appear, and all in good time.

This is a book of two halves. The first half is *Benind the Scenes*, with already existing figments of my imagination. The second half is a homage. A homage to my home city. A city of a thousand trades, and therein a city of a thousand stories. Gathered here are tales inspired by Birmingham. Tales, that try to paint the city in slightly different colours, other than those worn by the city's football teams. Tales, of everyday people-mostly-and their everyday lives.

As a whole, the book is a collection of short and not so short stories. That's a world away from writing a novella or a full-length novel. All in all, I hope that is a vibrant, intriguing and altogether interesting canvas that captures a city that I call home.

One thing, that I really want to add, is as follows. Some parts of this book were written during the self-isolation and quarantine that came with the onset of the global Corona Virus pandemic. A weird and wonderful time as a writer. A time where positing the notion of a Zombie Apocalypse was something you wouldn't dare make up.

Which is why, the notion of writing a Zombie Apocalypse moved from being at the top of my 'to write' list-a list drawn up six months before the pandemic-to being dragged to the end. There was a simple, but very particular reason for this.

I wanted to make it through. I want to live through this COVID-19 experience, in all it's chaos, confusion and fugue-like state, before committing to paper.

The key premise?

No one could make that up.

Not really.

To write about such an event, as it started, was all too close. I've waited nearly six months, to feel happy to write about it. Life imitated a form of art, and this was altogether strange.

Opening Salvo

Behind the Scenes was started as a writing project within days of completing Peace Betrayed: A Peace Novella. In this story, Devan Coultrie's ending in that particular universe allows him to cross over into the Fragments Universe whilst retaining his own identity and integrity as a character. The Devan we see here, and will continue to see, is beyond the romance of the Peace Novella Series. We also meet Hades, who was also a twinkle in a notebook at the time. His story had been sketched out, a writing plan made. Only, he would have to wait, and until Behind the Scenes was executed.

Hanging three freshly ironed shirts from the balustrades on the stairs, Padmi stood back to admire her handiwork. She smiled as she imagined the shirts swooshing around as though inebriated ghosts.

This was their deal.

He could deal with these when he came home. There was nothing in their agreement about putting them away. Her thoughts were interrupted by the ringing of the doorbell.

Padmi's brow furrowed. She wasn't expecting anyone. Mango was asleep, Gorbind would be late. He'd muttered something over breakfast, about a serial killer and chasing forensics. There was always half a story from her husband before his morning tea, that never made any sense.

She glared at the door. Her plan had been to flick through Netflix; to make her way down a rather pricey bottle of red wine. Staring at the door, she willed the unwelcome guest to get bored; to get gone too.

"Gorbind, are you in?" The letterbox rattled repeatedly. It moved with such ferocity, the hinges creaked and protested. There was a small chance it would fall free and to the floor.

Swearing under her breath, Padmi stopped forward to swing the door open.

Devan Coultrie's feet didn't touch the ground as he was hauled across the threshold. Five minutes later, he was sat upon the sofa, in something of a crumpled heap. Devan was drenched, having brought a storm with him.

Padmi's wine was in his hands. Much to her disdain, he had already glugged some.

"You and your pathetic fallacy," Padmi shook her head; there was barely disguised contempt in her tone as she spoke. "So it's over; your time in her brain is done. Deal with it. You know exactly where you come from, why too. Plus, Devan, you were only ever supposed to be around for one book. You got lucky, you got three."

"All of those pages. She got rid of all those pages, thousands of words. All that ink." Staring at the floor, Devan pressed the wine bottle to his lips. "Might've been four," he sniffed to look up, with something of a hang-dog expression. "Still could, one day, possible. There's a queue, a log-jam in her writing process. More writing with your Gorbind, there's the fella Hades, someone called Orca. Oh, and The Lady Aurelia, who sounds…. she sounds magic, to be honest."

"The Fragments Universe," Padmi half smirked. It sounded a lot more glamourous than it might eventually be. "You really should do one, Devan. You need to leave."

"Wait," Devan slugged more wine to sit up straighter. "You, only exist, Padmi, because I do. She wrote me, then Gorbind and you, to see if she could. The plan was to experiment and to test a hypothesis; could she write romance and of the contemporary kind."

"I don't like you," Padmi wrinkled up her nose, to spit out the words.

"You don't have, you don't count," Stated Devan, looking directly at the fourth wall. He may as well have been staring down the lens of a camera, trained to pan into his face. "They, on the other hand, do."

***

Thundering down Main Street, the Black Mustang-tinted windows, chrome finish, you know-couldn't have looked more out of place. As it turned into Oak Street, the vehicle slowed down. The vehicle shed it's visage to become a '63 Lincoln for all of three seconds.

Why? The local sheriff's deputy just happened to be sat in his car.

Passing through the gates of Oakview, the Mustang roared down the drive. Eventually, the vehicle stopped; it was parked at an angle upon the lawn. Hades stepped, to dart up the veranda. He rang the doorbell, his one finger jabbing at it, incessantly. He waited a whole minute, before kicking the door down in one fail swoop.

Devan Coultrie sat on his sofa, eating.

"Dude, you may want to get up…." Hades waggled a finger, to step aside. In a blink, he'd moved into the lounge. He picked up the t.v. remote and turned up the volume. He watched the report on BBC world service. He listened to something about the Dow Jones.

Hades, Lord of the underworld, had fingers in lots of different pies.

Behind him, another figure darkened the doorstep.

"Don't make a mess," Hades commented, turning his back upon what was about to happen.

"Gorbind, I can explain…."

Hoiking Devan from the sofa, Gorbind pinned him up against the wall. Devan hung at least three feet from the floor.

Gorbind Phalla was not happy.

"Do that again, and so help me, God. I will kill you."

"And I will," said Hades, looking over his shoulder. "I'll hold his coat and everything."

Eventually, Devan dropped to the floor. His pride was bruised, and his card marked. He made a mental note to send Padmi some Montana Moonshine. He had some rather interesting Blackberry wine that would replace what he had glugged. He'd got the message. No one messed around, and with Gorbind, his wife or Hades, Lord of the Underworld.

Hades and Gorbind left, the Mustang pootled down Main Street as stadium rock thumped against the windscreen.

Man and God, had somehow, gotten away with it.

***

In the beer garden, of the Gunmakers Arms, this seemed a good a place as any for a meeting of friends.

"Any minute now," Gorbind looked at his 'phone, before swirling his pint. "Don't wind him up."

Hades pulled a face, to sip stupidly fizzy lemonade. Technically, he was on duty.

"Bang on time," he said, nodding as Devan clambered into position at the picnic table.

The man looked harassed; all very black-eyed and unshaven.

There was also a scent….

Sliding across a glass of bourbon, Gorbind lowered his sunglasses. "You look like crap," he wasn't going to mince his words. That wasn't the way that this gang worked.

"You smell," Hades pronounced as he wrinkled up his nose. "You honk half way to hell, and I know that place. Has some rather nice rooms to rent."

"I feel like crap," raising his glass, Devan slung back the bourbon in a rather practiced manoeuvre. "Never mind the smell. She's done with me, with my books; I'm done. She's taking no prisoners. You're next," Devan fixed his haze upon the lord of underworld.

Snorting with derision, Hades slurped his lemonade.

"Seriously," blinked Devan, crossing his arms. "Tell him," He kicked Gorbind below the table. "She's coming for you. She's going to ring your bell and then some."

Pushing his glasses up his nose, Gorbind turned to look at Hades. His lips had twisted into a grimace at the now rather sore ankle. He'd deal with Devan's petulance later.

"Grab your coat, sir."

Sucking up the last of his drink, Hades rolled his eyes. Reaching below the table, he located his eponymous helmet. Hades rose awkwardly to his feet.

"It's a cloak, actually. This, aint over," he said, clicking his fingers. Hades, disappeared into speck of purple light. The red and white straw in the empty glass wilted in a rather dramatic fashion.

Meanwhile, in Gorbind's Kitchen, Padmi was catching up on the drama of being married to Devan Coultrie.

"Man alive," Padmi looked at Aditi through her fingers. "What on earth am I supposed to say to you? This, is why we, plus the readers, are all Anti-Aditi."

"It is what it is," As she shrugged, Aditi speared a yellow tomato with a fork. "Not my imagination, not my circus. We're done though. For now."

Nodding, Padmi checked her 'phone as a message had come through. The device clinked against a mug of tea. "She's moving on." Padmi's fingers tapped out a message to then press send.

"So I heard," Aditi smirked; her expression was all very cat-like. "Hades won't like that; the fact that he's her next pet project."

"He doesn't have to," replied Padmi, blowing into her tea. "Hades is cute, clever too; he's also something of a pain in the backside."

Shaking her head, Aditi waggled her folk; the tomato still on the end before it was munched clean away. "Now, now," she giggled quietly. "He gets a bad press, what with his siblings stealing his thunder. He's just a lonely, miserable f-"

"That was Prometheus, stealing fire, but yes," Padmi slurped her tea, to set down the mug. Her 'phone vibrated. "Gorbind's just told him. And so it begins."

Gorbind found himself in a dream. Her dream, as created by Hermes, at Hades behest. The two of them, watched from afar. To keep them libated, they even had a cuppa as they sat in Gorbind's kitchen.

"Touch that pen, Hades, and so help me, God. I will brain you." Gorbind dumped sugar into his tea whilst reading Mango's school report. She was settling into nursery; all his fears about her being in the middle band had proved to be unfounded. The little girl, had somehow ended up in charge of the class sand trays.

"I *AM* a God," muttered Hades, gingerly moving his hands. His digits had been hovering over a set of fountains pens.

Her fountain pens.

"Lord of the Underworld," continued Hades. "Say so, and in the job spec."

"Leave her hemisphere's alone," Gorbind looked up, he'd paused on Mango's real name, "Leave her. She can't see us, hear us or smell us, when consumed by a lack of writing mojo. Right now, she doesn't want us; she doesn't need us. She's sent us all to Coventry for a reason."

"Aint that the truth," Devan Coultrie appeared in a plume of blue smoke. He nearly collided with Gorbind's fridge. "Coventry. That flipping ring road has a lot to answer for. No, leave her." Taking his life into his hands, he poked Hades in the shoulder. He moved the pens away a little and into the middle of the dining table.

Gorbind returned to the school report. He tuned out as Devan whinged to Hades. There was something about moonshine, pancakes and how Aditi was arguing with his sister. Leftovers from the romance novella series, that whizzed around in the ether.

Hades, was all ears; distracted by Devan Drama.

Neither noticed as Gorbind slid the pens away, into his coat pocket.

For now, their destinies could wait.

Melee

When most of the boys from Fragments get together, and decide to make a bet. A rather unsavoury one.

"This won't end well," Aldo arched his brows to open his wallet. Two, crisp, ten pound notes slid out of the leather, to be placed upon the dark brown table.

"Nope, we know that much," Shaking his head, Chris scratched Draco, his dog, between the ears. With his other hand, he counted out twenty, newly-minted pound coins and pushed the pile toward Aldo's stake. The money clinked against a pint glass as it moved. Draco leant his muzzle against the table.

"If we get caught," Matthew chuckled, as he rooted around in his coat pocket. "This will rumble on for eternity. Here, mine." A flurry of crumpled up bank notes landed near Draco's snout.

The dog eyed the money in curiosity; his pink tongue lolled between his teeth.

Sipping chardonnay, Daniel shook his head. "I shall pass," he declared, pulling an unamused face.

"And me," Joel nodded in agreement. "I shall plead ignorance. I like them; I like all the girls and don't like this one bit."

Raj Anand also shook his head. He had no idea why he was here, why he had been conjured from the furthest corners of her imagination. He'd been happy there; happy to just gather dust and do nothing. This whole thing, made no sense to him; he had no idea who half of these people were.

"I can deal with it, I'm cute," Hades appeared in billowing plumes of purple smoke. He landed a sheaf of notes onto the table, sliding them across to the man in charge.

"Euros, Hades?" Gorbind counted the stash, tutting as he did so. "Three fricking grand in five hundreds. This looks like money laundering."

Hades grinned, all too wickedly. "Say the man who is pitting Aditi against the Acc-just take it." He huffed loudly, mostly for effect. "If Padmi finds out, and doesn't brain you, spend it well. You'll need it for the surgery, as she's likely to snap your spine in half."

Rising to his feet, Gorbind left to feed fifty pence pieces into the aged jukebox in the corner of The Gunmakers Arms. Tia and Maria, the Gunmakers cats both rubbed up against his legs. Their purring, tugged at the fabric of the universe; they clearly had a soft spot for Gorbind. Brandy and Monica's 'The Boy is mine' filtered out across the air in the bar.

Gorbind turned to face the group.

Hades sat back, as something dark flashed across Detective Inspector Phalla's otherwise neutral eyes. Reaching into the pocket of his waistcoat, Hades pulled out three gold coins. Each one hummed with divinity and twinkled in the harsh lighting of a Birmingham Boozer. One by one, the coins were plonked onto the pile of Euros.

"Tea time," Pronounced Gorbind. "Hold your bets. For the last girl standing."

Habemus Hades

I may refer to my characters as figments of my imagination, but to me they are as important, as three-dimensional as you and I. They have personalities and idiosyncrasies; they have a sense of being, as well as a face, for the most part. But what does that mean exactly?

Well, simply put, how I imagine them, as I write these figments, these people, in their own little worlds. If, through some random fluke, my work made the transfer to the television screen, I have an idea of what they may look like, how they may fill that screen. In my mind, the likes of Gorbind and Devan actually have a face that I might put to them. I shall however, for now, withhold that, so you can make your own mind up. You can decide for yourself, as to what the characters look like. The imagination is a powerful thing.

Hades, on the other hand, has been and continues to be a little harder to capture. I remember binge-watching Sleepy Hollow the television series, and thinking that the leading man appeared to be just the ticket. That was however, a transient thought, that eventually dissipated. Hades is elusive and evasive when it comes to giving him a face. He is theory, a myth from millennia ago and trapped in the sands of time.

Having said that, in this snippet, Hades is fleshed out a little; this is in anticipation of his own story. There are some echoes, of the Sleepy Hollow T.V. show leading man. One of the important facets that I focus upon is his clothes. Most specifically, I was interested in his waistcoat. I remember wandering around the Birmingham Museum and Art Gallery, trying to find inspiration as to what my rendition of Hades, Lord of the Underworld, might wear. The answer, reader, came in the form of William Morris and his sketches for embroidery and print. There were floral motifs that resonated with the idea of Hades falling in loving with Persephone, the daughter of Demeter. When Persephone resides on Earth, there is abundance, prosperity; harvests are plentiful. Yet, when she returns to Hades, Autumn and Winter grip the world.

That, and I envisage Hades to be rather dapper; smart, sophisticated and something of a glint in his eye.

Savouring the taste of the ragu in a pan, Padmi pulled a face as her palate registered flavours. She dropped a teaspoon into a blue bowl, to reach for a pepper mill. As she ground the contents, the mill squeaked and groaned as though being tortured.

She was alone this afternoon.

Gorbind had taken Mango out. He was enduring jelly, ice –cream and party rings.

Padmi and Gorbind were also in the middle of a fight.

Football, be damned.

Padmi had no plans to concede defeat. She was currently holding Gorbind's Jelly Baby stash hostage. Until he gave up, bent to her view and her view alone, the sweets would remain in her custody.

Her husband could stew a little longer. Not unlike the ragu that she had just sampled.

Behind her, the kitchen door swung open. Padmi felt a cold, cutting breeze bloom across the back of her neck. She then saw a reflection flutter across the surface of the kitchen cabinets.

"Finally," she said, lips parting into a heaty smile. "Sweetie, you have a face." Lowering the heat beneath the pan, Padmi turned to face her visitor.

"Meh," pulling at his own cheeks, Hades shrugged. He then passed a hand over coarse, rather dense stubble that clung across his jaw. "And a get-up," he parted his teak-coloured jacket, it was all neatly tailored and very form-fitting. Beneath, was a waistcoat, covered in finely embroidered pastel-pink poppies. The workmanship, with delicate stitches that made the poppies look as though freshly-picked, was divine and exquisite in equal measure.

"It's a start," he said with a languid sight; Hades tucked his fingers to the waistcoat's pockets. He glanced at his toes, to stop his feet. Feet, of the human size ten variety, that were housed in brogues that matched the colour of his jacket.

Hades twirled on the spot, his jacket billowing. Much to Padmi's delight.

"And we know how this ends, Hades," Padmi looked over the Lord of the Underworld, in admiration and amazement at how well he scrubbed up. "You're a bit....rakish." she inclined her head, to squint as she continue to scan him up and down. "Skinny. Not my cuppa tea, I'm afraid. You should be a little...beefier."

"The feeling is entirely mutual," Hades poked his tongue out in childish pique. "I'd worry, Padmi, if I was your cuppa tea. It really wouldn't work. You know that, I know that. Reckon you'll ever have one, a face. Aditi, the other women of the Fragments Universe too?"

His question was a distraction. Hades suddenly felt all very vulnerable in having a face. He tugged his coat a little closer; an attempt to sooth himself. He now had an identity and something beyond only his name and title.

"No, never," replied Padmi. "We're any woman and every woman. Oh, and we channel Dracula too," she crossed her arms to lean against a worktop. "You don't have to see us, hear us, to feel our thrall and our magic. It hangs in the air; our presence is pulled taut and into being as though the fabric of the universe."

Raising his brows, Hades was caught; he hung on her every word.

Any woman and every woman.

Padmi was right. They both knew how his story would end.

At least now, Hades had a face.

Kangana Out Loud

Over the last few years, I have been welcomed by local authors to events where I have been able to read my work. One such time, was when I read Kangana out aloud, for the first time, at the Gunmakers arms. I was really nervous, and I had no idea what the audience might make of the story. I had previously, read bits from Postcard from Peace and Retreating to Peace. I did have some idea therefore, of what I would have to do. That had been an okay debut. This particular evening however, I experienced really bad collywobbles; with heightened anxiety, I rather tripped over my words a great deal. I hadn't practiced as much as I would have liked, and this became my undoing.

However, I had an idea in the run up, whilst tying myself up in knots. What if my characters, the very figments of my imagination were sat in the bar? What if they were in the audience, how might they experience the event?

Someone had caught wind of a reading. Someone, had then persuaded his wife that they ought to go pay a visit to the event. Perhaps loiter in the bar, by way of moral support. This whole supporting local artist's thing, was the all rage these days.

"For now, place nice," Hades blew across the top of his Guinness. He pulled a face having taken a hearty mouthful. "Dionysus lied about this stuff. Muppet."

"Can't make me behave," Devan pouted as he swirled a wheat-coloured IPA. He had two black eyes and a plaster across his nose.

"Can and will," replied Hades. "Be good, or I shall turn you into a horse's behind. Only without the romance of a Midsummer's Night Dream."

"Of all the places in Birmingham," Padmi arrived, clutching a large glass of merlot. She grimaced at Devan, to sit next to Hades. "Never been here; didn't realise it belonged to writers and such. Nice place, though. Just seen their two beautiful cats."

Hades kicked Devan to attention below the table; he'd looked as though he was to keel over. "If Moody Knickers here can make it, you and Gorbind will enjoy it just fine. Gunmakers Arms Birmingham. Looks good to me."

"Moody knickers who?" Gorbind wasn't too far behind his wife and set another glass down before Devan. He himself, had half a pint of lemonade to drink.

"Don't trust yourself?" asked Devan, pulling the glass close. "Scared, what with the reading and all?"

"Just a bit," replied Gorbind, inhaling deeply. "So is she." He looked at the Maroon5 Hoodie that hung on an empty chair nearby.

He knew what she was about read. Thing is, he hadn't told his wife. That, was what scared him. That, was what had him drinking lemonade. For now.

Later, there was some time to reflect.

"Do I kiss you, perhaps kill you slowly?" Glaring at her husband, Padmi pressed the cool rim of her wine glass to her lips.

"Slowly, ever so slowly," Hades laughed as he wiped tears from his eyes. "Either way, we all want to watch it happen."

"You got laughs," Devan went to shake his head, but got caught in a wince from the movement. His nose throbbed something rotten. "You actually made me people laugh, and in a Birmingham Boozer. Welcome to the club," he slugged his pint to put a hand to Gorbind's shoulder. Something of a brave, but also diplomatic, move.

"Talking to me now, are you?" Slurping his lemonade, Gorbind took his own turn at not playing nice.

"You may have broken my nose," replied Devan. "But you'll need hell to freeze over, before you break my spirit."

"I can do that, HIC!" Hades momentarily looked abashed. He pressed a palm to his mouth, to look less than his a couple of thousand years and more like a like a naughty toddler. "God, Padmi ought to nail your bits-"

"You scared her," Padmi cut off the Lord of the Underworld, to pin her husband to his seat. "She took a chance on you; she read you out aloud. She tripped over almost every word, to try her best. She kept going too. The pair of us; she gave us reason for being. Remember that."

A sudden hush had descended and unfurled around the table. The lights crackled; darkness fell.

Then, they were gone.

Bide thy Time

"This is infuriating," Hades tutted to slug bitter coffee from a red travel mug. "How can you stand there-oi, ref!" He lurched forward toward the touchline. His eyes flickered lilac and the soles of his shoes smoked. Hades was ready to dole out some divine justice.

The thwack of Gorbind's arm across his chest had Hades rock slightly on his heels. The notes of a supernatural whistle were suspended in the icy air. Visible only for a millisecond, purple in colour and beyond human comprehension.

Gorbind curled his hand around Hade's shoulder. Not everyone was brave enough to stop the Lord of the Underworld from starting a pitch invasion.

"Stop, Mango is learning about the off-side rule," chided Gorbind. "If she doesn't fall into the trap, she'll never know where it is. Oh, and one more eff-bomb, Hades, and you can walk back home. You're one warning away from being sent off. You really need to behave, and don't you dare sulk."

"She's thinking about him," bellowed Hades. A murder of crows screamed to take flight from a tree. "Not me, as her next writing project, but him."

"This will take time," said Gorbind. He affixed a smile to his face as his daughter ran down the wing and waved at them. "She spent three years mooning over Devan.I got eighteen months through sheer fluke."

"And became her ring-master," Hades made no attempt to disguise his growing unease. "The Gatekeeper of the Fragment Uni-REF!!!"

Ten minutes later, Hades was back in his Mustang. The driver's side window was wound down as Hades, Lord of the Underworld sulked at being sin-binned.

"You were warned," hissed Gorbind, wagging a finger. "You literally turned the air blue. Now I have to go flirt with the coach; see if she'll overlook this, so that Mango can stay on the team. If she gets dropped, 'cause of her favourite Unco Hades there will be hell to pay."

Unco Hades snorted loudly, despite his deep-rooted discontent.

"Bide your time, Hades," continued Gorbind. "She mourning the end of a rather weird relationship. You and I, mate, we are rebounds. It's also nearly Christmas, there will be magic. Right, you sit there and sulk." He looked at the touchline. The coach was headed towards the Mustang.

"She has nice eyes," offered Hades, watching the woman with some sadness in his chest. "Tell her that; you'll make her smile. She doesn't do that often these days. Not since her brother died. It was an accident, a tragic one. He and I talk trains. Nice fella."

The tinted window whirred closed shut.

Gorbind absorbed the information, turned on his heel and went to talk with the weary-looking coach.

Every Story has a Start

This is a very important Behind the Scenes element. It sits here, to serve as a reminder. This is to remind me of how Gorbind and Hades are to meet in the retelling of the Hades Myth. A story that sits, on my desk, waiting, for me to get to it. Here, in Benind the Scenes, we observe these two characters as having a deep and enduring bond that transcends the being of one man, the divinity of a God. It is a meaningful relationship that explores how two extremes might meet in the middle. I will get to the story. It is next on my list. This particular extract fore shadows somewhat how Hades and Gorbind are destined to meet. This was written with the Birmingham German Market in mind, by way of background atmosphere and when I feeling as though I couldn't write anything.

"What take are we on?" Yawning, Hades stretches his eyes wide open. He blinked a few times, as they were dry and tired too. "I'm cold, wet and that Christmas Market is altogether trippy." Pulling up a fur-lined hood, Hades slunk is hands into the depths of deep, cavernous pockets. He'd overlook the fact that it was maroon, toggled and made him appear to be some form of Hipster that was trying too hard. It wasn't his cloak, but he felt that he carried it off reasonably well.

"Cold, wet?!" Screeched Gorbind, loudly at that. He was hoarse as he was staving off a cold. His eyes narrowed as he thrust open his coat jacket. His shirt, soaked the rain, was also streaked in scarlet. There were slashes across his abdomen; deep, angry looking gouges that didn't particularly bode well. There was also a red, roaring gunshot wound in the centre of his sternum. "You've not been shanked and shot, having ran down the stairs of the Floozy, trying to catch bad guy."

"That's true," nodded The Lord of the Underworld. "I tend to just evis-"

A glare from Gorbind told Hades to quit whilst he was ahead.

"Take six, seven, eight, nine and a half," Grumbled Gorbind, He pulled his own coat closer. Knee-length, blue and quilted, it was somewhat sombre compared to the one that Hades wore. Rain was coming down in sheets, it had been all day. "She won't commit to anything," he said, a little tentatively. "Unless she has a proper sequence of events for the opening salvo. This, this whole me and you thing, the bit where we meet; it's all snatches for now. She's waiting for a tipping point, where she'll be able to stitch all the fragments together. Then, and only then, will our paths collide and in your notebook."

"Meh," Hades shrugged to root around in his pockets. He grinned, all very wickedly, to pull out a hip-flask and a packet of Jelly Babies.

"Those," snipped Gorbind, "Are mine," he grabbed the bag, to tear away a corner. Hungrily, he scoffed a good handful. "Tell Padmi about those, and you're a dead man"

Scoffing, Hades snapped the lid of the flask to glug away.

Gorbind bit the head off of a green jelly. He felt something was a little off, as he looked left and right. The rain, it seemed to be falling in some form of delayed motion.

The Muse. He had disappeared.

"It's okay, Mercury, slash Hermes, is otherwise engaged in something called a retrograde," Hades rolled his shoulders, with no clue as to what he was talking about. The specifics at least. "He's had a rough patch lately. The world, his wife; every single writer in this world, is out to brain him. So he ebbs and he flows when he can."

"Gunmaker's?" sighed Gorbind, stuffing the packet of jelly babies into a pocket and making a move.

"Gunmaker's," nodded Hades, following the man who was fated to become his wingman. "But pop into that Indian Street Food place first, for some papdi chat and some samosas, perhaps. You really need to line your stomach. I'm good, I can drink till Hell freezes over."

Rolling his eyes, Gorbind walked passed Tesco and into the blurry mass of Christmas Market Goers.

No one would see them, hear them. They may have felt like a biting breeze, a buzzing that came out of nowhere, and was hard to decipher.

A Zombie copper and the Lord of the Underworld.

An unlikely alliance, yet to be forged.

Cabinet Meeting

Tapping his toes along to a blues riff, Gorbind nodded along in time as he stared into his pint. He'd been asked to get to the Gunmaker's once he had put Mango to bed.

It was his daughter who had relayed the message. Something about the cat speaking to her, having had a fight with a squirrel.

The squirrel had lost. Padmi had then screamed blue murder at the carnage that covered the kitchen floor.

Gorbind had made a joke about calling forensics, about appointing a scene of crime officer to come have a look. He'd grabbed a few food bags from the kitchen drawer, and asked if she fancied gathering the evidence.

His wife had not been best pleased.

Given who had sent him the message, it wasn't as strange as it sounded.

"Ah you came," Hades pulled up a chair on the opposite side of Gorbind's table. A tumbler of Kraken rum slid across the shiny surface to almost kiss and collide with Gorbind's drink.

"That cat of yours," pronounced Hades, "Is a sandwich short of a picnic." Taking off his mulberry-coloured coat, he draped it and with great care, over the back of his chair.

"Not my cat," said Gorbind, swirling his pint before supping it. "Can't stand him. He's a doughnut of the N-th degree. He's Padmi's. Send her your feedback, see what she does to you. Whatcha want?" he asked, sitting back.

"To tell you, that you were right," Hades pulled his rum closer, to cradle between his hands. "Christmas, Advent, and the Mr.Bleu De Chanel adverts. It all brings in the magic, to help her think creatively. Oh, and she's doing that thing..."

"She looks at all the pieces," Gorbind uttered, all very softly. "Puts all the corners in place, to start putting things together. Fragments had diagrams. Kangana, was long walks to Sare hole Mill. You, Hades, are a weird thought that often crops up when trying to plan lessons. You just wait til she adds the human condition to your contents and commas."

"I'm not human-"

"No, you're a God." A third voice carried through the air. A soft, tempered voice that seemed to echo through eons of existence.

A woman in scarlet had appeared by the Gunmakers piano. She moved towards them; her silken skirts rustling as she moved.

Hades snapped to his feet, there was even a courtly bow that was all rather amusing. He got even worse, to take the woman's gloved hand and press a kiss near her knuckles.

"The Lady Aurelia," Hades beamed, his eyes glimmered and he stepped aside to pull out a chair.

"Shit, the vampire," Blind-sided, Gorbind shot to his feet. His pint, held firmly albeit just about. His own knuckles had somewhat blanched.

"Stand down, Detective Inspector Phalla." Aurelia wore a wry smile as she pulled off her gloves. "I have no inclination to eat you. His Unholiness here, tells me that you are one of the colours on the wind. A thread, in the fabric of this universe, and something of a White Knight sent by Divinity Undefined." She lifted a veil from her eyes, to unpin the hat to which it was attached. A hat, which was unanchored, she placed upon the table. "I know of you. Gorbind, of your wife, your young lady Mango too. Her real name, is inspired, my dear boy and reminds me of where I came from. A beautiful name, that really captures her essence and also her whole raison d'etre."

Clicking her fingers, Aurelia conjured up a fluted glass. It was a quarter full, and with a scarlet-hued merlot.

It was definitely merlot, given the lack of ferrous in the scent that both Hades and Gorbind inhaled.

Wiping his hand across his jacket, Gorbind remembered his manners. He tentatively offered his hand as his heart rate became elevated. It was part worry, part excitement. "How lovely to meet you," he added a smile, gave a nod as his hand was shaken.

The Lady Aurelia knew about Mango. That would do.

"Take a seat, Gentlemen," Aurelia flashed a toothy grin. "We have much to discuss."

Unco Hades

Hay fever. This story was inspired by suffering from hay fever. Oh, I was also still trying to figure out to dress Hades. There is also the bond that is formed with Gorbind's daughter; a bond that will be explored in more detail when it comes to capturing Hades' own story.

"Atchoooo!" Blowing his nose, Gorbind stretched his eyes wide open. He made a mental note to speak with Hades; there was far too much pollen floating around. The Lord of the Underworld knew a woman with connections.

(Or so the myth, would have it.)

Hanging onto the kitchen counter, he sneezed three more times in quick succession. His temples throbbed as his brain turned to blancmange.

"Holy Mother of-" Uttering a string of expletives Gorbind went to sit at his table. Only a crack of lightning striking it had him recoil back. He had to make a grab for a spatula in defence.

"GORBIND!"

Cross-eyed and full of bogey, he focused on kitchen door as it was flung open. Padmi looked at him, her hands on her hips. She too was suffering; her eyes were pink, her nose puffy.

"Hades, have you seen him?" Padmi was just about able to speak; she covered her face to sneeze. "He was baby-sitting."

"Hold-"Gorbind's face contorted as he resumed sneezing.

"Merrrm!"

A fairy wand, all sparkly and purple flew out from beneath the kitchen table.

Padmi and Gorbind looked at one another as their daughter crawled out on all fours. She stood up, adjusted her costume-she was Batman today- and padded barefoot across kitchen whilst pushing hair away from her face. The little girl was also covered in glitter.

Mango pulled on a mask, flashed a knowing grin at her parents and left the kitchen.

"Hades?" Gorbind snorted into a kitchen towel; he edged towards the kitchen table. The spatula was jabbed in the dark, and eventually hit something fleshy.

"If I come out, promise you won't laugh?" The Lord of the Underworld sounded wary.

Sniggering, Padmi joined Gorbind. In her hands, she held her 'phone.

"I promise nothing," replied Gorbind, eyed Padmi. "Come on, we're all grown ups."

Padmi pulled Gorbind to her side, 'phone primed to record the evidence.

Flecks of glitter were jettisoned from beneath the table. What followed was the well-built, six foot two(and a half) frame of Hades, Lord of the Underworld.

Only he was dressed in a black Ramones T-shirt, a red tutu, rainbow tights and blue Dr.Martens.

He was covered in glitter.

With mouths agape, Padmi and Gorbind stared. Their necks craned as Hades moved across the kitchen and in the same direction as Mango.

"Tea-time, with The Justice league," he stated, all very poker-faced. "Give me another half an hour. You two look awful." Reaching into the tulle of the tutu, Hades pulled out a packet of anti-histamines and handed them to Padmi. "Laters." Off, he went, waving.

"Did you-" Gorbind blinked as he watched the door closed.

"Tights," stated Padmi. "I want that man's tights."

Poop and Puke

Dumping tea-bags into two mugs, Padmi clicked the kettle on. She was tired, beyond weary as leant against the kitchen worktop.

Last night had been spent battling puke and poop.

Both Gorbind and Mango were incapacitated. It was October; the bug faerie was out in force. Mango had picked something up from nursery, shared it with her father and all hell was breaking loose.

"One of those for me?" The back door creaked open, bringing with it a gust of wind and a flurry of leaves.

Padmi rubbed her eyes as Hades, Lord of the underworld swooshed into Gorbind's kitchen and headed to the freezer. She rubbed her eyes to squint; this did happen from time to time.

This morning, Hades was standing there barefoot, dressed in Claret and Blue silk pyjamas and a matching terry towel dressing gown.

"You're a Villa fan?" Padmi asked finding a third mug.

"Long story," he replied, pulling out a box of rather expensive ice-cream. Hades pulled up a chair, clicking his fingers. A spoon rose out of a drawer and landed in the ice-cream.

Padmi had opened her mouth to protest. That wasn't just ice-cream. That was Gorbind's 3 in the morning, "I will catch that bastard, damned if I don't" ice-cream. She was too tired to put up a fight.

"Talk, Hades," she tutted, making tea. "And you'd better replace that."

"She's dumping Devan," Hades scooped up ice-cream. "Breaking up with him; it's all over."

Splashing semi-skimmed milk in a mug, Padmi joined Hades at the kitchen table. Hell had a thing about black tea.

"The last time her world changed, all plate tectonics and stuff, we ended up with Fragments. Devan was a rebound," His speech had quickened to a crescendo. "What if she goes thunderbolts and lightning again? We all know what's sat on her desk. I'm genuinely worried about her."

"She won't," Padmi blew across her tea. "She's come too far. Devan gave her the courage for Kangana.

To write Rainbows. As for what's on her desk." She sat back a little to look at the man, the God, opposite.

"It's not her," she offered, sipping her tea. "It's you. You're scared. The Lord of the Underworld is scared!" Padmi laughed, wiping away a random tear. "Oh, Hades, sweetie..."

"What if she turns me into a fluff monster?" Asked Hades, pouting. He'd gone a little pink too.

"Gorbind is the defender of the galaxy. Devan, the hooch baron."

Oh, she laughed. Giggled, hysterically.

Composing herself, Padmi dunked an index finger into the ice-cream. Hooking her digit, she scooped out a blob and ate it.

"Hades," she said smirking. "You're descended from Titans. There's nothing fluffy, about you. Now, how do you feel about puke and poop?"

A little later.

"DADDDDYYYYYYY!"

Pushing the bathroom door open, Gorbind stood aside.

Running across the landing, Mango was headed towards the sink at full pelt. Her legs were little, but she had pace. The little girl was a blue blur as she moved. Her dressing gown could very easily have been a superhero's cape.

Blue. Somehow, he and Padmi were raising a Bluenose. For the moment, Gorbind could rest easy. Mango's bedroom had yet to become a shrine to St.Andrew's and was all pink and yellow.

"Woah, you look hideous."

Shuffling towards the bannister, Gorbind curled his around it to look down the stairs. His head throbbed a little harder with the sound of the rather abrasive tone. The voice, wasn't usually a problem.

"Unless you want a dent in your immune system, go whistle," Gorbind flipped Hades the bird and rubbed his own jaw. He needed a shave. Gorbind had been in bed, incapacitated, for two days. His loving daughter had shared her germs all too selflessly.

"I'm a God," Hades retorted, as he ambled up the stairs. "I don't have an immune system."

"UNCO HADES!"

Mango-Gorbind much preferred her real name-had bolted out of the bathroom. She was now wrapped around some rather knobbly knees.

Gorbind had seen the said knees, once upon a time. They weren't pretty, not really. All that stuff about perfectly formed Greek Gods? It was embellishment and then some.

"Ah, my favourite moonbeam," Breaking into a smile, Hades scooped Mango up into his arms. There was a genuine affection between them. She would always be his favourite moonbeam. Hades had been there-well just after-when she was born.

It was he, who had given Mango her real name.

"How do you pair fancy an adventure?" He asked. A glint of mischief burned and glowed in the depths of his lilac and lavender eyes. All it took, was an astral flash.

Mango and Gorbind watched with mouths agape as Hades stood upon a boulder. His feet were shoulder-width apart, as he wore a look of concentration.

Then he swung.

In his hands, was a nine-iron. Something hefty, and wholly inadequate as the Lord of the Underworld had just teed off. A blue golf ball hurtled around, before slowing down. It was pushed and pulled in the fabric of the Universe before pinging off the rings of Saturn. Hades had thwacked it and then some, turning this in a game of pin-ball.

In a heartbeat, the game was over.

"What did you do?" Padmi watched as Gorbind and Mango slept, all cuddled up, on the sofa.

"You should sleep," Hades gently nudged Padmi up the stairs.

Hearing her stomach gurgle, Padmi blanched. She snapped worried gaze towards Hades.

"I'm a God," stated Hades. "I don't have an immune system. But I do have a family. I'll look after you. I'll look after you all. Run."

And so she did. Up the stairs, and into the bathroom.

The Lady Aurelia

"It feels altogether a little strange," Aurelia pursed her lips together, before letting out a deep breath. She passed the tip of her tongue across dry, chapped lips, so as to try and gather herself.

"It will get easier," said Gorbind. With the tip of his fingers, he slid a hi-ball glass across the table. "Have a drink of that. It'll help."

Frowning, Aurelia eyed the glass with some level of suspicion. The contents, were deep red and looked as though the liquid was oxidised.

"Go on," Nodded Gorbind. "Struggle all you want in your reality. Here, Benind the Scenes, you don't have to. "And hey," he rolled his shoulders which some degree of nonchalance. "The barkeeper," he said flicking a finger towards the young man behind the bar at the Gunmaker's Arms. "He had it on tap. Has to, what with Birmingham having a Vampire community. Badger and stoat. Fresh keg, apparently."

Aurelia squinted at the police officer; she couldn't help but look at him with curiosity. She barely knew the man. Yet there was a connection between them that she really didn't understand or therein explain.

"Stoat," Aurelia smiled, to start giggling. She picked up the glass, to gently swirl it life. "I know," she said, nodding. "There are vampires in Birmingham. Some of them, are nasty, evil creatures who make me look like the tooth fairy." Putting the glass to her lips, she took a slow sip.

She could taste the stoat; it was wonderfully subtle. Badger, was known to be earthy. This concoction, that she imbibed, was light, frothy and not in the least bit dense to drink. This, tasted like a vintage that she could get used to.

"And out of the blocks goes Aurelia, chin chin!" Gorbind raised his own glass. He was on the fizzy pop for now. "You've got your plan, Hades too. I couldn't be happier. Neither is she…." He glanced momentarily skyward. "She likes having a plan, something to focus her figments and help them coalesce."

"Indeed," said Aurelia, passing a palm across her mouth. She plucked a handkerchief from the pocket of dress to wipe her hands and dab at the corners of her mouth. "There is some commitment to a cause, to see her universes eventually get off the ground." Aurelia took another mouthful of the blood. "I'm familiar with the plan, how it all works out for me. Glad to be part of the Fragments universe."

"Good," agreed Gorbind. "It'll be a change of tact for her, a good change. It's more relaxed, more hopeful too."

"True," sighed Aurelia, reclining in her seat a little. "Hope, is a powerful and wonderous thing. Unless your name is Pandora."

"Don't. I can't stand that woman."

Aurelia and Gorbind both looked towards the bar. Hades had appeared, and in lilac flash. He was handed a glass by the barkeeper. He ambled towards them-he never moved in a hurry, not really-as he removed his helmet. With the other hand, he sipped Kraken rum.

"Well," he said, settling down at the table. "I've made it to the Lickeys. She's written bits for me, and I am positively over-bowled," he was almost bursting with glee. "Things are looking up," he added nodding towards Aurelia. "For us both. She's managed to write a small dissertation-sized portion for us both." He really was glowing with warmth.

Aurelia looked at the Lord of the Underworld with a wry expression.

They had history. Interesting history, which appeared in her plan as well as his. History, that made the earth move and kept them both warm. For a Vampire, like her, that didn't happen often. For a

Greek God like Hades, that usually involved siring of unwanted offspring.

Fortunately for him, she wasn't of the child-bearing type.

For a moment, Hades and Aurelia looked at each other with a frisson of contentment.

The Lord of the Underworld clicked his fingers.

***

"He'll never know, Hades," Aurelia whispered, blowing a kiss.

"I have no plans to tell him," stated Hades, "A gentleman never kisses to tell."

"One hell of a kiss," commented Aurelia. "I could eat you."

"Wasn't it just…." Hades winked. "Stop. I know you don't bite."

***

"Long may it last," Gorbind didn't see Hades click his fingers for the second time. "Long may the writing flow last."

"It's all a bit tentative," commented Aurelia, "As though she's searching, and trying to find her feet as a writer."

"She is," Hades was nodding in agreement. "After three years of Devan, this is all about exploration. Even

this, Benind the Scenes, is a big leap. It's all beyond her
initial aspirations and ideas. She's playing with us, as
figments of her imagination."

"Will he be back?" posed Aurelia. "Devan?"

Gorbind shrugged. "No idea," he replied. "Never
say never. He appears in, pops into Benind the Scenes.
But never say never. He might not come back with a
bang just yet, but it is what it is. She does rather tend to
get invested into her projects, in her plans and
notebooks. Goes all very deep; gives a writing project
her all. After this, she plans to take you two on, Aldo
too as Pencil Sketch. All her other scribblings, are well,
Benind the Scenes."

"And she always sees each one as a big gig," stated
Hades. "She really does commit her all to it."

Sitting back, Gorbind cradled his fizzy pop. A big
part of him was glad. He looked at Hades, at Aurelia; he
could see sparks of something new. Sparks of creativity
that went beyond what he was, what he knew Devan to
be.

He smiled, with hope, at the glimmers.

What he saw, was something new. Something brave.
It was beautiful and full of hope.

Interview Panel

"What in the blue blazes are you two doing? Have you lost your minds?"

The kitchen door had flung open, letting in a glittering, purple cyclone. An eddy of twigs and leaves circled at the base, before settling to form the shape of one man, and one man alone.

"I'M A GOD!" yelled Hades, rolling his eyes at the omniscient narrator. "I'll get to you later," he added, waggled a finger in the general direction of the extractor fan over the stove.

Aditi was sat at Gorbind's kitchen table as she watched Hades remove his helmet and tuck it under his arm. She herself wore a grey and white, knitted bobble hat. Her nose was rather pink as she had travelled from a rather chilly Oakview, all the way in Montana.

Holding on to a cup of tea, she flipped her gaze towards Padmi.

"What?" asked Padmi, coiling her dark tresses into a neatly formed pony tail. Between her teeth, was a black hair band; it contrasted sharply against her teeth. She was dressed in a blue coat, and looked ready to leave. A cherry red, rectangular handbag sat nestled between her feet.

"I'm about to kick off," said Hades, putting the helmet onto a work, he then rested his hands on his hips. "Me, Charon, the river Styx. The chariot is waiting, I want to go to the Malvern hills; my story is all set to go. But no; you've had an idea. SHE'S had an idea," his finger once more gesticulated at the extractor fan. "You've taken her brain from me. Don't do this to me, Padmi. I am ready to go."

"We're off to do an interview; with The Red head." Aditi grinned somewhat menacingly as she drank her tea. Mischief and mayhem were etched across an otherwise unassuming face.

"What Red Head?" Hades looked at each woman in turn; his brow furrowed. "Can you do this later perhaps? Let me take the ferry, get to the hills. Give me her brain, for a couple of hours. Her brain, her soul; practice your questions, do your whole Kangana beats a retreat thing. Then you can have her; all of her."

Padmi exhaled deeply, to pick up her bag. She looked directly at him, but thought of Gorbind's beard, his feet too. An unpleasant thought, which would prevent Hades making eyes at her, through her own soul.

"No," she said, all too bluntly. "You've waited a year, two nearly now, what with Benind the Scenes. You can wait another couple of days. It won't kill you. And you know what," Padmi flexed an index finger. "This interview, is actually for your benefit. I want to make sure about her. Before you get hurt, and sink to your knees."

"He'll do that all right," Aditi spoke into her tea, but tipped Hades a wink.

Hades, Lord of the Underworld, blushed.

"Go wait on the ferry," Padmi pulled her handbag into crook of harm, to retrieve her keys from its depths. A woman's handbag, really did contain a bottomless pit. "Hold your horses, and the rest of you."

Hades glowered; he glowered at them both.

"Go," Padmi pointed at the back door. "Or I take away your babysitting privileges."

Hades clicked his fingers, to turn back into a glittering, purple-leaved eddy. The swirling mass exited, with the door slamming shut all very dramatically behind.

***

Padmi's heels clip-clopped across rain-splashed paving slabs. The heavens had opened, dumping a deluge across the city of Birmingham. Pulling up her fur-trimmed hood, she skated around the puddle that stretched out across the door of St Martin's in the Bull ring. At her wrist, her handbag swung side to side as though keeping time. It was an altogether expensive, but glamourous metronome. A gift to herself, having been recently promoted.

Padmi Dharam-Phalla has appeared as though out of thin air to make her way up some stairs. Stairs which bisected a cubed water feature sat at the base of the hill that led to The Rotunda.

"Stupid heels," she tutted, chiding herself. "Should've just worn trainers; stairs, the chuffing hill." Nelson, with his Victory, looked on. He may have rolled his eyes, or shaken his head. From way up on his plinth, he had seen it all. Heels, drunken brawls; lost-looking folks wandering around as though zombies lost in the swirling mists of time. He'd seen the true colours of Birmingham, in their full technicolour glory. Some of them were beautiful; others were tinged with sadness and despair.

Weaving and out of pedestrians, Padmi made her way slowly up hill. She really didn't fancy breaking her neck. Everyday life, streamed passed her. Mums, dads, buggies; an elderly couple, wearing cagoules and holding hands.

She smiled as they walked by. "Perhaps," she told herself. "That's what Gorbind and I will have. Provided he stays away from those stupid jelly babies. Send his glucose levels completely the wrong way."

The gradient of the hill flattened out as she to the Birmingham Bull at the top. She cut across the space diagonally, to head towards The Rotunda. The Bull, was beautiful in bronze. The Rotunda, an unmissable edifice at the centre of the Birmingham skyline.

"If ever there was an apocalypse," she said, muttering to herself. "Those two would have to stay standing. The last two bits of Birmingham. God forbid though, if anything were to happen to St. Martin's."

The thought made her shudder, as she opened a tall, glass door using a metal handle. The possible destruction of the church didn't bear thinking about.

Taking the lift to the ninth floor, Padmi gathered her thoughts. She was here for a good reason. To protect someone that she cared about, someone of such great value in that they were beyond both friend and family. As a mortal, there was in reality, precious little she could do. However, Hades was important to her, to Gorbind and to Mango. There was just something, about the way that Hades related to the little girl. Tenderness, affection and protectiveness imbued the relationship between the Lord of The Underworld and a very human child. That reminded Padmi, that with all that existed in the world, the drama and the chaos; Mango was a sign of all that was good. All that could bring you joy and happiness.

In a world, where a red button could be pressed on a hysterical whim, her daughter brought light to a being who very often lived in the dark.

That, was worth fighting for.

She was here, to stand up for a God. To protect him, at all costs.

"Padmi, great, you're here!" The lift door pinged open, and she found herself being dragged out by Aditi. She was led towards a set of double doors.

Aditi had ditched the bobble hat from earlier. Attired in a neatly tailored dark blue suit, she exuded confidence and power. She looked every inch the sophisticated and learned lawyer that she had trained to be. There was just that something about Aditi's power, presence and persona that sometimes made Padmi feel unsettled.

It was something more than that, in fact.

Aditi, made Padmi feel inadequate. A feeling that Padmi quickly filed away. She could it bottled up now, and it would simmer away quietly inside for now.

"Rained. Made travelling that bit harder," Aditi shook her head whilst wafting a black clip-board. They were headed towards an office. She pushed the door to shepherd Padmi in.

Dumping her bag onto a table, Padmi lowered her hood. She slowly but surely absorbed the office space. Three grey chairs were nestled around an ash blonde coffee tale. The room itself was air, with white washed walls over a blue carpet. Through wall to ceiling windows, you could absorb a panoramic view of the second city.

"So how do we do this?" asked Aditi, her eye-lashes fluttered to accentuate eyes and emphasise curiosity.

"As practically as we can," replied Padmi, untying her belt and unzipping her coat. "The aim is simple; protect Hades. Beyond that, to ensure that The Red Head doesn't hurt him. She must know, how much he means to us. That we won't stand by, if she were to so much as sneeze at him."

Aditi nodded as she listened. She'd been writing the brief down onto the file paper attached to the clip-board.

"This interview, Aditi," Padmi took off her coat, to fold it up. It was then dumped behind a chair that she claimed for her own. Her handbag was tucked in below. "Really is for a role, a job. As such, it comes with duties and responsibilities. Did you find it?"

"Uhuh," There was more nodding from Aditi, as she slid passed to take up a second chair next to Padmi's. Lifting the file paper, she looked at a second document. "It came in an iron-clad chest, was bewitched to Kingdome Come and was delivered by some fella called Hermes."

Padmi smiled, hopefully, at that. She expected nothing less from the Gods. Nothing less, from the people that Hades begrudgingly called family.

Hades was the middle child.

That explained most things, but not all. Least of all, his ability to form meaningful relationship. Despite the time that Hades had spent with her, with Gorbind and Mango; he still had a lot to learn. This interview was part of that learning experience.

It had to be perfect. It had to work.

Over the next twenty minutes, there was back and forth over the aims of the interviews; what the most equitable outcome should be. Different parts of the job specification were underlined, circled, with black liquid eyeliner. There was even some blood as Padmi suffered a papercut. Given the current millennium, she modified some of the duties and responsibilities that would come in being involved with Hades.

If Hades wanted steak and chips for dinner, he could make it himself.

That or ask an underling, slash minion, to do it.

At two o'clock exactly, the interviewee arrived. They were dressed in a powder-blue suit; knee-length skirt, a crisp white blouse was teamed with nude stilettos. They took up the third chair, before Padmi and Aditi.

Her hair, it was beautifully red; the colour a breaking dawn. There was a link and a curl to it, but it was tamed for now in a neatly formed chignon. Her icy blue eyes, could have pierced an armoured tank. There was something really very foreboding, in the way that she looked at her interviewers.

There was also a serenity in the way that she smiled, that somewhat quelled the storm that stirred in her eyes. In her eyes, Padmi saw hope and in very delicate measure.

(Though if anyone was to mention hope to Hades, he had tendency to go positively apoplectic.)

The young woman was nervous; she bit at her rosebud lips. A flush, of child-like vulnerability bloomed across her otherwise porcelain skin.

"No need to be nervous, "Padmi poured water from a green-tinged jug into three hi-ball glasses. "We're not going to eat you," she said, offering a glass. "Just a case of getting to know you. I'm going to ask you some questions. Aditi here, will be taking some notes as we talk. Is that okay?"

Taking the glass, The Red Head nodded. She took a sip, before balancing the glass on her knee.

"Persephone," Padmi uttered the name, to sit back in her chair. "How would you romance an introvert? Someone who really doesn't like human company, tends to be aloof. They don't particularly want to give their heart, their soul to a random person, but craves connection so as to feel part of something."

"I guess I would have to take things slowly," replied Persephone. She put her water down. A droplet glistened upon her lips. "Try to understand perhaps, the cause of being aloof. Human company, and the contact it brings, is hard. As a mortal, I can't imagine how it might be, for a God, to be so above and beyond."

That was the opening gambit. Padmi wanted to do this properly, and as such, would take no prisoners. Ever. She watched, she listened. Padmi was trying to engage her own head, heart and gut to scope out the woman sat before her.

Aditi raised a brow, but smirked to write down the response.

"I did my homework," Persephone had the floor. "Hades isn't some lost little boy. He doesn't require all of this softly, softly nonsense. This, isn't some romance novella, with a country squire and a milk maid."

"Careful," Aditi looked up from her notes. As far as she was concerned, there was nothing wrong with being part of a romance novella.

"So, what would you do?" posed Padmi. "With a God, with all that power."

"Find out, about his pleasure." Persephone's expression softened somewhat, but something flickered in her eyes. There was no longer any child-like naivete to be found. "All work and no plat, would make Hades a dull boy. I guess, that's the case and point here. I'm not here, to be a bauble or a trinket. I don't think, for moment, that Hades, Lord of the Underworld wants a trophy wife from The Stepford range."

Padmi threw her head back in laughter.

"You have hubris," she said, squinting at Persephone. "Not bad, in small doses, but deadly in excess. Shall we just cut to the chase here? We're just dancing around."

"Sure, why not," Persephone picked up her glass once more. With another mouthful, she locked gaze with Padmi.

"Forget for a moment," stated Padmi, her head tilted to one side. "The pantheon of Gods from which Hades comes. It's not the, that you have to worry about. There is more than one type of family."

"That you, is it?" Persephone was always going to counter this directly. A tapered index finger jabbed between Aditi and Padmi. "You two, are his family, are you, of a kind?"

Aditi put down her clip board; face-down to conceal her notes. Notes, that were highly vitriolic. There was a rather cutting comment about the size of Persephone's feet that was better kept secret.

"Hades is far more than a God; we are far than family," Padmi pronounced. "As such, there is a bond, a connection that goes beyond blood, beating heart and the stirring of the soul." She kept Persephone in her cross-hairs, she wasn't going to roll over, least of all for this up-start. "Hades deserves to be happy, to be loved. He deserves to be a part of a world where there is happiness, hope and love; he should not be condemned, resigned to a world of darkness. If was somebody, anybody, who compromised that, then yes. There would be hell to pay."

"And he knows a thing or two about hell," commented Aditi. "Says so in his job spec. However. The hell, that Padmi and I, the rest of the Fragments Universe may cook up, is far greater than anything that a God might conjure."

"We're human, like you," Padmi took a mouthful of her own water. "We know hurt, anger, despair and pure unadulterated love. We have the sort of experiences that tear hope apart; squish it, smash it, to turn it into smithereens."

"So we're protective," Aditi cocked her head a little. "There is a sense of duty that not many would understand."

Cradling her water, Padmi continued to eyeball Persephone. There was something between them, which at that precise moment, was horrible overwhelming. Every inch of Padmi bristled; every sinew was pulled taut with affection, the bond she felt Hades. At that moment in time, Hades was staggeringly important.

Whatever it was, that kept Padmi locked in the moment. It was far beyond getting to know one another; far beyond the simple mechanics of an interview.

"Perhaps that's the problem," Persephone pondered, out aloud. Standing up, she drained her glass to drop with a clink to the table. "Perhaps Hades needs somebody else; perhaps he wants somebody else. Someone, who is well and truly beyond what you offer him. This isn't good," she tutted to gesticulate at the room. "An interview, masking an attack. This isn't about Hades; this is about you. You're scared, and of losing him. Scared, of what he might gain."

Padmi and Aditi got to their feet.

"He's a grown-ass man," Persephone laughed as she shook her head. "A God too, but that's neither here nor there. He's going to do as he damned well pleases, he has no need for you. He doesn't need you pair, to vet others in his world. You really think that matters to him?" Still she laughed, crossing her arms.

"This interview," she said, pointedly, "Is a joke. It's irrelevant. I do respect your tenacity, though. If I loved someone-and you clearly do, he really does mean a great deal to you-I would fight too. I'd want to protect that person as well. But you've made a mistake. Two mistakes."

Aditi curled her fists, anticipating an assault. She didn't make mistakes. Ever.

"You thought that I was a child, an innocent," Persephone raised her brows, to shake her head. "I'm not, trust me. Then, you infantilised Hades; you've taken away his autonomy, whilst harping on about his power, his divinity. Imagine, if he knew; would you still be his family then? He avoids The Olympians for a reason, the same reason. You should know better. The relationship, the bond that you have with him, might have told you that."

Padmi fumed. Her nostrils flared at the indignity of it all.

"This," grinned Persephone, "Is over." Clapping her hands together, Persephone disappeared in a plume of yellow daffodil petals. These fluttered to the floor into a heap.

Aditi looked at Padmi, horrified.

In a fit of pique, Padmi lobbed her glass at the wall. Mistakes. They didn't make mistakes.

Gorbind Suspects Devan

This is a cross-over, a curious one. In his Peace Novella Series, Devan Coultrie goes from being fairly ordinary, to being one hell of a piece of work as a would-be Hooch Baron. There's a lot of character development, and not all of it is cute and cuddly. So much so, it has ripples; ripples that reach Gorbind in the Fragments universe. In this story, we see how Gorbind tries to understand Devan and his actions. I won't tell you what he did, you may want to go find out, and make your own judgement. This story, does to some extent, echo my own meta-cognitive and

*experiential attempts to understand my own character. Having
Gorbind turn the thumb-screws was an interesting way of
broaching that exploration.*

Gorbind inserted silver coins into the drinks
machine. A pound coin, fifty pence and newly-minted
twenty pence piece were slotted away to rattle down the
innards of the machine. He really needed a cup. One
for himself, and one to be given to the interview, by
way of courtesy.

The machine clunked and churned noisily to make
the first cup. The whole process sounded apathetic and
hard-pressed; as though the machine had something
better to do. Gorbind rolled his eyes, whilst tapping his
toes in impatience. With a tinny ping, the machine
spewed amber-coloured liquid into a being plastic cup.
He grimaced to lift it from a latticed, grimy-looking tray
and set it aside onto a nearby table. Whilst he was there,
he picked up a sugar shaker. Lifting it to elbow height,
he dosed his tea with an unhealthy amount of
sweetness. Gorbind pulled a face, to stir the sugar in
with a rather stained, woebegone teaspoon.

The machine continued to clunk and churn as it
made another cuppa. It shook violently, causing
Gorbind to shuffle back across the blue linoleum. He
belted the machine, squarely and in the middle, with a
flattened palm.

"Get on with it," yelled Gorbind, adding a swift kick
for extra impetus.

The machine whimpered, subdued into submission.

"Good," nodded Gorbind, "Do that again, and I switch you off forever."

Crackling and zinging suggested a level of unwilling compliance. That, and if Gorbind could overpower a machine, he could probably overpower anything. The toaster in the refs room knew that all to well. It's every present companion, the microwave, was also something of a Gorbind survivor.

Chirruping, the machine released the second cup of tea.

"There, that wasn't so difficult, now was it," he was cooing almost to take the second tea. Picking up his own, Gorbind made his way to the interview room. He pushed the door open with his knee, to lean back and shoulder it closed. He'd picked this place for a reason.

Navy-grey walls made the room feel constrained and oppressive. It was a bear pit of a room, that was in fact a bear trap. A blue table, edged with a brown veneer, jutted out from the wall. Either side, tucked underneath, was a plastic chair. The seat of which was covered with a coarse fabric that made long, drawn-out interviews, even more painful to endure.

"Here," Gorbind set down the two cups of tea. Removing his coat, he hung it on the back of his chair before sitting down. He pulled a board across the table. Wedged beneath the metal clip was a black biro. He lay it before him.

"All right," he said, unclipping the pen, he removed the lid. He wrote his name on the form. Slowly, deliberately. "You've been charged, so now's the time for the details." He filled in a second box; this time with the name of the interviewee.

"Destruction of a marriage," Gorbind read off the sheet attached to the clip-board. "Flouting of associated vows. Blatant disregard for fidelity, trust and integrity. Does that sound about right to you?" He looked, to glare with a steely gaze at the interviewee.

"Yes," Devan Coultrie gave a flat, unequivocal response. He let out a breath, to pull his tea towards him with his left hand. His palm then curled around the beige cup. "Why you?" he asked. "Why are you interviewing me, and not some other random copper. Is there not some conflict of interest here?"

"Probably," nodded Gorbind, looking at the sheet again. "I'm nosey," he said, flicking his eyes back towards Devan. "And I'm not just your imaginary friend. I want to know the deal is, the real deal and not some fairy tale. Not the conjecture that you presented in Peace Betrayed. Actually, was there conjecture, did you actually say why you were such a muppet?"

Devan took a few mouthfuls of his tea. His lips puckered with the last, as though he was about to say something sour. "No," he said grimacing, as he gulped down tea. "I didn't say a word, to be honest. To be honest, I don't even remember confessing."

Gorbind put down his pen. He reached under his seat, with both hands, to hem himself in, under the table.

"Right, to be honest," Gorbind steepled his hands on the clip-board. "That's a good start, the best place to begin. Tell me then, why. Why did you do it?"

"You going to tell Padmi?" volleyed Devan. "I could, I could tell you everything; be honest to a fault. But if you tell Padmi…"

"Right here, right now," said Gorbind, "It's just me and you. Padmi, is elsewhere, doing what she needs to do. Perhaps you can take this up with her later, if you want to. If I recall correctly, you pair have something of an interesting relationship."

"No thanks," Devan's stony expression said it all. "Interesting, Gorbind, is an understatement."

"So, talk," Gorbind could match Devan for curtness. "Speak to me. I am all ears, ready and waiting, to hear your side of things. Why cheat, Devan and on your wife, Aditi Rao."

"Because I could," Devan spat out the words. "Because I could push the button on something that was otherwise pure fantasy. Aditi, was never there. I would wait, for her to turn up and our relationship was always on her terms. I…never once asked, for her to stay. For her not to fly off."

"Fantasy," echoed Gorbind. "You had a fantasy in your head, but you actually made it a reality."

"On a whim," Devan stated, in a very matter of fact fashion. "I sent a text, having slept in my not so loving wife's arms. I did it, knowing that she'd be gone, and I'd once more be left to my own devices."

Gorbind shook his head as he wrote down Devan's responses. "Having your cake and eating it too?" he snorted in dry derision. "Far from original, Devan. You were thinking with your…a whim?"

"We want what we can't have," Devan momentarily rolled his eyes before fixing his gaze upon the man opposite. A man, who despite being his friend, was deliberately trying to get under his skin. "I didn't just want my end away. This was far more than just thinking with my…"

The pair of them looked at a flickering strip-light; it crackled and rankled in censorship.

"Ellipsis?" Asked Gorbind, only to tut. "All for implication, leaving to the readers imagination. This is all very frustrating."

"D-ongle," Devan's face contorted. "Oh, come on!" he yelled, "Even that doesn't get passe the strait-jacketed sensibilities."

"Shiest," groaned Gorbind, using his pen to write an expletive across Devan's statement. He slid the clipboard across the table, the pen was tossed towards Devan.

Devan, took the pen, to write a few more choice words across the page.

"It was her idea," declared Devan, throwing aside the clip-board. "Not mine, not Aditi's, or the accountants. But hers," he jabbed a finger towards the strip-light. "To turn me into bit of a sh-"

Gorbind rolled his eyes.

"That's why!" Devan fumed, as he crossed his arms. "I was vanilla, pointless and all too fluffy. Something had to give, and it just happened to be the accountant."

The two men looked knowingly at one another. Reaching forwards, Gorbind scooped up the clipboard. Using the pen, he added a few more bits of information.

"My infidelity was an experiment," Devan shook his head, before licking his bottom lip. "How could change me like that, turn me into a toss-pot?"

"You weren't supposed to be a toss-pot," Gorbind looked up from scribble.

"No," sighed Devan. "She was trying to flout the maxims, turn the tropes around. Only it all got a bit blurry."

"Spice," Gorbind grinned broadly, all too incongruously. "Of a weird sort. Did it work, and for you?"

"Tore me apart," Devan declared, uncrossing his arms. He lay his palms flat upon the table. "I became someone that I'm not. Someone, that I never wanted to be. She forced me, to be a different man, to be a different character. I was in her hands, at mercy of her ink pens, with no where to run. I did as I was told, Gorbind. As, I was told."

There is it was. That was the answer.

"We are but players," Gorbind put down his pen, to slide away the clip-board. "We cannot be masters of our own destinies. We simply tell the stories. Pub? We can get a pint at the Gunmaker's. This is all but a fiction."

Devan nodded, getting up from his chair. "We'll never win," he muttered.

"We're not supposed to," Gorbind stood too, and made for the door.

"We are but players," Devan turned out the light as he followed Gorbind out. "And this is all but a fiction."

Shakespeare Day

This was inspired by Shakespeare's birthday on 23rd April; which is also St.George's Day. I am rather partial to a bit a Shakespeare, and rather enjoy watching productions by the Royal Shakespeare Company when the RST is open. It's been strange not seeing plays during Lockdown, with many of the plays being streamed on line. There are thirsty six plays, and I must have seen at least half of them, in one shape or form.

"Any idea why we're here?" Devan rubbed an eye as he sat on the walled dais at the back of Gorbind's Garden. Sat next to him was a ham and cheese croissant with a mug of chai.

"No idea," yawned Gorbind. Sat next to Devan, he held a bowl of cheerios. His own tea, was on the floor before him, in between his polka-dotted socks. "Six in the mornings, Daddy, tell De Uncos and bring my dressing up box. I love the girl to pieces, but I swear she's going slightly mad. Lockdown, is driving us all around the bend."

A breeze picked up a clutch of leaves. The eddy swirled wildly. Before long Hades appeared, as the leaves crackled away. Another day, another set of claret and blue silken pyjamas. Clutching a pewter goblet, he sat next to Gorbind.

"You're a Villa fan?" Asked Devan, whispering as he craned forward.

"Deadly Doug…"answered Hades, slurping Ambrosia. "Long story, bad bet. Gorbind had a spare ticket. Oh, look. Mango!!"

Gorbind's little girl was traipsing across the patio and down the lawn. Her dressing up box was sat on the dais with her dad and two uncles.

"Daddy, you another beast Dogberry, all day. Today." She rooted around the box, to pull out a flattened, Police man' soft hat.

"Dogberry is a doughnut," grumbled Gorbind, putting on the hat at a jaunty angle.

"Unco Dev, you beed Hamlet," she shuffled forward with a sword, a skull and what looked like a pair of oil-stained over alls.

"Hamlet?" Devan laughed to shake his head.

"He is vey vey complicated, and over over…" stated Mango. "He's always so grumbly as well."

Devan and Gorbind looked at one another; both shrugged.

"Unco Hades.." Mango nearly fell into her dressing up box. She scrambled out, to hold a battered, yellow gold, plastic crown with what looked like jelly beans attached. "You beed all the Henry's, Richard the horse and spider man. You have lots to give. Now go pease play. I having my breakfast. Bubyes."

And off she pootled, back into the house.

Technical Gremlins

In the first instance, I write most things long-hand. I have some rather nice fountain pens and box of lovely inks. I enjoy writing stories by hand, and end up filling lots of notebooks with my rather, not so neat and cursive handwriting. It is only when the first draft of a story is complete, that I go to type it all up. I find that in writing long-hand, my writing is more organic, and I am better able to harness my imagination and all the ideas that scramble around my cerebral cortex in an effort to get out.

Typing, is something that I find difficult; my brain has been known to freeze at the sight of a blank page. So imagine my horror when my trusty laptop went a bit kaput; it sang it's final song and ascended to cyber, tech heaven. I was saddened, frustrated and angry; this happened right at the beginning of lockdown. I was also a bit stoic. I still had my pens, my notebooks too. I didn't need it for this-this book-just yet. I was annoyed that a device that I had used for nearly a decade had given up the ghost, it had discharged its duty all too impeccably.

This snippet comes from that particular experience. Thank goodness for pen, paper and ink.

It was green. Ultra Green. This snippet was written in Ultra Green.

"Mummy, that a horse...?"

Thundering down the road was a mustang. With hoof-beats thundering from hell, the animal whinnied as it made quick work of Acacia Avenue. Tarmac burned and blurred.

"Meerrrrm, git daddy...." Mango jumped off the sofa, away from the window as the horse pulled up outside next go Gorbind's brand-spanking new F-pace.

One minute it had four legs, then four wheels.

(He was going up in the world, but that was another story).

Gorbind ran down the stairs. His face half-full of foam.

"Since when do you use front door?" He asked as it flew open.

"In a friggin' disaster," replied Hades, Lord of the underworld. "Hence the riot gear. We've got trouble."

Gorbind watched as Hades came in. His helmet shone, his breast plate glimmered and his boots thudded towards the kitchen. Embers flickered from his spurs.

Stood in the kitchen, Hades filled the kettle from the sink.

Hermes," he said, racking up mugs. He even found squash for Mango. "Useless donut had kiboshed her devices."

Frowning, Gorbind crossed his arms. "What on earth is the matter with you?" He asked, squinting. "Hades, you never talk like that."

"Hermes, frigging Mercury," uttered Hades, dropping tea-bags into mugs. "Buckle up, and Batter, up. She's not best pleased, and she makes Ares look pretty."

"You'd think she'd write this all down...." Hades grumbled as a plate of chocolate digestives landed with a thud onto the kitchen table. He half jumped, whilst trying not spill his coffee.

"Oh, be quiet," Padmi, huffed, and sat down opposite. She glowered as Gorbind sidled up to Hades. "And stop pulling sour-puss faces; you're none too pretty when you have a face like a smacked backside."

The two men looked at one another, picked up a biscuit and dunked into their respective beverages.

"Why is my wife upset with you?" Gorbind nibbled away, all very wary of Padmi. "Me, she'll banish to the sofa. You, she'll send to Coventry and the Ring Road."

"Just saying, that she's the only writer not writing whilst in lock-down," Hades licked each of the fingers of his left hand. Wiping them across his William Morris waistcoat, he found another biscuit. "I'm gathering dust..." he stuck out his bottom lip, and batted his lashes.

"Oh, you'll live," Gorbind tutted as soggy biscuit landed with a plop into his tea. "I remember Fragments. Man alive...she was a woman possessed...."

"Right," Padmi huffed still, she crossed her arms to look her husband, and Hades too. "Hold on, be thankful. Right now, she's obsessed with socks. Her brain, her soul is charging with something completely out of left field. But when she finds her fifth gear, you'll know about it. You're still there, Hades, and you make her grin. Hold onto that. Not even Gorbind, or Devan, have that impact."

"I really don't," Gorbind sounded all very wistful.

"You're a fantasy," Continued Padmi. "The sort, that is like a decent cuppa."

Hades and Gorbind both squinted.

"Well worth brewing," said Padmi. "Well worth waiting for. Mark my words."

Sharlene

Knows

"Uhoh, incoming," Padmi clattered crockery onto a drainer as she looked out of the kitchen window.

Devan Coultrie was running down the lawn and towards the house. Only he was half-dressed, unshaven and rather red in the face.

"Meh?" Gorbind, still suffering from brain ache, sat at then kitchen table as he tried to drink ginger broth.

The back door swung open, Devan slid in across the tiles. Striped Boxers and a pair of polka dotted socks.

"Whose gonna kill you?" Asked Padmi, reaching for a checked tea-towel

"Sharlene," Devan looked around, for somewhere to hide.

"Sharlene," Gorbind tried to smile, to laugh. "Sharlene," he repeated, peering at Padmi. "Sharlene Sharlene. Powers that be, Sharlene."

"Oh," smirked Padmi, "She found you." Shaking her head, she watched Devan slide under the table. "I hope she canes yer ass."

"Call Hades," grumbled Gorbind, sliding sunglasses up his nose. "He'll want to sell tickets for this."

"Here's to the front row," laughed Padmi, reaching for her 'phone.

Pencil Sketch: Core Conditions

Here we meet not one, but two characters. There is Aldo, a very new character to the Fragments universe. He like Hades, waits in the wings, for his story to be written. In Benind the Scenes, he sets about blending in with all the other figments; his destiny is also tied to that of Gorbind. There is another character here, who is not so shiny but is somewhat significant. His name is Dhillon Havane.

Dhillon Havane was one of the first fictional characters that I wrote. I had the immense privilege and most wonderful tome being part of a writing group that wrote Star Trek Fan Fiction. A group that helped to inspire each of it's members and fire up imaginations to take writing to Warp. Dhillon was an anti-hero, a real piece of work that was written to be mad, bad and dangerous to know. The complete opposite, I guess, of the ideals that Star Trek embodies. I really didn't want to write a nice boy, and that is ultimately what Gorbind is, as well as what Devan started out as being. As such, he appears in this story as a shadow. A warning to all the other figments of my imagination. I quite like that; the potential to write a character that is unpalatable by design. Aditi Rao, Devan's wife, circles somewhat closely to that. I don't think for one moment, that readers should always be enamoured by the characters that they stumble across. Every movie, every pantomime, has to have a villain. Having a bad guy as part of the narrative, is what allows us to focus on the good guys. It is what causes us, to pledge allegiance to the would-be here.

Pencil Sketch continues to develop. There is one underlying principle to Aldo Armande, and it's really very simple. We have the potential to be bad, to embrace it whole heartedly and with reckless abandon. We all have the capacity to show our dark side. What holds us from doing so, is the existence of boundaries. Boundaries, that we touch, fiddle with using our fingertips and stretch; yet we dare not transgress.

All we have to do, is flex and flick our finger tips, and test those boundaries.

There were some sounds that really shouldn't be heard. One or two of them were made by the human body.

Standing at the bathroom door, Padmi grimaced. Her ear was pressed against it, as her mind boggled.

Her husband didn't sound match fit. He had slept badly; tossing and turning in fits that had led Padmi to decamp to the sofa. At one point, Gorbind had snatched the duvet and disappeared into it. Leaving her cold and resisting the urge to roll him off the mattress.

"Oh, boy," Padmi took a deep breath to shoulder barge the door. In her hands, she held a hi-ball glass of mint and ginger tea. "Sip this, slowly," she said, taking in the view. She placed the glass onto the floor, next to a foot.

Gorbind, prone and on his knees, was half way down the u-bend. He waggled a hand towards the towel rail.

"Migraine?" She asked, dragging a blue towel off the rail and dropped it onto Gorbind head. "That man Pencil-Sketch, has a lot to answer for," Padmi tutted as she sat on the edge of the bath.

"Remind me to brain him," muttered Gorbind. He grunted and groaned to flush, and lowered the toilet seat to sit. "He's...."

"A pain in the backside," Padmi smiled weakly. "In more ways than one."

"She's...."Gorbind mopped his face with the towel. "Pencil-Sketch," he added, letting out a deep breath. "An experiment. Again."

"Aren't we all experiments," Padmi slid off the bath. "He's not as cute as you, though. You're not a Shit, either." Wrapping her arms around Gorbind's shoulders, Padmi narrowed her eyes.

Pencil-Sketch. She'd have words with him.

***

"This is all rather unexpected."

Rolling up her sleeves, Padmi tied her long hair into a pony tail. A black band pinged at her wrist to tame her tresses.

"One sick as dog, hasn't eaten in days husband," she said, rolling her eyes as Gorbind pulled a duvet over his head. He was slumped in an armchair, with a bucket next to it.

"One slightly stoned Lord of the Underworld," Padmi's stretched her eyed wide open. Hades, was doing a headstand in the window. He'd turned up, completely toasted and singing show-tunes. "More than my human brain dares to conceive. And the Hooch Baron..."

Curled up under a blankey, Devan Coultrie held onto a stuffed elephant. He was dead to the world, having not slept in 3 days. He'd landed in the garden, uttering something about bogey monsters.

Then the doorbell rang.

"Oh no, not another one..." Swearing under her breath, Padmi stomped towards the front door.

"Peasedontbepencilsketch. Reallydontwantneedpencilsketch."

"Hello..." The door had been thrust open, letting in a tidal wave of cologne.

"Oranges," muttered Padmi, stepping aside. "Satsumas. You smell of satsumas. Why, I mean..."

"Edible, no? You look as though you might hit me," Pencil-sketch wiped his feet across a hessian mat. Before sliding his size tens out of a pair of Italian boots.

"Oh, I might, hold that thought..."

"At your service," Pencil-sketch grinned over his shoulder, as they both headed into the living room.

"Never," tutted Padmi, cuffing the back of his head. "Really not my type."

"Donthitonmywife," Gorbind surfaced from the duvet, to glower at Pencil-sketch. "Or I'll send you to Coventry. Without an expense account."

Pencil-sketch paled as he landed on the sofa next to Devan. Wiping the smile off his face, he made a mental note to behave. In a fashion.

***

"This has to be the most pointless exercise known to man." Pencil-sketch pouted as he wiped crockery. A stack of six plates sat next to the microwave.

Padmi, stopped mid-pace, picked up the stack and then dropped it into the bubbles that filled the sink. Turning on her heel, she continued to pace.

Rolling up his sleeves, Pencil-sketch shook his head to go through the motions once more. He'd done this three times already.

"Don't go call me grass hopper," he said quietly. "It would be a cliche. You're annoyed, and I don't know why."

"Because I know," Padmi pulled out a chair, then another from below the kitchen table as she stopped pacing. "Shut up, sit down, and look pretty, Aldo."

Aldo. Pencil-sketch dropped a dinner plate. He liked being Pencil-Sketch. He'd been Pencil-sketch since forever.

Doing as he was told, pencil-sketch pulled out his arms; there were bubbles everywhere.

"I know what happens," Padmi steepled her hands on the table. "What happens in Geneva, in Verona. All the stuff you get up to, in being an asset. I know, how Gorbind brings you here broken, battered and bruised. How I have to mend all the bits at the dining table, with the first aid kit. With all the stuff you do; being a..."

"...a shit," pencil-sketch pulled a tea-towel from the worktop. "You know then, where I come from, where I will go and all that happens in between. Let it be. I'll live. And I have a request."

Padmi inclined her head, to listen. That and she really didn't like the watery sheen that had drifted across his inky-blue eyes.

"Don't call me names," he stated. "Pencil-sketch. I am and always will be, Pencil-Sketch."

***

Standing in a lift, clutching matte black Thermo mug, Pencil-sketch squirmed a little.

"I do wish you wouldn't eye-ball me so much," he threw a side-ways glance at his creator. "I'm not a lamb Biryani."

She was here, at Waterloo house, headed to the sixth floor to 'use her imagination.'

"There aren't many people in your head that scare the life out of me," he said, huffing a little.

"But Dhillon Havane. He takes being a cretin to a whole new level."

She couldn't help but smile. Dhillon Havane. Now that had been an interesting few years.....

Still nursing his coffee, Pencil-Sketch watched through the glass as she sat in the boardroom, There was a blue notebook open before her, a straw-coloured wooden box of ink and her pens.

"What do I need to know?" he asked, a 'phone pressed to his ear. "About Dhillon Havane."

"Wow," Gorbind replied with an audible breath; it crackled across the line. He was still out in the ether for the time being. "Not heard that name in years. Man, he's way before my time. Way before Devan's too. But he's pertinent."

"Yeah, he feels it," Pencil-Sketch nodded as she waved. Again, she looked at him as though she was peeling him slowly. Not like a grape. As though, she was trying to get down to his bones, through his epithelium with a scalpel. Carefully, systematically.

"He's the first," replied Gorbind. "The first, son of a batchelor, make your eyes water, deck him if you're The Alpha male. An anti-hero."

"I got that bit," Pencil Sketch, slurped coffee. "Provenance, details that are relevant."

"Star Trek," Snipped Gorbind. "Long story short. He arrived with a bang. There was torture, mud, a tin-shack and he was dragged out of it barely conscious having been beaten to an inch of his life by A Romulan Splinter Group. Twisted, misogynistic and a narcissist. His entrance, it's branded on her memory. She went in with a plan; a hypothesis test. Came out with a character who to this day, brings out the worst in people."

For a moment Pencil-Sketch, concentrated on the ink box.

"Devan wasn't even close, to what Dhillon is, was," continued Gorbind. "You, are a slightly different kettle of fish."

"How so?" he asked, inhaling the scent of brown sugar.

"You, Pencil-sketch," replied Gorbind. "Have a heart. Oh, and soul. It's tattered around the edges; but it's there. Mind your back. You meet Dhillon at your peril. Stay away, from darkened alleys and dodgy pubs."

With that, Gorbind hung up.

Something moved, through the glass.

He saw a pink post-it; being waved at him.

Scrawled across it in Imperial Purple, was a letter.

T.

***

His head throbbed. Rubbing the nape of his neck, Aldo slowly opened his eyes. He tried to breathe, as a rash of white-heat pain spread across his chest like wild fire. Catching a glance at this knuckles, he saw scuffs, scratches and a blood.

Kicking his heels, he wriggled to sit up right. His baby toes, throbbed.

The boardroom. He was laid out on the boardroom table, with no idea how he got there. Gingerly turning his head, he saw the barely -five foot splodge looking out through the window and at the floozy.

You don't go looking for trouble, Aldo. Trouble, comes looking for you.

Then it came to him. How he had got here.

***

A circle of chalk had been densely applied to a dirty yellow tiles. Noise bounced and bounded around, as a crowd bayed. Each and every one, wanting blood, sweat and a little bit of entertainment.

Aldo wrapped his left hand-his dominant hand-in bright blue fabric. The edges of a silver and brass knuckle duster were quickly, tightly tidied away. That was interesting. Of all the things to use.

"In the blue corner, the young pretender......" A mic swung from ceiling, nearly colliding with a dirty, yellow bulb that had clearly seen many, better day days. His name was declared, with a scoff and something of a sneer.

Then came his opponent. He saw the hood of a grey sweatshirt fall back. He heard boos, hisses; the herald of a panto villain.

Aldo stepped forward. He held out a hand, he was going to remember his manners. Some sportsmanship too. There was a referee somewhere.

A spitball hit a spittoon.

There was a smirk, a laugh from the former fighter pilot.

The two of them stripped to the waist.

Stepping back, Aldo took up his stance.

His fists curled, close to his face.

"And?!" Pencil-sketch swung his legs over the edge of the table. "You can't leave it there," he hissed, putting a hand to what felt like three broken ribs.

The splodge turned around, to blow across her tea.

All, in good, time.

***

"Here take this," Bryony handed over a steaming mug of black coffee. "You're going to be here a while. This is just a snap-shot, a bloom, She's having an idea. The Muse, is being a-"

"Thank you," Pencil-Sketch took the drink carefully in his hands as he sat back in a dark-blue armchair. "Do they all look like this? Counselling rooms. All have to fit into a pro-forma, template or schema." He looked around, the walls were pale blue, the carpet duck-egg and the windows looked out to a blue sky. Dotted around the room, were other dark-blue bits and pieces; albeit fuzzy for now.

"Just the ones in her head," replied Bryony. She too had a drink; tea, and even a biscuit. A ginger-nut. It was perfectly, congruently incongruent.

"This going to be thing?" he asked, blowing across his coffee. He could smell the two teaspoons of brown sugar. "You, me; counselling sessions. In here."

"Yes," nodded Bryony, looking straight at him. "And yes. There's such a thing as an Ethical Framework. I've done my homework, for this particular role. So no. I'm your counsellor, Pencil-Sketch, nothing more. Nothing less. That IS what I'm supposed to call you? Pencil-Sketch."

"Yep," nodded Aldo. "Pencil-Sketch. That is exactly what I want you to call me."

***

Aldo had been pacing since the crack of dawn. Pensive, didn't cover it. He'd effectively sat on her shoulder during breakfast.

With each and every cup of tea, his agitation and eagerness ratcheted up a notch. How many cups of tea did one woman need? And bread?

His mind boggled.

When that happened, hers boggled too.

Sat, in the yard, somewhere between an Art Gallery and Zombies, she was wasting his time. His nerves were stretched taut.

For days, snatches and tableaus had floated like confetti across her visuo-spatial sketchpad.

Her imagination. He'd been trying to faff with her imagination.

Hades had done a bunk, which helped. But Hades had left behind a lingering blue-print that all too annoyingly pulled at her heart strings.

She was torn. Between the pair of them.

Right now, crisp, white, lined paper was appearing every now and again. So white, it was almost luminescent. Ink too. Not that he liked Deep Magenta.

Sat on the lawn, propped up on his elbows, Aldo tried to squint.

He had a vague idea, of what he had to do. What Devan, Gorbind, and even Hades had inadvertently done.

An idea, a thought so perverse, he pulled a face.

Damn it to hell.

He'd have to seduce her. Pervade it all. Imagination, dreams; sense of being.

That got her attention. She looked up, but blew a raspberry. Straight at him.

This, was going to be harder than he thought. Collapsing backward, Aldo lowered his sunglasses and spread out like a beached star fish.

Would Gorbind Cheat?

Slicing mushrooms, Hades glanced over his shoulder. "You're vibrating," he couldn't help but arch his brows as Aldo paced up and down Gorbind's kitchen. "What is it, you're going to wear a hole in the flooring and my patience." He returned to the mushrooms, scooping them up in both his palms to drop them into a pan.

"The whole gorbind gets propositioned, does the walk of shame in the morning, thing," Aldo stopped pacing to flump into a chair. "Did he, didn't he, his fan club will kill him, if we don't..."

Hades flew across the kitchen to slam closed the kitchen door. Padmi was upstairs with Mango.

"Sit with it," replied Hades, lord of the underworld, sliding back to the stove. "She is. Until she inks it. We're okay."

"And then...?" Aldo sat forwards, his hands steepled across his knees.

Hades shrugged.

So did she.

***

Hades rubbed his eye with the heel of his left hand. He was swaying side to side, with a pale blue bundle attached to his shoulder. Looking through the kitchen window, Hades watched Gorbind pace up and down the lawn as dawn broke over Birmingham.

Rain, was coming down in sheets. Making this scene altogether more surreal. Gorbind, in his pyjamas, was getting soaked.

"Is he still out there?" Devan appeared close by, and faffed around to warm a bottle. He did it with his eyes closed. "He won't do it. He's a good boy."

"So were you," stated Hades, the bundle had started to mewl. "Look what happened."

"True," Devan conceded, sighing a little. "So he could. Cheat."

"He could, indeed," Hades cradled the infant. "What's that look on his face?" He handed over the child as Devan waggled a bottle.

"He's figuring out the mechanics," replied Devan, pulling faces at the child. "And so is she. Damn you, counselling book. Again."

Hades half-smirked. "Yeah, don't tell Eros," he commented. "Cited all the way through. Keeps him flipping employed."

Rolling his eyes, Hades scattered Parmesan into his risotto.

"Excuse me, for being a little pissed," Devan Coultrie, stood by the fridge with his feet shoulder-width apart, grasped the neck of a bottle of wine to pull out a cork.

There was a wonderfully squeak pop as Aldo held out two glasses.

"When I became a shit, there was a four-man focus group," continued Devan, pouring Chianti. "There was pacing, tossing and turning. Gorbind does it, doesn't do it, and nothing." He thumped the bottle down onto the table. Padmi's dinner service-from her wedding trousseau-bounced and vibrated. "I'm angry."

"Why are we doing this here?" whispered Aldo, his eyes darted to the closed kitchen door.

"What's wrong with..."

"I have kids," replied Devan, sitting down at the table. "You don't exist yet."

"I'd have to kill you," replied Hades. "Lord of the underworld, says so on the tin. Currently in a good mood....ish."

"And we couldn't go to the Gunmakers?" offered Aldo, sipping wine and scooping up risotto.

Devan and Aldo both looked at Hades.

Why was he here, and always?

***

"This one of those 'Yes, dear, No dear' moments, isn't it?" Gorbind turned down the hob as he watched Padmi empty the freezer. At her feet, was a black bucket that she had half filled with ice.

"The sort where I stand here, and go with it." He arched a brow to check that his Aloo Gobi was cooked through. Grimacing, he tossed in a handful of coriander. Stirring, he switched off the stove.

Then the back door flung open. Gorbind dropped his spatula.

Hades, Lord of the Underword ran in. His feed slid across the tiles. There was squeaking as he came to a full stop. Dressed in Claret and Blue silken pjyamas, Hades was wild-eyed and bed-raggled.

"Injury!" He yelled, "Knitting related Injury. Who knew that socks, could be so dangerous."

Padmi slammed a drawer shut, then the freezer having moved the bucket. She slid it forwards across the floor, until she stood toe-to-toe with Hades.

Gorbind pursed his lips. His heart was racing.

"She'll have to play now," screeched Hades. "How hard, is it, to fill her pen, open my book, and..."

Hoiking up the bucket, Padmi poured the contents over Hades. He was over six foot tall. By half an inch.

Padmi didn't flinch. She was all very poker-faced.

"Oh, wow..."Gorbind started to laugh."Bucket of cold...."

"Tie a knot in it, Hades," Padmi plonked the bucket onto Hades' head. "Or put a sock in it, Do it with bells on. But take Mango with you. I need Gorbind for a bit."

Gorbind's feet barely touched the floor as he was dragged across the kitchen.

"Yes, dear, no dear," Gorbind was beside himself laughing. "If I have to be someone's fantasy...."

***

"I don't mind being Mr.Vanilla," Gorbind slurped his tea, before dunking a digestive into his mug. "I have room to grow."

"Mad, bad, dangerous to know," nodded Hades, slugging banana milk shake. "Whilst being a complete mystery and therein a fabrication."

"What does that make me?" Asked Devan, dropping sugar into a tall mug of black coffee

"A squirrel," replied Gorbind. "You're the fricking squirrel."

Mechanics

"I'm not going mad, am I?" Devan tutted, before shaking his head. He ran his fingers through his hair before putting his hands on his hips. "That would be slightly crazy? Not to mention a bit of a palaver."

He was standing right in front of t.v., buffering the sound of Zombies running amok in the centre of Post-Apocalyptic Birmingham.

"Two seconds," Padmi was also stood in the middle of her living room. She and Aditi were poring over the dog-eared pages of a Harlequin/Mills and boons.

"Rotate..." muttered Aditi, following Padmi's finger as it travelled underneath the words. "Plane A, needs to be equi-distant...."

"Right, one lamb biryani, three portions of yellow dhal and a bottle of Jack-" Gorbind walked in carrying their dinner in a plastic bag.

Only Padmi had snatched her gaze straight at him. She looked at him as though he was the formula for nuclear fusion and there was a variable out of place.

Aditi, had walked past the coffee table and shoved Devan to stand next to Gorbind.

Padmi and Aditi looked at their respective spouses. Still they studied the book. Brows were furrowed, they twittered quietly.

"What did you do?" He asked throwing the blue bag of food into Devan's arms. "And why do I suddenly feel like a very expensive, will bruise in the morning, Lobster dinner?"

"Page 235," Devan hastily cleared his throat.

"It's biology, chemistry and a fair bit of physics," commented Padmi. She smirked, giggled and then held out Page 235 for Gorbind to scan.

"Twist, place...plane C will invert-"Gorbind grabbed the book shut.

He shook his head, to land it into Devan's arms on top of the take-away

"Crazy, but worth the bruises," he looked sideway at his wife.

She quickly scarpered, followed by Aditi.

"Just lie back and think of Ikea."

Hades Harem

"Of all the places to sit and sulk, Hades," standing on his lawn, Gorbind looked at his roof. He'd heard a clunk, as had Padmi.

She'd sent him out to look.

There, under a fizzing grey cloud, next to the Television aerial and chimney stack, sat Hades.

In his claret and blue, silken pjyamas.

"Whatsis problem?" Devan swayed side to side as he tried to soothe Junior A. Junior A was currently teething and slung over his shoulder whilst milk drunk.

"He's fashionable," sighed Gorbind. "Everyone but her, is writing a Hades story. Romance, sci-fi, fantasy , reverse-forward harem, yada yada. Only she doesn't do band-wagons. She's not best pleased either."

"Reverse harem?" Posed Devan.

Gorbind shrugged. "I have a challenge having a proper one," he laughed quietly. "What would I do with a reverse one? Get down here, before you fall off. You'll make a mess of the lawn."

"Your fan club. Think of the fan club," snickered Devan. "Hades Harem!"

Hades flipped them both the bird.

***

"Here, take that," sitting down onto a mulberry-coloured sofa, Gorbind handed Hades and Devan artisanal IPA's. The ice-cold bottles had been languishing in the fridge since Christmas. He'd tried one, and nearly puked. Right now, Gorbind had pinched Padmi's bottle of merlot.

She'd hidden it behind the mung beans, thinking he'd not look.

"This feels weird," Devan took his bottle as the three of them watched a television.

"That, is an understatement," Hades blew across the mouth of the bottle before taking a slug.

"Assume the brace position," sighed Gorbind. "Slug at will."

"Why?" Asked Devan, his mouth was full.

Hades picked up the remote, the image zoomed in. "She's reading. Romance...."

"Oh," Devan almost choked, as he laughed. "Eye-roll."

"DRINK!"

***

Somewhere, in a galaxy far, far away, Hades, Lord of the Underworld, is trying to adjust his set.

He'll need to get the angle right to watch Final Score. Those claret and blue pyjamas hang over the back of his stony throne.

If he had breath, he'd hold it.

Hell hath no fury, like a Villa Fan and on the last day of the season.

(All comes down to goal difference. Apparently)

Talk to me

"HADES, get your backside here."

A flattened out Birmingham accent pinged across the sky.

"Ah, boll-poop, Stay there," Hades plonked Mango into the swing-set in Gorbind's Garden. "Don't move, and don't talk to the crows. They're all stoned. I'll be back in a jiffy. Think of a new Colour."

Clicking his fingers, Hades disappeared across space and time.

He landed, on the steps of The RSC in Stratford. Scrambling up the stairs, he turned left and walked towards Door 6.

Hades, Lord of the underworld, entered stage left. He had a feeling he was about to encounter a bear. On the apron stage, was a table with two chairs. Sat in the middle was a pot of tea. But only one cup.

She sat the other side of the table, and watched him move.

Hades, took a deep breath.

"What's a boy to do?" he asked, sitting down and tying his gown. "Two years. Two flipping years, of being sat on your desk. Trapped within your cursive handwriting. I've watched Devan rise and fall; watched you plot, plan universes and then, stall. I've listened to Gorbind go all misty-eyed; he started out as bit-part character.."

I could take you off my desk. You, your notebook, stick you in a bin and burn you.

"You wouldn't dare," Hades blanched, his bottom lip started to tremble. "All that deep magenta ink."

Then get a grip. You're not doing yourself any favours. Padmi's right. You're a fantasy.

Rolling his eyes, Hades scoffed to cross his arms.

You've sat there, because I believe in you. I believe in your ability to mean something. If you've learned anything, you'll know that I hang onto that. If you mean something, you're worth holding onto.

If I believe in you. You'd do well, to believe in me.

Chewing the inside of his cheek, he watched her stand up. She drained the cup of tea, and picked up the tea pot.

Get back to the garden, Hades. Enjoy, this lull.

All that cursive; Sweetie, that's potential. You'll actualise it.

But on my terms. Without an ice-bucket.

The table disappeared. She walked down the length of the apron stage and into the darkness.

Clash

"Noooooo......"Hades pursed his lips, his brows had risen full mast.

Gorbind mirrored the expression, only he was about to take a sip of tea.

"Jeez, mother of...." Rolling his eyes, Devan swore before skulking off screen. "Wake me when it comes back."

Pencil Sketch laughed quietly, whilst shaking his head. "This is like watching England take penalties...."

"She pressed fecking delete," commented Gorbind. "She wiped the damned thing."

They were all stood around Hades, at a laptop, in Gorbind's kitchen. They had watched the page fill, the words scatter across the page in a haze of sky blue. With a collective gasp, they had been holding their breath. They'd only come by to see how the notes books were doing. There had been a message from Hades, to meet at Gorbinds, as he tried to channel her muse using a laptop and some dream serum that he had filched from Hermes. All of them were huddled around the screen.

"Why were you....Armour, chain mail," Gorbind elbowed Hades. "Four Horsemen of the apocalypse. I looked like Galahad. "

"Damned if I bloody well know...."Hades stood, rolling his shoulders. He needed more tea. "She doesn't type. She never has. She'll ink it. Then we'll know."

"Blue-eyed floozy," Aldo laughed as he also shrugged. "It's now stuck in my head; stuck on the visuo-spatial sketchpad, like a flipping post-it. Knitting with one needle...."he frowned as the lyrics danced around in his imagination. "Someone, is going slightly mad."

"She will too,"nodded Gorbind. "Ink it. Let Midsummer's Night pass."

Hades, Gorbind and Aldo looked at one another in turn.

"Avoid the donkey," sighed Gorbind, slurping his tea. "And that flaming Wall."

"Layla," Hades stirred tea, to nod at Aldo. "And falling in love with someone you shouldn't. You just wait, till you have a playlist. You dream in orchestral movements punctuated by guitar riffs."

Gorbind smirked. His playlist was actually very straight forward. He had this horrible feeling, they'd back in his kitchen, and it would eventually make sense.

***

Aldo lowered a shiny black zipper and peered into a suit-carrier. If Gorbind's get up was anything to go by....

"Stop looking at me as though I was steak," Gorbind wasn't best pleased as Padmi looked up him and down. "This isn't as cute to wear as you might think." He stuck out his bottom lip, to tug down an oatmeal coloured tunic that peaked out below a chain-mail. "You can hang that Galahad fantasy, and with bells on."

"Ssh," Devan elbow Gorbind as they both stood at Hades shoulders. "She's trying to sort this out, in her head at least. Let Padmi perv for three seconds. Might press delete yet." They were still watching her dream, watching it all coalesce.

Hades was also in full armour, his helmet sat next to a toast rack. He was back at the laptop. He could feel it, all swirl around in the mists and murk of time. Something was about to kick off.

"Let her perv," Hades followed the words, the scratching out, the loopiness and ink. "Insert something clever here about equality and objectification...."

"Uh-oh," whispered Devan, stepping away from Hades, the laptop. His heart had skipped several beats.

Hades rose, snatched up his helmet. His spurs sparked lilac across the floor.

Rolling his eyes, Gorbind followed, Devan too.

Aldo sauntered, as they all passed Padmi. He paused though; suit carrier draped over his arm. To glance over his shoulder.

"Go on," he said, wearing a barely concealed grin. "Someone has to say it. If only for the sake of tradition."

Padmi took a deep breath.

(Oh, balls)

***

Hades was right. It would eventually coalesce.

"Any idea what this is about?" Aldo removed a key from the lock as he was followed in by Devan.

Padmi had given each of the boys a key. At least then, she didn't have to worry about the door coming off it's hinges. Even though Hades had one, he didn't use it very much. He sort of just appeared in a purple flash, in the blink of an eye, and usually with a click of his fingers. He was also occasionally babysit, so the key was there to remind him of the human condition.

"None whatsoever," Yawned Devan, all very bleary eyed.

The two of them traipsed down the hall way and into Gorbind's kitchen. There, they found Hades.

Sat at a laptop, Hades wore a look of concentration. Either side of him, there were two suit carriers draped over kitchen chairs. Each one was labelled. One for Aldo, there was another Devan.

"Get dressed," Hades spoke, but without looking away from the screen. "Then get into the Mustang. Devan, I need you up front." He put his hand to a leather-bound tome, to slide it across the table. "You'll need that," he half-turned to look at Devan. "Where we're going, the whole satellite navigation thing won't work. It'll be a chocolate teapot."

"Where we going?" asked Aldo, as Devan picked up the tome with both hands.

"To Hell and back," Hades returned his gaze to the laptop. "But first, get dressed."

"This has to be on Hades' more…erm, interesting ideas," Padmi's voice carried from the hall way and into the kitchen. There was the metallic clunking to be heard as well. "You look all very brave, Gorbind."

Gorbind Galahad appeared in the kitchen. Boots, chain mail, a helmet too.

Aldo and Devan watched as Gorbind sat. His helmet was removed, to be plonked to the one that Hades wore from time to time.

"We're needed," said Gorbind, gesticulating at the suit carriers. He did however, glare at his wife as she looked him up and down. There was nothing so disarming, as being mentally undressed by your own spouse. Being eyeballed was always bad enough. Padmi seemed to do with it uncharacteristic lewdness and it made him feel rather uncomfortable.

"Upstairs is free," Padmi told Devan and Aldo. "If you want to get dressed too."

"We have no time," huffed Hades, getting to his feet.

Devan edged forwards to read the screen. Words would appear, the cursor flash, before the words were deleted. This happened a few times in the space of a whole minute.

"Uhoh," Devan had a weird feeling of déjà vu. As though he had said that before.

With a flourish, Hades clicked his fingers. Devan and Aldo were kitted up in the blink of an eye.

"Let's go," said Hades, gathering his helmet and making for the door. Gorbind followed, Devan too.

Aldo made up the rear. He stopped in the hallway, as Padmi put her hand to his elbow.

"Come back," she said softly. "All of you, Aldo. Together, and in each in one piece. You're a band of brothers; you'll have to look after one another."

"We will," nodded Aldo, before kissing her cheek to check. "Musketeers of the Modern day. Hades has his reasons, for asking us along. He wouldn't want us to get hurt, but I guess he need a hand for once. Who'd thought it," he said heading to the door. Aldo glanced over his shoulder.

"A God, and in need of human help."

A few moments later, Aldo pulled the right passenger door closed. Gorbind did the same on the left. Both had to use two hands to pile into the big, beefed up, black Mustang.

"Right, let's do this," Hades turned the keys in the ignition, curled his hands around the wheel.

Devan blew his cheeks out to open the massive great big leather-bound tome that Hades had entrusted him with. Some kind of celestial, all very divine A-Z that now sat across his lap.

Aldo hung onto his seat. As did Gorbind.

"She can't write this in one sitting," said Hades, sliding the gear stick and taking off the handbrake. "Brace."

Off went the mustang, rubber burned and tarmac melted.

That blue pen.

Ran out of damned ink....

***

He'd drove days, through several nights. Hades had put his foot down in leaving Acacia Avenue, in literally being hell-bent to get where he wanted. The Mustang had roared across continents, through a couple of rather interesting dimensions too. In the back, Aldo and Gorbind had slept through that last bit. Up front, Hades had been compelled to briefly smack his co-driver around the head. A smack, that was the imparting of divine insight, so as to be his navigator.

Devan had been literally cast askew in his seat, but a left-hook that he really didn't see coming. Aldo and Gorbind had lurched forwards, only to be shoved backwards without a second glance.

"You'll probably have a really bad headache after," he had said, returning to the wheel. "But it will pass. On the way back, let Gorbind take the wheel." He flicked a finger backwards, to make Gorbind rub his eyes and act as though he was stoned for a good hour or so.

Hades couldn't look at Devan after. He knew what the fates would demand from him, having temporarily dosed the hooch baron with divinity. Gorbind, was on another account together; Hades wasn't so worried about him. The least that could happen on this sojourn, is that there'd be a coupe of broken bones. If Hades knew Gorbind half as well as he thought, the copper would have a fix already on the speed dial.

Devan had spoken in tongues at time. His otherwise muddy brown eyes had gleamed and glowed pink and yellow as delivered directions. On his lap was the leather-bound tome, handed to him in the kitchen. That was the Helios Almanac, a sort of celestial A-Z that would show Hades were to go.

As it were.

This was a journey to hell of a different kind. One thing was for certain. The Lord of the Underworld was never boring. Not if he could help it, anyway.

Eventually, the Mustang roared across an ochre-coloured plain that was pinned in place by a lilac-coloured sky. The engine's thunderous drone quelled as the vehicle came to a stop. Hades pulled up the handbrake. Pulling the toggle under the dash, he opened the boot. He then turned around to fae all the boys.

For now, whatever would unfold. They were his boys.

"You three stay here," his eyes flickered, far more than normal. The lilac was deeper, more incandescent. "You won't be here alone, for long. When that happens, fight, Gentlemen. Fight, for your life; for mine. For every thing that you hold dear. The world as you might know it, depends on that; depends, on you. Once you're done with that, wait for me. Whatever you do, don't come looking for me."

With that, Hades slid out of the car. The driver's door thumped closed behind him. He snapped his fingers to temporarily cage the boys.

In the boot, he found his helmet and his pronged weapon. Forged by divinity, it made the air hum with the sound of the universe. Hades ran a finger down a tine, to smile as he levelled the vibration. A reminder of how it wasn't as innocent as it looked. In the right hands, it could be used to devastating effect.

Sliding on his helmet, Hades held on the bi-dent with a firm grip. He stepped away from the car, clicked his fingers to unlock the vehicle. The boys all poured out. In the blink of an eye, amongst the protests, Hades was gone.

What happened next, between God and Malevolence, was all too much for ink, pen and paper. All too much to be fully understood and therein relayed by a mere more mortal.

But first, the mortals had to experience it.

***

A wave of pain jolted Gorbind awake. He opened his mouth to breath, to get some air into his hot, dry and pained lungs. Only to choke and feel grit daubed across his lips. He was lying face down in dirt, and it was every-where. In all his nooks, crevices and crannies. Gorbind felt the grains grate with a coarseness against his skin as he gathered up his limbs. Each and every bit of him hurt; his muscles roared as he bundled himself to his feet.

Gorbind staggered to get upright. Shuffling on his feet, he moved all very awkwardly. He rubbed his eyes; not a clever thing to do when wearing a grimy, hot, leather gauntlet. Opening and closing his eyes a few times, he tried to focus. His eyes, like the rest of him, hurt. Being dry didn't help things either, as everything was a bit blurry. Squinting, he surveyed ochre tundra that seemed go on for miles without end.

Overhead, the sky was gun-metal grey. He shook his head, trying to take it all in. His heart raced, with his mind well and truly boggled. This wasn't earth. Or at least, not how he knew it. He continued to look around; spinning on the spot. Boulders, rocks; that was all that littered the land. Behind him, a craggy rock face loomed across the horizon. The surface of it, was scorched, with clearly visible burn marks.

"DEVAN!" He yelled out, as much as he could. His throat ached in throwing the name out into the air. Gorbind had no idea of how or why had ended up face down in the dirt. "ALDO!" he tried to yell louder, as he fell to his knees. Fear, crept over him to make his skin feel cold.

"Where are you?" he asked himself, his head in his hands. "Where the bloody hell, Hades, to have damned us to die here. You really did drive us to hell."

"GOR-BIND!"

That got his attention.

His head snapped up, as once more Gorbind scrambled to his feet. Shuffling towards him were two figures, hanging onto one another. Slowly, they crept towards him. Gorbind broke into a sprint to meet them.

Aldo was upright, but he propped up Devan against his shoulders. Devan's one foot was being dragged in the dirt, the other was raised to ankle height.

"I'm not dead yet," grumbled the Montana Hooch Baron. "I think I broke my leg. Again."

"Hades?" Asked Gorbind, taking up the other side of Devan.

Aldo nodded toward the rock face, and at what looked like the open mouth of a cave. "Dancing with another Devil," he replied. "Hades drew him away, having watched us be knocked clean onto our asses. He was in some sort of divine or devilish chokehold. Said to hold back, to wait for him."

"Like a bunch of daisies?" scoffed Gorbind. "That fella is bananas."

"Didn't think so," grinned Aldo.

"The damned devil broken my bloody leg," groaned Devan. "I want to beat him with it."

The three brothers-in-arms walked slowly toward the cave.

***

And when Devan, Aldo and Gorbind shuffled into the cave, it was all a bit blurry around the edges. Except for Devan, who was dumped to bear witness, onto a rockpile.

He saw everything. He was supposed to. Hades had made sure of that. He yelled to Aldo and Gorbind, to fall in with Hades. The two of them clambered to stand either side of him.

Shoulder to shoulder. As they set to wrangle with a darkness.

A darkness with minions, at that point. Aldo and Gorbind had to make up the numbers. Cyclones of energy with toe to toe with both of them. Unable to move, Devan sat on his perch, pinned into place.

No part of him understood why he had to watch; other than having a damaged limb. As much as he liked Hades, Devan couldn't think why Hades would have trusted him first have divine sight, or to sit there and watch.

"Gorbind!" yelled Devan, watching him be picked up by a cyclone before being dumped to the floor with a crash.

Landing in a heap, Gorbind was soon on his feet, albeit shaking his head and holding onto this helmet. He went straight back into the melee.

The two cyclones merged. Aldo and Gorbind banded together. Together, they were stronger. Together, they could give Hades a fighting chance.

Devan saw every fist fly, every blow land. He saw Gorbind hurl a mace at a swirling, spectral mass of black and blue. Aldo, was throwing balls of fury to give some form of cover.

Then time felt as though it had slid to a slow stop. As though treacle, the fabric of space and time became dense and overwhelming. Even his breath, felt as though it was trapped inside his chest, and unable to get out.

This was no ordinary dimension.

For Gods, mortals and all those in between, there was a stand off beyond both language and comprehension.

Devan felt his skin tingle; his blood was running cold and crystalline. He watched still as Aldo and Gorbind knocked to the ground with heavy, unmeasurable clouts. Both were dazed, confused; mortally disorientated with the faculties jangled.

Hades stood ten feet in the air, nestled in a swirling mass of black-blue, grey plumes. Sparks flew from his fingers, his bi-dent glowed.

The air in the cave turned electric. A God, glowered into the eyes of an abyss.

***

Somewhere in the ether, the three sisters of fate held their breath. A wheel sat in silence, measurement paused. The two steely blades of destiny paused in their cruel, karmic pre-disposition.

They wouldn't. They couldn't, honestly?

***

Surely not, this was all too much. Devan wanted to breath, for this all to over. He clutched his chest, for he didn't like what he saw.

***

They couldn't do that, and to one of their own.

That would be sacrilege. Complete and utter sacrilege.

***

A flash of blinding light had Devan thrown back. He'd managed to shield his eyes with a grimy palm. It would feel like eons, before he rubbed his eyes, caught his breath and tried to focus. As the smoke cleared, his eyes adjusted. He held his breath.

He scrambled to sit; his heart in his mouth. Devan saw Gorbind and Aldo scoop up a battered, broken-looking hades into their arms.

All of them heard the mass of malevolence vibrate and implode into a noisy fireball. A fireball that caused the stony walls to rumble and shake. The whole place was ready to cave in.

"We've got to get out!" Devan had crawled towards them, on his hands and knees. He had to do the same to leave the cave.

Hades was dropped in the boot; his helmet and bi-dent thrown in after him.

"He can sleep tight for a bit," commented Gorbind, slamming the boot down.

"Is he dead?" Devan had hopped into front passengers' seat. "He's Hades, he can't just die."

"You'll need a splint," Gorbind dodged the question, to pick up bits of dead tree that littered the area around the car. He and Aldo did their best to reset Devan's limb.

"You'll have to drive," said Devan. "I have a horrible head ache. Hades said to let you take the wheel."

Gorbind did just that. Rolling his eyes at how far back Hades had his seat, he turned the keys in the ignition. Home. With a God in the boot.

You couldn't make this up. Not really, and in a million years.

***

"PAD-MI!!"

He didn't often yell her name. But Gorbind had no choice.

He, Aldo, had shoulder-barged their way into the kitchen as lightning cracked across the skies of Birmingham. Thunder rolled. Black clouds swirled with menace.

They both cleared the table, in a frantic hurry to dump almost lifeless Hades, with a splat, across the surface.

A toast rack bounced off the floor.

Upstairs, a door clunked. Padmi thundered down the stairs.

"Oi, wait up," Devan hopped in, a make-shift splint plopped as he moved.

"DON'T YOU YELL MY-"Padmi threw open the kitchen door, ready to brain Gorbind.

"Get the 'phone," Gorbind pressed an ear to Hades chest. "Not that you have a beating heart..."

"How do you call nine nine nine for God?" Padmi scrambled to get the 'phone. They still had a land-line. "Can't take him to A&E..."

"Press seven," said Gorbind, checking the God's eyes. "That would be the Necromancer in Small heath."

"We have a necromancer on speed dial?" Padmi shook her head, but threw the phone at Gorbind. She flew off to find a first aid kit, for all the good might do.

"Aldo, call the hag in Digbeth," Gorbind held the phone to his ear. "She's the one with the uber magic and not a testosterone-fuelled megalomaniac."

"Sir," Going into Asset mode, Aldo also put the kettle on. Then there was locating the biscuit barrel.

All the while, Devan watched; more than a little helpless.

"I have a job for you, Mr.Morbid," said Gorbind. "How d'you fancy raising hell?"

***

"You can't let a God die..." Padmi hissed as Gorbind paced in the hall. "Your Nani would never forgive you. History, wouldn't forgive you. Cannons of Myth, would go kerboom. And stop pacing."

She lurched forward to pull him back by his shoulders.

"Thunder and lightning?" She asked. "This is neither Macbeth or The Tempest."

"Fiction, nonetheless," grumbled Gorbind, breaking loose to head back into the kitchen.

***

Hades rapped gently on the kitchen door, before sliding his head around. Not hanging about for consent, he sloped in to edge towards the kettle.

Sat at the table, Padmi was hunched over a glass of bourbon. Two hours ago, he'd be lain across that same table, lost in the fabric of space and time. Only for the hag, and Necromancer to pull him back. The pair of them had been thrown across the kitchen the minute he'd opened his eyes.

(They'd also fixed Devan's leg so Aditi would never know. Her or his fan club.)

Hades, drew water and filled the kettle. Grabbing two mugs, he put tea bags in both.

Then as he turned, Hades found himself pinned against the worktop.

"You put Gorbind through Hell," Padmi stamped on his feet, kicked his shins and then punched him in the stomach. "Literally. Me too. Who do you think you are?"

Blows rained. Everywhere.

As he doubled over, Padmi landed a right-hook across his jaw.

"You do that again, and I swear," gasped Padmi. "I'll chop you to pieces, sink you ten feet under and feed you to your own Kraken."

He believed her. Straightening up, he curled his fingers around Padmi's wrists.

She'd only end up hurting herself. As Padmi fixed him a with a glare gilded with impassioned fury, he saw it.

Hades saw that very thing that made him a God. The very thing, that all mere mortal men believed they could harness to quell the female of the species.

In the blink of an eye, he saw divinity made woman. He let go of her arms immediately.

Then he heard his name. The jangle of bracelets.

And two very choice expletives.

In Punjabi.

The sound and more importantly the weight of footsteps-those footsteps-filled his otherwise perfectly, purple soul, with dread.

There wasn't much, in heaven or hell, Horatio, that did that to Hades, Lord of the Underworld.

Gorbind's grandmother swept into the kitchen and towards him. Straight towards him, with the precision of a nuclear war-ahead.

Ordinarily, she was lovely. Hades and Nani had somewhat adopted one another.

(How he managed to deliver pitch-perfect Punjabi was best left unsaid.)

Padmi reverently, stepped aside. As though she knew exactly what was about to happen. Then there was the smirk.

"Ah, edour," nani beckoned.

Hades obeyed. His feet, moved of their own accord.

"Kabardar, tu edha pher kita," Nani half turned, before raising her and cuffing Hades around the back of the head. It was a full-scale thwack, that only a Matriarch could land. "Mar ke ayah, you-should-know-better-because-you're-God-akhal hai nai."

"Pattah nai, mundah kitoh ayah...." and off swooshed Nani to the living room. "Phirvee sada hega."

"Well, that told me," said Hades, wincing as he rubbed the back of his head.

"Moral of the story?" Padmi poured hot water into the two mugs.

"Don't piss off women," grumbled Hades. "Especially Punjabi ones."

He howled as a hot, soggy, scalding tea bag smacked across his nose.

I'm leaving you

Padmi stood at the bottom of the stairs. There was a mug of tea in one hand, a jammie dodger ready to dunk in the other.

On the last step, were a pair of deep mahogany-coloured Chelsea boots.

Hearing foot fall on the stairs, she looked up. She saw his feet first. Today, was a yellow polka dots on pink day.

Dressed in a dark-blue, three-piece suit, Gorbind ambled down the stairs as he fiddled with his cuffs. He stood in the middle, avoiding eye-contact. Having spent nearly a week in state of incapacitation, he was match fit. Showered, shaved; Gorbind smelt a bit like the top of Mont Blanc.

"Where are you going?" She asked, biscuit poised. "Dressed like that. You look as though you're about to take The Road to Wembley."

Stepping down, he sat on the last step. Gorbind started to put on his boots.

"This is it; this how it ends?" Padmi sat down beside him. "You're leaving?" She asked, dropping her biscuit to the floor.

"For now," replied Gorbind. "I have to go; there's no room. Devan, is done and dusted. Hades, is waiting in the wings. Aurelia, postponed. You and I, have Pencil-sketch to play with. My other story, gathers dust. Every player, has their part."

"When will you be back?" Padmi, gulped and bit her lip. A single tear edged down the bridge of her nose.

"To walk Mango down the aisle," he replied, all very quickly. "To sit at the dining table, when I bring you Pencil-Sketch." Gorbind got to his feet. "When Hades and I meet, for what feels like the first time. I'll be back for my birthday. I'll never miss that."

Only for Padmi to pull at his hand.

"I can't stop you, but that doesn't mean I won't try," she sniffed and wiped away tears fell freely.

"Come back, and in one piece. If it's several, I will never forgive you."

He gave her fingers a gentle squeeze and made for the door.

Out Gorbind went, to the Fragments universe.

He didn't look back.

With Mango asleep, Padmi sat on her daughter's swing set with her head in her hands. Halfway down a rather pricey bottle of Merlot, she'd been crying for hours.

The bottle, a stained empty glass were close by.

She'd found it, on the kitchen table nestled inside a bouquet of white roses. There had been a post-it too.

"Walk through the storm."

He'd also left behind his wedding ring.

This was all Gorbind's fault. He'd done this before, years ago. The pain was the same. For Mr.Vanilla, he knew exactly how to tear her heart and soul apart.

To leave his wedding ring behind.

Muppet.

"Oh fer the love of all things pink and fluffy..."

Snorting, Padmi looked left and a pair of knobbly knees.

"This hurts," grimaced Hades, standing next to swing. He was dressed in full armour and clutching his chest. It was all very dramatic; something of a tragedy.

"Pfft," Padmi threw her hands in the air. "And what the bloody hell is YOUR problem?" She wiped a hand across a a stream of bogeys and grabbed the bottle by the neck.

"Oi, that won't help," Hades took the bottle, to hold it aloft. "Heart burn, thanks for asking," he added, pressing the rim to his lips to glug. "It's a metaphor, what with you being in pieces. Aphrodite is a bit pissed, Eros in a sulk. All demanding an explanation. I got sent down here, up here, to see what happened. Divine intervention, of a sort." He shrugged to drink more merlot.

"I liked you better when you were stoned, Padmi clambered to her feet, using the chain of the swing.

"Ah, there she is!"

Padmi groaned as Pencil-Sketch bounced down the lawn towards her and Hades. In his hands was a radio.

Hades winced.

"Pencil-sketch, you half-baked numpty, how are you?" The Lord of the Underworld offered his hand anyway. Apparently, this next character was here for a good reason, not yet fully formed or clear.

"Half-baked and a numpty," replied Pencil-sketch. "That's the politest from you yet."

"Yes, well, I know you're a..."Pulling a face, Hades exhaled. "You make me look pretty, what can I say. And that's saying something."

"You should dance," Pencil-sketch took Padmi by the hands, to drag her to the middle of the lawn. The radio had started to blare

"What, no, did you miss the bit where my husband walked out?" Trying to resist but failing,

Padmi was twirled around a few times. Then she found herself fox-trotting across grass.

Hades watched. Carefully and in silence for ten minutes.

"Tell her, Lord Hades," Pencil-sketch eventually poured Padmi back into the swing. "That she's here, Queen Regnant, keeping Gorbind's Kingdom safe.

That this all hurts, but will go away. He'll be back. In the meantime, we're here to be looked after. Minus a round table, and dragons."

Looking at pencil-sketch, with his foppish dark hair and vapid grin, Hades absorbed the observations. He was ill at unease with this new fella. Hades knew, knew exactly where the pencil-sketch moniker came from and why.

"What he said," Hades slugged more wine. "It's true. You know you're the real boss. We all pretend that Gorbind's the gaffer. You have his home, his hearth...and...." he thumped his aching chest. "His achey breaky heart." Hades squinted as Padmi stood up and ran to a rose bush.

The merlot was plonked with a clink onto the swing.

As Padmi puked, Hades pulled Pencil-Sketch toe to toe. Equal-footed in height, they squared up to one another rather neatly.

Hades looked Pencil-sketch in the eye. Lilac versus inky-blue.

Then he grasped pencil-sketch by the collar to raise him from the lawn.

"I'm not that stupid," stated Pencil-sketch, dangling. "I can't. She saves me. Mends me. Every time."

Releasing his grip, Hades let the man fall.

"Good," said Hades, straightening up Pencil-Sketch to dust off his shoulders. "But if you did; if the thought even blooms in that chaotic brain of yours. You'll be eating your own spleen for eternity and a day."

Back for the Birthday

Throwing his jacket over his shoulder, Gorbind trudged out of the darkness and onto the lawn. Dusk was falling across Birmingham. He smiled to see the sky over his hometown turn blush-pink. The softness, the colour, reminded him of sweet, succulent nectarines.

"DAD!"

Gorbind stopped dead; he held out his arms.

Mango ran towards him. Her long, caramel-brown hair ran loose behind her; her crowning glory, it billowed in a gentle breeze. glory, it billowed in a gentle breeze. Before long, Mango had engulfed him. She was even hoisted aloft a little from the ground, as her father made the most of the hug.

"What a welcome," declared Gorbind, hugging his daughter close. He held her tight, for what like an eternity.

His little girl. Only she wasn't so little anymore; she was a grown woman. Mango, remained however, the apple of his eye. Though his son did make for stiff competition, from time to time.

"Like clockwork. I'm so glad you came home," Mango took Gorbind by the hand, to head towards the centre of the lawn. Plastic garden furniture was arranged around a table, in a semi-circle. The table was covered with a yellow cloth and laden with food.

"Birthday tea time, Dad," beamed Mango. Scooping her hair into a pony-tail, she secured it with an elastic tie that pinged from her left wrist.

Gorbind smiled softly; his wife did the same thing. Their daughter was the spitting image of the woman that he loved and with every fibre of his being.

"Happy, Happy Birthday, Dad," Mango enveloped him in yet another hug; each one was always deeper, more meaningful than the one before. Then, she landed splodgy kisses across his face. "Dad, did you do that thing; the thing that I asked?"

"Yeah, I did," Nodding, Gorbind draped his jacket over a garden chair. "About that. Sit with me a moment."

"Oh?" Mango's expressions changed, from being delightful to anticipating despair. She pouted a little, to pull up a chair and sit.

"It's okay," he said gently, putting a hand to her shoulder as he sat. "Clean as a whistle. Not a single thing to worry about."

"Right, well," tutted Mango, "But you said sit with you, Dad. You're not that convincing, to be honest."

Laughing quietly, Gorbind grabbed a bottle of wine, by the neck, from metal bucket. It was cool to the touch, with condensation forming across the label. He poured them both a rather large drink, into plastic, fluted glasses.

"Sweetie, go kiss a few more frogs," Gorbind was shaking his head as he handed over a glass. "And there are always frogs; this world is full of frog. There are plenty of frogs floating around. This one, Mango, was so cute, I went looking for a Papal Knighthood. As your father, my solemn advice and guidance, is for you to give him the speech. It's not me, Mister Ex-Why-Zed, it is most definitely you."

Giggling into her drink, Mango shook her head and also rolled her eyes.

"Go date a doofus," continued Gorbind. "Get hurt, get an idea of how to bounce back. Mango, my darling; go take a risk." He let out a deep breath to the inhale the crisp, rather zingy wine. "As your father, it is my job to protect you; I always will, that is my job, forever and a day. Yet, you need to do things for yourself. It was pointless me doing a background check; the boy is vanilla. I know a few things about being vanilla, I assure you. You don't need me to tell you that."

"Frogs," stated Mango, sticking out her tongue as her nose wrinkled up.

"Frogs," echoed Gorbind, as his wife and son came out to join them.

Later, as the stars started to twinkle, Gorbind was back out on the lawn once more. Only now, he was dancing, with Padmi in his arms. From inside his breast pocket, his 'phone shuffled through songs that he curated for their own special playlist.

A playlist, that he had also downloaded and sent with a postcard, some chocolate too, from Geneva. A playlist, that when he was missed, was played at full volume in the car, the kitchen whilst preparing Sunday dinners and for some daft reason on the first of January to get the hung-over kids out of bed.

"You'll be gone in the morning," Padmi kissed his ear lobe. Her hands sat snuggly between his shoulder blades. "But always around for your birthday tea time."

"Come hell or high water." Gorbind had found the familiar route of kissing Padmi's ear to her jaw. He wasn't going to forget; not yet. "Wild horses couldn't keep me away. You, the kids. You're all my birthday wishes, rolled into one, to be my beautiful family."

As an instrumental version of 'She's The One' ebbed away into the moonlight, Padmi peeled away. She took Gorbind by the hand to lead him into the house, and to their room.

He knew what was coming; repeatedly, at that. There was more than one way, to make a birthday wish.

Zombie

Apocalypse

First

Instance

This was written in the days leading up to lockdown; the COVID-19 pandemic was about mess with life as we knew it. I think, this was inked about a week before. I had spent a day at a writer's retreat in Central Birmingham, having taken train in. That would be the last train I would take, before it was reserved as transport for essential workers. Two reading events had already been postponed at this point; being a writer in the time of COVID, was now a big deal. This was also the same day that the annual St.Patrick's Day parade was meant to happen.

However, that was cancelled. Birmingham had descended into something of an eerie, very sombre silence that was incredibly hard to walk through.

The world was on the cusp of something rather untoward; something, altogether unexpected. In my mind, it made sense to have Gorbind and Hades wander the city and absorb the sense of doom that was creeping closer and closer. A sense of doom and gloom that enveloped us.

In this snippet, there is uncertainty, as well as a war room. This is quite deliberate, given the rhetoric that would be espoused by politicians in particular, in the coming months.

The world had gone to war.

With a pandemic.

Pulling up his collar, Gorbind looked out across Birmingham. He placed a palm over his eyes, to dim the view a little. On the horizon, the sun was setting; as an orange-red orb, it was very much like a fried egg as sank down. As it moved, the sun looked as though it was being sucked in by the mass of buildings the formed the city skyline. Gorbind squinted to take in the view of the BT tower. It was covered in graffiti and scramble netting.

Graffiti and scramble netting.

How things had changed. The tower now stood in no man's land. A neutral zone, between the different factions. Even he wouldn't step foot in the place. At least, not alone or unarmed.

"Here drink this," Hades appeared at Gorbind's left shoulder. He held out a thermos cup, filled with chai. It was definitely chai; the scent was unmistakable as it permeated the descent of dusk.

"You made Chai?" asked Gorbind, taking the cap to blow across the surface. He inhaled the heady, spiced scent. He could feel the warmth permeate to his hands and flavour wafted deep into the darkest recesses of soul. "How the flip did you manage that?" He closed his eyes, to take a long, drawn out slurp.

"Black market," Whispered Hades, pouring a cup for himself. "There's an interesting bartering system in Small Heath. I made this, but I kept back some spices to put them into The Vault. You, me and the family: we're covered."

Hades wandered off towards his black Mustang. It was parked on the hard shoulder, of one of the many roads that formed The Gravelly Hill Interchange. For now, the whole thing was deserted.

Gorbind smiled weakly. The family; such a curious turn of phrase for Hades, Lord of the Underworld. Hades really was family. He had bonded with Mango, becoming the little girl's chief babysitter. Padmi chose to tolerate him as well.

He'd met Hades in the rain, in Needless Alley. The whole thing had been fairly surreal. He owed Hades his life and had been trying to settle the debt ever since. Hades had become his de-fact bodyguard, his trusty lieutenant but also his most loyal friend. Having the Lord of the Underworld be your wingman was well and truly other worldly. It was also rather comforting. Gorbind's relationship with divinity had become altogether curious. He finished up the capful of tea as Hades returned.

"Padmi sent these," Hades clutched at the thermos still, with one hand. In the other, was a cloth bag. "Sandwiches, parathas. Even threw in some Indian sweets."

"Sweets, really?" Gorbind almost squeaked and with sheer childlike delight. "We're in the middle of a Zombie Apocalypse and she made sweets?"

"Well, it is your birthday," sighed Hades, handing over the thermos. "She'll brain me for telling you. Padmi, nearly smacked someone trying to get caster sugar. She traded some candles, boot polish, a litre of shampoo to get the saffron. I was there," he said calmly. "I made sure that Padmi stayed standing. The while going to Hag Country, and on her lonesome, was never going to happen."

Hag Country. Gorbind bristled to look at Hades. Birmingham was split into so many factions; it had never been so divided and at war with itself. Some, were okay; he'd managed to twist a few arms and extract allegiance. Others weren't so easy to grapple with. Hag Country, was precarious. He'd heard stories about that place, that made his blood run cold.

"Who'd thought it," Hades rooted around in the cloth bag. "The would-be King of Small Heath over there, trying to expand his borders. The mad, bad and dangerous Hag of Digbeth over there. Their minions. All converging here, for a battle. Too many souls went through that day, Gorbind." He pulled out a circular bundle of waxed paper.

"The Battle of Birmingham. The Battle of Gravelly Hill Interchange," stated Gorbind, pouring more tea. "A horrible battle, involving the undead. With a necromancer, slap bang in the middle of things."

"Well, I'm standing here," grinned Hades, unwrapping the bundle. "Me, the fella from Greek Mythology. In this universe, Gorbind, anything is possible."

"Hades, the Lord of the Underworld," Gorbind let out a slow breath. "The one being, who is an eternal optimist. We should eat all of that."

The two moved to the bonnet of the Mustang. Hades set down the parcel, to also unpack the rest of the bag. Gorbind put the thermos next to it.

"There's just something about ladoos," said Hades, plonking a paper bag onto the bonnet. "Apparently, Padmi used your Nani's recipe." A stack of sandwiches followed.

Biting his lip, Gorbind unwrapped the parathas. Each one was dripping with butter. Home-made butter. He, himself, had churned it.

Churning butter. A skill, that had never been part of his training to become a Police Officer.

"You really want to be out on patrol," asked Hades, unwrapping the sandwiches from their tea-towel packaging. "You have people to do this. Scouts, scavengers and trackers. You have people in all most every camp across the city."

"Being in the tunnels, in the map room," said Gorbind, "Is okay for a while. It's all very safe. But I like coming out into the day. I want to see the city that I've sworn to protect. The city that I fight for, every day. A city, that law enforcement, made my responsibility. I could stay, Hades, in the map room and the whole damned thing could be burning to the ground. Here, standing here with you; I can see it all, breathe it all in. It is all alive, and far more real than a map in the room."

"It's all really quiet," Shaking his head, Hades selected a sandwich. The sliced bread was wonderfully rustic; coarse and crumbly between his fingertips. "Curfew in the city. The mind boggles."

"Deathly quiet," Gorbind tore a paratha in half. "Except when the scouts are out. You can hear the sirens. Sound a bit like a constipated vulture."

Hades half-choked on his sandwich.

"Mango," laughed Gorbind. "She told 'em that, and it stuck. The trackers, are drunk donkeys. We had to tell the kid something. Especially, when she had nightmares. Three weeks, Hades; Padmi and I didn't sleep a wink."

Brushing away crumbs, nodded in empathy. "I remember," he offered, quietly. "I've never been hugged so hard in my life. She told me all about it one might. Pease, Unco Hades, the Ombies are making my deams go bad. I'm scared. Pease hep daddy meks them stops."

One day, at the close of that three-week window, Hades had heard Mango call out. He could hear that little girl, all the way from the Underworld. Such was the bond between them. He'd slipped Hermes some nectar, to bounce into a dream. He'd seen the night terror in full flight. Hermes had conjured it away, relieving the terror that caused Mango such pain and misery. He'd also put Gorbind and Padmi into a divine sleep to give them some respite. Hades had sat with Mango, soothed her to sleep and made sure she was settled.

"Didn't think you'd ever get hugged," chortled Gorbind. "Least of all, by a child."

"Chief babysitter, all right!" Hades jabbed a finger into the bonnet. "And I know how to hug perfectly, thank you, and adults too."

"Really don't need to know," Gorbind was laughing now. "Genuinely, really don't. Anyway, how did your trip go, with the scouts?" He licked his gingers as he finished one half of the paratha, to munch on the second.

"Okay," replied Hades, nibbling on his sandwich. "Not bad. They gave me a tour of St.Martin's how the whole place is functioning. We missed a fight in the Rotunda, involved that woman Felicity. We heard about it though. Took a walk to the Gunmaker's. Nothing to report there, for now.

"And the library, the nerve centre?" asked Gorbind.

"Still standing," declared Hades. "You really can't miss it. It's fortified and robust."

"Good," Sighed Gorbind. He drank some tea, had more parartha. "The City of Birmingham shall stay standing. It must not fall."

A plan

forms

"Colin, Brian?" Hades pulled his sunglasses up as he walked down the corridor.

Something out of the forties, the corridor was yellow-tiled tunnel in a bunker, below the depths of Birmingham.

Two zombies looked from their teas, smiled macabrely and grunted their greetings.

"Not bad, thanks," replied Hades, returning his glasses to the bridge of his nose. "She did have this on her list. See you at half-time, eh?"

Turning on his heel, he pushed open a claret door to enter a map room.

A map room.

In the middle of the room, was an aerial view of Birmingham. Littered with little boats, it really did have more canals than Venice.

Stood in the middle was Gorbind. He surveyed the Fragments universe. Each and every bit of it.

Dressed in a long, dark blue, woollen coat, he looked commanding. Even down to the epaulettes on his shoulders.

Hades saw movement below the table.

"Devan?" He asked, tilting his head to side. "Who you hiding from exactly; Aditi or the accountant?"

"Mama F," Devan's head, sans long locks poked out of darkness. "Didn't give my sister any rakhi day money. Long story, lots of little ones; a three-part saga."

He promptly disappeared.

"Colin and Brian?" Hades sidled up to Gorbind. "Those two rocked up? You couldn't get Anna, she's pretty crafty for a Zombie. When her brains go ka-boom, it's a piece of art. I'll find her. You need Anna."

"Call her," Gorbind threw another boat onto the map. This one was covered in stars and stripes.

Hades grinned and walked off to find a telephone. A red one, rotary dial and cord too.

"Anna? Hi, Hades, Lord of the Underworld. Sweetie, how do you feel about Birmingham? No, not Alabama..."

Waiting in the Wings

Sipping from a red travel mug, Hades ambled across a courtyard. Around the outer edges, were portacabins. These were neatly arranged in a horseshoe to cope with the demands of the set. Two of the portacabins functioned as hair and make-up. The last few days had seen an in-flux of supporting artists, all hoping to be part of the big scenes. Hades tapped on the door but carried on regardless; he closed the door with his shoulder.

All the while, he didn't look up from a sheaf of paper. A script covered in inky annotations to clarify bits of the screen play. There was a set of scribbling from the director-one roped in at the last minute to get production of the ground. That and something about wanting to save his soul as he was worried about paying the ferryman. The previous director had been something of a megalomaniac with more than just a diva-like artistic temperament. Who in their right mind, would give Hades stage directions, to flounce?

The second set of jottings were from the author. Scribbles in deep magenta that looped the loop in all the right places. Hades had come by to share them with one of the characters in this *Behind the Scenes* production. The character in question played a not-so-small part in the Zombie Apocalypse section.

The artist playing the character, had been asked to participate at the pleasure of the author. As such, Hades took his own personal pleasure in delivering the notes to someone who he rather had a soft spot for. He wanted to come by himself, as this related to his own story, his own development as a character. He was only too aware of how the deep magenta impacted upon his own sense of being, the kink and the curl. He did, however, wish that scarlet was used from time to time. He cared less for deep magenta, than he did for the colour of blood; he knew that at Oxblood Ink was available for the author. Oxblood was all to sinister for him and his sense of being. That particular shade of ink was best left for The Lady Aurelia.

"Ah, Hades!!!" A squeal, a clap of hands, rather made his name ring out in a rather delightful fashion. A bit louder and at a higher pitch than expected, but lovely to hear, nonetheless. "I heard you were on set. I rather hoped I'd bump into you."

"Hello, Anna," His eyes rose from the script, flickering with glee. There was even a zing, a flash of pure, unbridled mischief in the depths of the lilac hues. "I was rather hoping too, sweetie," Hades set his cup down, to loot at her reflection in the mirror. "Woman alive, Anna. You look hideous."

Anna grinned, her reflection did to; she was glowing with pride. "Thank you," she was positively overjoyed as her shoulder rose a little as she laughed. Anna patted hair that was wound tightly around curlers. "I really do look awful," she added. Her face was made tattered, torn, decaying in places too. "My," she gasped to pull a lower eyelid down. "I even have black-blue eyes and didn't have to throw punch in return. I have bits of flesh falling of an everything," Anna sat back, resplendent in her decay. "Scuffed and scratch beyond recognition."

Hades listened as he pulled up a chair. It was wheeled, the coasters screamed across the portacabin's linoleum floor. He sat down in a heap; the script bundled to his lap.

"You brought notes?" Anna's eyebrows waggled, as she peered towards the script.

"I did indeed," Hades wheeled himself closer to Anna, to hold the script between them. "Here this is where you have your big scene," he ran finger over the text. "The author would like to you stagger around with all the grace of a drunken sailor. The director agrees."

"Heavy footed?" she asked, looking in directly in the eye. Her tone had depths of conscientiousness, of wanting to do the best job possible.

"As a yeti," nodded Hades, tapping at the director's scribble. "Feel free to make noises, laugh as you have lost the plot, not to mention your soul too."

"I can do that," Anna listened as she uncurled a lock of hair. She then fiddled with another, that was already half to her shoulder.

"Here, lemme help," Hades tugged at another curler, to uncoil Anna's blonde-brown hair. "Don't break anything. I can do the rest, whilst I'm here, if you like."

"Sure, carry on," Anna waved a hand, as she continued to read the script. "Don't light match though, whatever you do. Enough hair lacquer to set this whole damned trailer alight. Sparky as you are, Hades…."

"I've been called worse," laughed Hades, "Far worse, and by people far more malevolent. Think you have one hell of a scene."

"Oh, my, Gorbind!" Anna squealed once more, there was even a gasp as she shook the script. She looked at Hades, all very wide-eyed. "He makes it through, right?"

"Passes through," Hades carried on unwinding curlers, to tug a lock into a sprightly corkscrew. "He will, in some fashion. Hell would freeze over, before Gorbind Phalla ceases to exist."

"Well, yeah," Anna chortled heartily. "Hades, Lord of the Underworld. Sort of in your job spec, young man, you know what I mean." Reaching into her crown, Anna tousled her hair to hoick out a curler. She handed it over to Hades.

"Thanks. You okay with the back story," he fiddled with her hair still, carefully unwrapping curlers. He had to concentrate with a particularly challenging one that was being resistant. "American tourist…"

"Got caught in the Apocalypse," Anna flicked back a few pages. "Shopping in Selfridges. Got set upon…cold kiss of death, its embrace." She flicked forward. "A battle at Gravelly hill Interchange. Oh. I don't get that far…but there are bits of me everywhere. Squelching and underfoot. I can live with that."

"It'll be messy," Hades pulled out the last of the curlers, before tugging and teasing at Anna's hair. "Beautiful. You really do look like death warmed up." He put both hands onto her shoulders.

Anna looked once more at her reflection. She placed a hand to Hades'. "You're a good man, Hades," she said softly. "For a God."

"Thank you," He gave her hand a gentle squeeze. "Secret though, Anna," Hades tapped his nose. "Don't go telling anyone."

"I won't," Anna's cheeks dimpled as she smiled. At any other time, the smile would have been beautiful. "I promise. Oh, and I'll die quick. I'll be gone in a flash."

"Hold that thought," Hades kissed the top of her head; the lacquer was irrelevant. He picked up his tea and clicked his fingers.

In a flash, Hades was gone.

THE CITY OF BIRMINGHAM IS SINKING

Referral

This story is inspired by two things. The first, is the parish church of St.Martin in the Bull ring. The second, is my stint there as a volunteer counsellor with the counselling service attached to the church. I really enjoyed my time there; I had a phenomenal experience in developing my self and my practice as a newly qualified person-centred counsellor. I gained a wealth of knowledge, skills and experience. All of which allowed me to appreciate and further understand the true colours of Birmingham. A part of my counselling journey that will also stay with me.

In the knave of St.Martin's is a stained glass window. It features healing in the City of Birmingham, after the second World War. To this day, that window inspires me to be a better counsellor and better author.

The first line of this story is very real.

I heard it one day, being shouted out aloud by one of the many street preachers that would often be found in and around the fruit and veg market. It was a striking, fearsome sentence that really stopped me in my tracks-I had been pacing, before seeing my next client. There was power, hell and brimstone, loaded into each and every syllable.

This sentence stayed with, I made a note of it, adamant that it was a story waiting to be written.

"The City of Birmingham is sinking." The preacher man bellowed as I crossed my counselling room. I was in between clients, and needed to stretch my legs for a few minutes. I felt a bit at unease too. I had done for days. I'd been thinking about giving all this up, to re-consider my profession. My mind was not exactly cogent at that moment.

Heading to the window, I pressed a finger to the slats of the window blind. Feeling grime and dust against my skin, I had to pull a face. I also made a mental note to give the whole room a thorough going over.

I'd get around to it. Eventually.

Outside, in the shadow of the fruit and veg market, the preacher was starting to pace. His hands flew around, ten to the dozen; he was gesticulating wildly. His face was framed by fury, and contorted to display it.

Or at least it looked like fury. Fury is often confused with passion. My eyes followed his movement. The way in which he strode around, it was erratic. I felt really quite unsettled by it; my stomach had started to churn. Something made me put my hand to it, to sooth away the unease. Then there was the pain.

Was that mine, or his?

He had my attention; it was brimming with confounded curiosity. A big part of me wondered, had questions about why he was there. What was it, that motivated him, to be standing there as he yelled himself hoarse? Another part of me, bristled. His message, the one he wished to spread, was that of peace and love.

Yet, there he was, yelling. The volume and force, at odds with the would-be peace that he was trying so hard to peddle. The brutality of the delivery boxed both my ears and my soul.

"The City of Birmingham is sinking," He proclaimed once more. Fire, fury and passion coated each and every syllable.

"So is Venice," I told myself. "We do have more canals."

I watched as the impassioned preacher man thumbed through a dog-eared Bible. The pages fluttered in the breeze, and were getting damp as fine rain started to fall. The paving slabs that he paced, took on a grey, silvery patina as the rain became heavier.

From on high, at the window, the preacher man had hit my radar. I could hear him, feel his feelings. The fire and the brimstone made my soul throb somewhat. I would feel it every week; every Thursday, at 1pm. At that exact moment, preacher man would take up his spot and start to communicate his message.

I would watch, listen; observe as the seconds, souls and souls would slowly tick by. A tide of treacle, that would keep me enthralled for a good ten minutes. Long enough to forget about the cup of tea that I had left to languish in the kitchen.

It is my job to listen and without prejudice. The confines of the counselling room are a safe place. For the most part, the walls are built upon trust. The trust operates at different layers; the trust that is put in me. The trust, that clients put in themselves to come see me. When someone enters my room, they help me to enter their world.

I walk with them. Alongside them. I do my best to hear, to feel; to understand the way in which the experience the world around them. There is a connection, a bond; the therapeutic alliance.

It's not always easy. Not everyone, will let you in and so readily. It takes time, as well as trust. It takes feeling safe to know what safe is.

Attention, and therein paying it to also get it; that is incredibly important.

I try to do it with purpose; a positive intent too. That said, my unwanted attention in peering through a blind, may echo the experience of a client. They may not welcome such an intrusion. Yet, I am paid to do it. I am paid to bring things out into the light. At times, this is painful, too hard to process; there may be resistance.

Anyone and everyone, could come here; this counselling room does not discriminate. It's open for all. All that find themselves here, are treated with respect. With an unconditional positive regard.

Even those, who speak, full to the brim with fire and fury.

Mr.Preacher man. For weeks, he would spread his message. Standing at the foot of the war memorial, he would pace. As he spoke, the paper poppies on the monument would appear to tremble and quake with his every word. He would be there, come rain or shine.

Then he disappeared. One Thursday, I would notice; notice the overwhelming silence as I paced in between clients. I checked the time, the day. Thursday, would then quietly ebb away. I would continue with my client work. I would deliberately keep that slot, that appointment free. Something told me to hold fire. Something, told me to wait and see.

Then the referral came through.

"Marcy, that one o'clock slot?" the administrative assistant was tentative in her query. "Don't suppose you fancied filling it. Only someone asked for you, Marcy; they asked for you specifically."

I looked it over, albeit briefly. It seemed straight forward, within my competence and area of interest. I'd glossed over it, avoiding the three words that might have made the penny drop.

It was all set. Thursday, 1pm.

I stepped out into the waiting room, I called out a name, hoping to find the right person. I saw the face and took the briefest of moments to fully register it. My heart thudded heavily; my throat suddenly tightened. I blinked, convinced that my brain was having a damned good laugh. A joke, perhaps?

Alas, this was no joke. The brain, was not taking the rise.

"Marcy?" He uttered my name. His voice was free of fire, of brimstone and fury. It was strangely beautiful, but sounded somewhat at sea.

"Yes," I said, taking a breath; I too felt as though at sea. "Please," I continued. "Shall we go through?"

Thursday. 1pm. Preacher man was sat there before me.

I set aside his file. There was an assessment in there; an outline of why he was here. I knew that much, but I let it sit having had a passing glance. As I looked to the here and now, that passing glance had shown me three words. How, I wished that I hadn't seen them.

I looked instead, at the man sat before me. The word, his words, about the City of Birmingham sinking, were etched across my mind.

"What is it," I asked, having gone through our working agreement, "That brings you here today."

"Loss of faith," he uttered; there was only a shadow of fury, of brimstone. "Loss, of faith."

Team Meeting

The Birmingham Museum and Art Gallery is one of my favourite places to visit, especially when it comes to looking for inspiration. So much so, it features a great deal in Kangana. Also, the whole notion of wanting to write a Hades story came from seeing Prosperine by Rosetti, there at the BMAG. The pre-raphaelite gallery is wonderful to walk through. I was gutted, beyond measure, to one day go looking for Prosperine-to inspire the Hades story-only to be told that she was on tour. I long to see her back, and in Birmingham.

The first thing that you see, on arriving at the first floor, is Epstein's Lucifer. It's a huge imposing feature that greats you. I say greets you; but I swear that Lucifer stands sentry, as though weighing up whether you should be granted access. In this story, I *wanted to explore and imagine what happens in the gallery after hours. When the denizens of Birmingham have gone home, there has to be something that happens with the occupants left to their own devices.*

This is also a story, that six months into lockdown, fills me with sadness. On writing, the BMAG is still closed, with no word as to when it might re-open. Something, that really saddens me, and frightens me too. Birmingham, and indeed the world, needs the BMAG. The colour, the vibrancy there, stirs the soul and inspires the mind.

Would you believe it. The BMAG is set up re-open this October. I am positively over-joyed. The news has come in, just this moment; as I set forth to type this story up!

I've seen most things, whilst stood up here on my round dais. Most things, most people too.. In the Round Room, of the Birmingham Museum and Art Gallery; I watch and observe. The first thing that people see, once they have ebbed up white, marble steps to the first floor, is me.

I am Lucifer, Nineteen Forty Five. Created by Jacob Epstein.

You really can't miss me.

I've been here a while. To be perfectly honest, there is nowhere else, that I would rather be. I've got the perfect spot, to watch the world go by. To watch the people of Birmingham come in and absorb a bit culture. I have seen the true colours of Birmingham. The good, the bad; the slightly disorientated, with no clue where they are or what they might expect. I stand here, frozen in eager anticipation, my hands held out to bid all a hearty welcome. Technically, my hands are held out to hell, but that's just semantics.

This place, the BMAG; it couldn't be further from hell. This place, is home. It's nice, it does the job. I can't complain, I choose not to. I would rather be here, safe and sound, than in one of the many scrap yards dotted around the city. I heard a story once, about the King Kong that used to be in the City Centre. Rumour has it, he disappeared, and into a scrap yard.

That was enough to be put the fear of....Now, where was I?

I would rather be here, standing in majesty and welcome. Then festering below a grotty tarpaulin whilst waiting to be smelted down, or crushed by the jaws of death. I was after all, an Angel once.

I, was the Lord of Hell.

I'll take the majesty. It is far more fitting for a being of my creation and station.

Oh, that's it. The lights are going out. One by wall, the lights on the wall snap off. The scarlet walls of the Round Room take on a darker, more sombre tone.

With the lights going out, that means the real lifers are going home. Their toil and grind is over for now. Even the day of rest, is anything but as Monday soon rolls around.

The real lifers are gone.

Now the other lifers, can have a little fun.

***

"Psst. Lucifer, you up?" The voice is gentle, over the sound of twinkling, tubular bells and rustling, silken skirts. "Team meeting. You might want to come down."

Hearing my name, my shoulders relax from their held high, fixed in place position. It's harder than you think, to look poised; especially when you're at full mast, all the time. I couldn't be seen at half-mast; that wouldn't do at all. My fingers soften too and I hear my elbows crack.

I wiggle my right foot. My ankle clicks as I do my best to shake off cramp. For a moment, I do the hot shoe shuffle, crossed with a bit of disco, to ger rid of stubborn pins and needles. The cramp lingers though. It's been there since the sixties, and nothing works for me to be rid of it completely.

Then and only then, do I open my eyes.

Treacle brown. In case you wondered.

As is the rest of me, to be perfectly honest. I could do with a bit of buff, a bit of spit and polish, actually. Tickles though, when it does happen. All in good time, I suppose. I was away, and from my adoring public, for such a long time during that ghastly Zombie Apocalypse. The real lifers, I can forgive. The germs, not so much.

Oh, and the Commonwealth Games are scheduled to arrive here soon. I want to look my best for then. I will want to look all sweetness and light. It's not a complicated request, not really.

"Hello, Night," I smile at the woman standing to my left. She's waited all too patiently as I come around. My wings whistle as they too descend from on high. The feathers rustle as my wings fold down to retreat into the holding space below my shoulder blades.

"Good evening, Lucifer," Night beams at me; her eyes crinkle up at the corners. In her arms, is a sleeping babe; safely nestled in the folds of her Azure blue cloak. There are also a dozen or so cherubs milling about her legs. They are her train of cute, clever and rather twinkly stars.

One of them, blows me a kiss.

I catch it and press it to my heart.

I'm not entirely evil; I was good once.

I just happened to make an interesting choice.

Making a choice, is not always easy. However, being able to, is powerful. Having a choice, is far more important than being an automaton with no free will whatsoever.

As to whether the choice is God given.

Chicken and egg.

The jury remains out.

"C'mon, let's be having you," Night turns towards the Museum shop and beckons me with her free hand. Her train giggles with childish glee, her blue silken skirts rustle as she moves. It's those tubular bells again, punctuated by triangles. She has been known to mix it up, and add a xylophone into the mix.

"Right behind you," I say, adjusting the barely there straps across my groin. "Just need to get dressed," I add, pulling up and around the skirt that generally keeps the draught out. Generally, and only just.

"Medea will be with us soon," Night rocks the babe in her arms. "Just a check in, this meeting. It's been a fairly quiet week, truth be told. Things are still picking up, post what-sit-thingy-magi-jig."

"I noticed," I nod as we walk through the shop, the industrial gallery and into the Edwardian Tea room. A puddle of penguins has escaped their frame. One, wears a banker's visor. The second, chews on a cheroot. Number three, counts out a stack of pink chips.

Night shakes her head. I shrug.

Penguins, playing poker. They are not as innocent as they look. Only last week, they fleeced a fella from The Audience in Athens. For something so ordinarily pretty as a picture, they had certainly evolved somewhat.

As we walked into the tea room, a light flickered into being over a booth. I clapped my hands to conjure up a pot of tea, a Sicilian lemonade and a very creamy looking latte, with a biscotti on the side.

It was nearly always my round, when it came to these meetings.

That and I really don't trust Medea. She was known for spiking drinks, with there being rather tragic consequences. The tea was for me. Normally, I go for Typhoo; a proper Brummie Brew. You couldn't go wrong, or end up dead, with a bit of Typhoo.

To think, that it was first sold in a pharmacy. Your average apothecary has come a long way since dabbling in tea leaves.

I slid into a pink cushion; it was all rather squeaky, and not to mention a bit cold to the touch. Night slid in alongside me. Her train disappeared, crawling away to tables nearby. They chattered amongst themselves, all very excitedly. Clapping my hands once more, I set their table with milk, cookies and a couple packets of party rings. They were good kids, and looked a lot like Angels. That all rather made me feel a bit homesick. A spot of party food, was the least that I could do.

I drew my tea close, to splash some milk into the bone china cup next to the pot. Taking the lid off the pot, I stirred the leaves to inhale the fragrance. The scent wafted into the corners and crevices of what was a very tattered soul.

Yes, I have one. It's a bit ropey, but it does exist. In a fashion.

Darjeeling. The King of Teas.

This stuff was rocket fuel if left to brew for too long. If left, it had the tendency to be acrid, unpalatable and downright offensive to the sense of taste. It was best served only just brewed. Placing a strainer over the rim of the cup, I poured myself a healthy dose.

Next to me, Night slurped her lemonade with her eyes closed. She looked as though she was achieving some form of nirvana. Seeing that she had in fact drained the glass, I tapped it gently, to refill. Night, was okay. We'd been friends for what felt like an eternity. We shared a darkness within. It was something, rather than nothing, to have in common with one another.

"Oh, I'm sorry! I was in the middle of something," Medea blustered into the tea room. In her hands, held aloft, was a gold-rimmed crucible sat on an ivory-coloured tripod.

This was why I had no faith in the woman. She was always, interminably, in the middle of something; it was never good. There was always some malevolence that she was cooking up and that crucible of hers.

"Lucifer, love, you got the drinks in," she smiled sweetly, bearing her rather square teeth. "Thank you, aren't you sweet, such a lovely thing to do," trilled Medea. She set the tripod down to slid into the boot. Her equipment clinked against her latte.

Over the rim of tea cup, I looked into the crucible. The contents, looked altogether sinister and not to be trusted. A blue-green sediment cling to the inside of the dish, and to the unwitting eye, looked harmless. Knowing better, I saw Copper Sulphate when I saw it.

My smile was somewhat uneasy as Medea picked up the biscotti to dunk three quarters of it into her drink.

Our eyes met, and I saw it as plain as day.

There it was, in the depths of her soul. A spikey ball of ill intent and maliciousness that came from used tainted magics.

Pure darkness.

As the light-bringer, this ball of energy, frightened even me. Me, Lucifer, The Fallen Angel. That which scared me, the very Devil himself, was something that simply didn't bear thinking about.

Yet, here it was. Medea crunched down on the biscuit, licking her fingers in turn.

I knew, she knew.

A battle of wills would have to wait. Until the Apocalypse at least. A proper one and not the sort with germs or the Undead. I've seen one before, I know what I'm looking for.

"The summer weather hasn't helped us this week," Night broke the silence to open the team meeting. In her hands, was a sheaf of rough, dog-eared parchment. Night kept notes on everything. It made sense to keep a record of all the comings and goings. She pushed a pair of ebony-rimmed glasses up the bridge of her porcelain nose. Her inky blue eyes momentarily flashed towards Medea and then back to her paperwork. "People would rather go sun themselves in Pigeon Park, go slightly crispy, than stay indoors."

I giggled quietly into my tea. Night also had a thing about berating Day. It was quite funny at times. When it came to the on-going battle between Night and Day, there was antagonism abound.

Ne'er the twain shall meet.

"Something about first dates though, Lucifer," Night turned slightly towards me, to address her statement.

"Several, yes," I replied, putting down my tea.

"Anything, er, promising?" posed Medea, her lips pursed in anticipation, as her eyes grew wide in anticipation and excitement. Rumour had it, she had once poisoned a beau. Medea and romance, were therein, a worrying combination.

"Yes, one or two," nodded I. "Nervous starts, stumbling conversations for the most part. There may be proposals, the would-be ringing of wedding bells."

"Persephone wittered on about that proposal for months," Medea pulled a face; there was no disguising her disdain. "The one with Gorbind, The White Knight. How he sank down to one knee, was all bit slushy, if you ask me. Bit of a soft sap, that one."

The White Knight. Gorbind Phalla.

"He's anything but!" I snapped, feeling my eyes burn and flash with irritation. "By virtue of being a White Knight, he is stronger than most. All those years, Medea, when he would come here as a boy; him, his brother in tow. The grandmother too." There was a burr to my voice, which I refuse to apologise for.

"Gorbind found his missing puzzle piece, the woman who makes him whole. She too, is special. Padmi, the Lotus Flower. Purity derived from The Divine. All of your tinkering," I waggled a finger at the crucible, has rather addled your brain. "Perhaps it is time to be rid of such poison, to come up for some air."

"Purity is all too boring," sneered Medea, slurping her latte. Yet, her gaze was trained upon me, as though she had me in her vindictive cross-hairs.

"You, Lucifer," she said, her lips twitched into a conniving smirk. "Are the original rebel. You broke all the rules, so I don't have to. Don't you ger bored, Lucifer? Up there, on your dais, in the Round Room? Say one night, when all the real lifers had gone, your unfurled those beautiful wings of yours to take flight into the city. Think of all the light that you could bring. I hear Gravelly Hill Interchange is simply delightful and to die for."

I was set to rise, indignant and in a fury. My knuckles had somehow darkened too. As Madea loomed large. Only Night had stretched out her arm across my chest, blocking my way.

"Enough, Medea," she uttered, quietly. "Lest your return to renovation and restoration be hastened. Persephone blinked at the dear boy and was sent to North America.

Chided and chastened, Medea sat back down. As did I.

So that was why Persephone had left. I'd put it down to child-like naivete. That was her too a tee, apparently; or so the story went. Her flirting and frivolity were all rather amusing, as though she was playing at grown-up. She wasn't my type, not really. Night had thought so to, I guess.

Night shuffled her parchment, before placing a few pages onto our table. She elbowed me, and pointed to her empty once more glass.

I duly obliged with a tap. There was lemonade once more. Night, really wasn't a cheap date. I caught her glare, a raised brow. I'd forgotten that she could read my mind.

The darkness. It connected us, on levels that human kind would never be able to comprehend.

"You'll be pleased to know that Persephone will be returning," declared Night, sipping lemonade. "There are plans afoot, whereby she finds her own soul connection"

"Ooh," trilled Medea, how exciting. She clapped her hand together, all very dramatically. She'd cooled down from her fit of pique very quickly. "How exciting, a bit of Brummie romance."

Night looked up from her pages of parchment. Her eyes are had become hard; a darker, more intense shade of blue. She was woefully scary when riled. It was Night who could turn the sweetest of dreams into full-blown, brain-bending, soul-shattering terrors.

"The White Knight, he will help," she calmed, to scan her paper once more. "It is he, who guides the soul connection to its home. Helps the bond be formed," She traced a finger across the page. Letters of gold and red flamed into being; curled and cursive, they flowed into brightness. "Hades," whispered Night. "And the Moonbeam. Her name is Mango."

I sat back, to pick up my tea.

Moonbeam, I had to smile. That was an interesting form of light.

Feast day

Tugging down his jacket, Suraj cast his eyes over his reflection. His chest felt tight as it rose and fell; he was brimming with nerves. Tweaking the knot of his tie, he nudged it away a little from his throat. Suraj could just about breathe. He put his palm to the buttons of his waistcoat; as though trying to keep his breakfast down.

He'd had a big, hearty bowl of porridge; there was no Weetabix to be found. Yet there were still butterflies doing gymnastics somewhere around his spleen.

"Suraj, will you come down now?" His Grandmother called up the stairs. "It's nearly time; please don't make us late. Don't make me miss it either. I've never missed one of these yet."

"Coming!" he yelled, in reply. His Birmingham accent bounced around the room. Bounced off a bright blue pennant, and the poster of St.Andrews.

Grabbing a soft, bright blue Glengary hat from his bed, Suraj placed it upon his head. He nudged it into place and took one final look at his ensemble.

A dark jacket, trimmed with gold piping covered his slight torso. A pure, brilliant white shirt with mother of pearl buttons gleamed beneath a black waistcoat. There was chained sporran at his waist, fluffed up beautifully.

Then there was the piece de resistance.

His kilt; stiff, starched and box-pleated.

Calcutta Brave. That was the name of the pattern. It sounded all very romantic. There was however, a story attached to it.

There was Birmingham Blue in the weft of the kilt. Emerald green from Antrim. Orange, yellow and a dash of saffron to his echo his Indian Heritage. His Grandad had made it for his Shaanti, all those years ago, when they had first married. Two tribes, two families, intertwined with cultural threads.

Leaving his room, Suraj trundled down the stairs. He hummed as he moved, trying not scuff his freshly shone shoes. He hummed the chords that he would play, later and loudly at that.

"Oh, don't you look lovely!" cooed his grandmother. She met him at the bottom of the stairs. Given what day it was, she was dressed in a shalwar khameez of the deepest bottle green.Draped around her shoulders was a shawl. His grandmother, her name was Shaanti; she looked awesome.

The shawl was another dose of Calcutta Brave.

"Your Grandad would've been so very proud of you," stepping forwards, Shaanti cupped face with her palms. She landed a big, fat, splodgy kiss on his nose. "The Piper, in the Saint Patrick's Day parade, dressed in Calcutta Brave. Who'd thought it? Him from Antrim, me from The Punjab. Us settling in Birmingham, with your Mum and Dad making you."

"Even Saint Patrick travelled, Nani," Suraj beamed as Shaanti brushed lint from his shoulder. "Scared all those snakes away too."

"Come on, let's go," Shaanti tugged at his elbow. She held out a palm. In the middle were his car keys. "Your pipes are a-calling. I put them in your boot, next to some sandwiches and a flask of tea. Proper tea, to keep out the cold, Suraj. Spiced chai, to whet your whistle."

***

Birmingham had more canals than Venice. Not one of them was green.

Looking out, Aida exhaled deeply. She was feeling more than a little homesick. Last year, she'd spent Saint Patrick's in Chicago. The river had been dye green; it'd been all too trippy.

She'd been working that weekend too. Wining and dining clients, trying to persuade them to invest in the family business. Brexit, as well the impending zombie apocalypse, had made life a little difficult for the family business in Wicklow.

Here she was. This time in Birmingham. Still trying to coax and cajole investors to consider Patel-Tiernen Trade and Import as a jewel for their portfolios.

Leaving the Novatel in Brindley Place, Aida walked through the city. She was headed to Digbeth and would meet someone important on the way. Digbeth.

According to her dad, that was where had met Aida's mother.

In the Kerryman, of all places. Her mother had been there, having been stood up by a date. She was headed back to the Irish centre. In her opinion, they had a better shandy. Aida's dad, Amit, was newly arrived in Birmingham. He was newly arrived, in Britain. He had just got off the Gatwick bus at Digbeth Bus Station. Amit had been looking for a cuppa. A good strong brew. What he found, was a pint of Guinness. He also found Ida.

They'd both needed a friend.

Three years later, the two of them, newly married landed in Wicklow. They set up shop.

An Indo-Irish enterprise. In good time, Aida was born, following her three older siblings.

Aida mooched through the centre of town. It was quiet, but would eventually live up. It was only just yet twelve. There was greenery all over the place. A bug-eyed leprechaun dangled from a lamppost. His grin was rather unsettling. In the distance, a green hue hung across the shiny metal disks of Selfridges.

"Irish eyes are smiling," she told herself as she caught sight of the famous Birmingham Bull. Aida stood still, caught between Waterstones, Zara and Jack Jones. Head thrown back, foot raised. The Bull stood in the shadow of the iconic Rotunda.

"I'll meet you at twelve." Aida muttered. "By The Bull, don't be late."

The Bull. You really couldn't miss it. It was dressed in a furry green hat, complete with a furry pom-pom falling across a haunch. Then there was the matching jumpsuit.

Reaching into her pocket, Aida pulled out her vibrating 'phone.

"Where are you-oh, there you are," the voice had a tilt. A brogue, not too dissimilar to hers. It grew louder as the owner came closer. Complaining all the while about a hangover, before cutting out. A red-headed man stood next to her.

"You sure you want to do this?" he asked, he leant in to kiss her cheek. He nudged his nose against hers.

"Yeah," Aida gulped, to pull back and link her arm around his. "I want to."

"Kerryman?" he asked, rubbing a gloved hand across her fingers.

"Kerryman," replied Aida, biting back emotion.

It was at Manzils that Aida fell to pieces. Her face crumpled, she nearly felt to her knees.

Callum had scooped her up, kissed her once again. Pulling a bouquet of Shamrock from inside his coat, he handed it over. She smiled weakly. They kept walking. Slowly and steadily.

The piper had started. Aida wiped her eyes, to see the him lead the parade. Behind him, drums thundered.

What neither of them spotted was the shadow on the pavement. He watched them; he watched them all with a smile upon his face.

They won't see me. They never do. I'm not surprised, not really. Dublin, Chicago and Birmingham. It's all such a blast, I flit to and fro.

I've been coming to Birmingham for years; for centuries, in fact. It was the churches that brought me over. With every consecration, I wanted to see what the fuss was all about. I've been here, a shadow, ever since. Each year, it's gotten bigger and better; the sixties, is when it started.

Half of Wicklow, Mayo, Meath and Sligo all landed here. Landed here, looking for crocks of gold to call their own. I see the piper, his chest thrust out as his granny watches. She looks fit to burst with pride. The boy plays well, I like what I hear. I see the lost looking little girl, putting shamrock on the door to the Kerryman. Her mam and dad met there. Since they went to their rest, she's been awfully sad. They sent her Callum; well I did. As my divine, intercessionary blessing.

Here I am, trying to avoid the puddles of booze. The stray piece of ticker tape. Birmingham knows how to throw a party. I don't mind a shinding.

My name is Patrick. This? Is my parade.

Angels of Birmingham

Avoiding the yellow lines that prohibited parking, Hades slid the Mustang into an alley. No traffic warden in their right mind would find the vehicle to attack it with a ticket. Hades, Lord of The Underworld, didn't particularly care for parking tickets.

With the car secreted away, he entered a multi-story building through sliding doors. The building looked perfectly ordinary with its 1960's brickwork. In reality, it was anything but.

Hades, had entered Birmingham Women's hospital.

On the surface of it, that was rather unfortunate. Given his title, his whole raison d'etre. For Hades to be here, was probably not a good thing.

In the lobby, was a map identifying all the different departments. Hades paused, his hands delved into the pockets of his waistcoat. He scanned the image from left to right, top to bottom. Finally, his eyes centred on where he wanted to go. To make sure, he took out a hand. A finger was pressed against the cold, rather dusty surface, of the map.

He hadn't done this in a while. Hence having to look at a map. He'd needed to refresh his memory.

Maternity. He was headed, to maternity.

With what could have been Divine Timing, a nearby lift pinged open. A handful of visitors trundled out. Hades waited however, as two balloons bopped out, nearly hitting the low ceiling. They were attached to matching metallic ribbon. The balloons were blue, filled tightly with helium. A couple came out after the balloons, accompanied by a blonde-haired little girl. She smiled at him; Hades smiled back.

"Babies," she told him, pointing a little chubby finger at two baby seats that her father carried. One in each hand. "My baby brothers," continued the little girl.

"I wish them a long and happy life," he said all too courteously as they left. He watched them leave through the exit. Then he put his palms to his face; it felt different.

He was smiling. That didn't happen very often. When it did, he felt nothing but happiness, joy and love.

Sensations, which hc was still getting used to. Sensations, which weren't all that common in the underworld.

Seeing that the doors were about to close, Hades sprinted in. The lift creaked as it moved, the lights flickered too. Humming and whirring, the lift made its ascent.

He had his reasons for being here. Not one of them, was macabre. As such, Hades looked as though he might blend in. As though he too, was an expectant father, ready to pace the lino as his partner laboured.

With a ping, the lift stopped. The doors parted, Hades hopped out, to look left and right. There was always some part of him that was wary when he did this. A bigger part of him, felt the full force of being an imposter.

Born of Divinity, Hades was never actually going to pace up and down a labour ward. He could have been a father, impregnated a random naiad or nymph in the same vein as his brothers. Ravished some woman, and on impulse.

Yet, he chose not to. He really wasn't that kind of guy; that kind of God. Hades knew that he didn't have it in him. To ravish some random woman, felt reckless and an abuse of power.

Hades tepped out, just in time. The doors to the ward swooshed open, bringing with them a nurse. His uniform visible beneath a red jacket.

"Back again, Mr.Howden," beamed the nurse. "Hopefully not too much longer. First babies do tend to take their time though."

Hades beamed back, taking a hold of he door. "Mr.Howden," he muttered "That'll do," he wandered into the ward.

The name, Mr,Howden; it meant nothing.

As in walked in, Hades heard pain. He felt it too. Every inch of him vibrated, throbbed in waves and aches. He held out his hands; he was shaking. Hades looked aghast, as his form flickered. He juddered in and out of being, phasing. That would have confused the mortals, if their optic nerve had the capacity to register it. In the blink of a human eye, Hades was blurring in and out of focus.

He could hear screams, tears too. Then there was something else, right at the end. Something that made him snatch his hands into his pockets. At the ceiling, the harsh lights crackled; they flashed in a staccato rhythm that somewhat confused him.

The atmosphere, was quite literally pregnant.

Then he heard it.

The cry of a new born.

Hades felt vibrations again. These were however, different. These were pulses of pure energy that made him tingle from his toes. The hairs on the back of his neck were standing on end, his lilac eyes twinkled.

Hades closes those lilac eyes to absorb it. Absorb every little bit of it.

That was why he came, and here to the maternity ward.

The vibrations that he felt, hummed with life, with a happiness beyond comprehension. Each and every single cry was a thread from the fabric of the universe. Each and every thread, was hope.

"Hades, kin of The Titans. Lord and God of the Underworld. Leave. This is not your world. Let the living be. Do no harm here."

Well, that stopped the flow. Hades snapped his lilac eyes open. Flames danced across his irises, as he felt the abrupt ending in his connection to the universe.

Phasing in and out of time, standing next to the nurse's station, was another figure. He hadn't seen one in a while, Hades was genuinely surprised. It took one divine being, to know another.

Dressed in varying shades of blue was a dewy-skinned figure. Their hair was the colour of spun gold. They were gliding straight towards him.

As they spoke, there was a firmness to the tone. The voice, was however, remarkable. The voice sounded as though it was a symphony of strings, and had once been captured by Elgar. In the figures hands, was an oboe forged by divinity.

Raising his hands in quiet surrender, Hades bowed his head.

"My Lord Messenger," Hades half-smiled to lift his head and look up. "The conveyor of good news and bless. Gabriel; am I right?"

Gabriel mirrored he half-smile, to return his oboe to the folds of his voluminous cloak.

"Indeed," answered the angel divine. "This is not your place, Hades. Not today, I believe." Gabriel rummaged in his cloak, to pull out a piece of parchment. He unfolded it, to trace a finger down the pages. "Nope, no one for you, for Thanatos, either. Shouldn't he be here, rather than you?" Gabriel folded up the parchment, to tuck it away. "And put your hands down, this isn't a stick up."

"Ordinarily, yes," Hades lowered his hands. "I fancied a drive, a walk too."

Gabriel frowned.

"Things have changed, Gabriel," Hades stated, all very calmly. "My chariot, makes for a rather interesting four-wheeled, mechanised automobile. You should try it."

The Angel Gabriel waved a hand dismissively. "What are you doing here, Lord Hades?" he asked, irritation made his symphonic voice crackle. He also put his hands on his hips, which made him look uncharacteristically foreboding.

"Babies," replied Hades. "They remind me of all the good things in the world; of all that is full of hope. I see them, I get to feel their cuteness I see what is alive, ready to go and pregnant with potential. I live in the underworld, my friend. Forgive a God, for wanting something different. To see it, feel it and hear it. This, is as close as I can get."

"To err, is to be human," Gabriel nodded, there was even more of a smile. "To forgive is divine. Not my place; nor is it my place to judge. I'm happy," he said folding his arms, as his wings fluttered quietly into his shoulder blades. "That you mean no harm.

Hades nodded as the iridescent feathers were filed away having being hoisted to full mast. The lights of the ward flickered once more.

"A scan," replied Gabriel, momentarily executing the chicken dance to make sure his wings were tucked in. "Happen from time to time. The discovery of a peace-maker, aviator; the next leader of a revolution."

"In Birmingham?!" Hades threw his head back, to laugh and clap his hands together."

"In Birmingham," nodded Gabriel. "Ooof," he lurched from side to side, as his oboe fell out of his cloak. "Stay there. Two minutes, maybe less. Back soon."

Gabriel disappeared in a flash. In a heartbeat, the divine messenger was back. The oboe at his lips, rang out in a melodious note, before it was tucked back into the cloak.

"Annunciation?" posed Hades.

"In a fashion," Gabriel wore a rather excited looking grin. His face sparkled somewhat. "Since you're here, fancy a drink? This is going to be a long night. If you have nothing better to do. We can both go loiter in the canteen."

***

The canteen turned out to be closed. For mere, male mortals, that might have been a tragedy.

Pressing a palm to the front of the coffee machine, Hades waited patiently. He'd removed his overcoat. It was draped over the back of a chair sat at a round, Formica table. He glanced over his shoulder, to see Gabriel polishing his oboe. He'd heard about it. Never, for one moment, did he think he'd see it, or Gabriel, for that matter.

The two of them, were from very different worlds.

Hacking away a mechanical splutter, the machine clunked out two steaming hot beverages. Hades carried the two plastic, beige-coloured cups to the table.

"I've seen Thanatos a few times," commented Gabriel. "Never spoken to him. We were both working. Didn't feel right, interrupting. A couple of time, Hades, he's got in before me. In the delivery room. Damned near tore my soul, my wings, to shreds. I guess we all have a job to do." There was a sadness in Gabriel's voice, tingles of it that were akin to wind-chimes.

"Now the warning makes sense," Hades tapped his cup against Gabriel's as he sat down. "First time that I've heard it, to be honest. To be said out aloud, like that."

"Azrael, she told me about you." Gabriel looked at Hades, with eyes of corn-flower blue. "Our Angel of Death, has a whole memorandum; a dossier about you. Rules of engagement, what have you. The warning, is slap bang in the middle, written in capitals. That and something about equitable, division of labour."

"I've met her," Hades chortled, whilst sporting a grin. A grin that briefly filled the canteen with spot light of warmth. "The memorandum, the dossier; the product of a plague, a revolution and a lot of nectar. Nice lady, showed me her sword and everything. Equitable, division of labour. She wrote that bit drunk."

Cymbals crashed somewhere, as Gabriel blanched.

Hades looked at his tea, it was an awful shade of amber. He ran a finger around the rim.

"You get to deliver the good stuff, Gabriel," he uttered quietly. "It's the one that are born asleep, that tears me apart. Thanatos, he picks them up; gives them a hug and carries them onto the ferry. He sings to them, sings them lullabies, so they don't feel alone. They come to me, and it hurts. Some of them, I can send them back as moonbeams or sunshine. I like rainbows the best. Rainbows, are all I have to give back. It's never fair, Gabriel, ever."

Pulling his own tea forward, Gabriel put his other to Hades' wrist. In a rare moment of solidarity, Angel and God connected.

(Later, when Hades took off his coat to dump it on his bed, he found a white feather When he held it up towards a torch, it glowed to cast a rainbow across the stone floor. He'd be over bowled by kindness before placing it below his pillow. Hades, Lord of the Underworld, liked rainbows.)

***

"This is a really special place," Gabriel spoke in hushed, gentle tones as he conjured the both into a very small, closed wards.

Hades took in the sight of transparent boxes. Cocooned inside each one-there were eight in all-was a sleeping baby.

"I shouldn't be here," Hades was alarmed; his heart ached, as he grabbed Gabriel by the elbow. "I can't be here."

A flash of light. A rapid beeping broke the calm. Three nurses ran to an incubator on the far side.

Time slowed down, as Hades waved a hand. He could it for a while. Long enough to make a difference. He moved towards the baby, weaving in and out of the nurses.

"What about the Fates?" asked Gabriel. "They were in the memorandum. Can you do this, I though there were rules."

"There are," replied Hades, he unfastened a small door. He slid in a hand, towards the tiniest fingers that he had ever seen. "Occasionally, I bend them." He pressed his index finger to the middle of the baby's chest. A bright blue light appeared, buzzing across the delicate skin.

"Baby girl Anand, Junior," said Gabriel, reading the name tag. "I know her," he rooted around his cloak to find his parchment. "She's eight week early, but…"

The blue blur across baby girl Anand, Junior turned lilac, then pink. Slowly, the little girl's limbs filled with life. She even wiggled her legs.

"She's going to lead a revolution," Gabriel looked at the little girl, at Hades. "Her Mum and Dad, they've prayed for a fighter."

Hades undid more of the box. Gently, he took Baby Girl Anand, Junior, into his arms. He was careful, to cradle her close and support her head.

"So they'll get one," Hades had no idea why he did it. But he kissed the little girl's forehead. "She will inspire people, be a muse." Hades flicked a finger towards the name tag.

Calliope Anand, Junior. Spelt wrong, and on purpose. A bit like her Mum's. A fragment, from another world. A gift, from someone taken too soon. For someone, who was loved and more than words could say.

"She'll be a rainbow," he said, returning the little girl back to the incubator. "We should go. Both of us."

Hades nodded at Gabriel to click his fingers; the pair of them wafted away. The mustang went too. It was spotted in Edgbaston.

Nurses darted towards the incubator as time resumed. One of them, noticed a puddle of feathers. The one, looked as though it was made of a rainbow. Picking it up, the one nurse tucked it into the little girl's name tag.

Calliope Anand, Junior, smiled to kick her legs. Her brown eyes, flickered.

Flickered lilac, and for a heartbeat.

Pink Sari

Time flies when you're having fun. Or so the saying goes. I guess it does, in most cases. The exception to this, the rule, the cliché; is most likely marriage.

Parts of it have been fun. I've experienced my fair share of frolics within the nuptial institution. As for time flying. I'm not so sure. A T.A.R.D.I.S, a Delorean and a bit of H. G. Wells, would only make things complicated. The memories, would be the first thing to be corrupted, never mind my soul.

Memories. How we make them, keep them; make them a part of our worlds. That's what I'm hang onto. Each and every day.

Here I am again. A different suit, a different audience. Yet it's the same day, and most importantly. It's the same woman.

Bear with me a moment, as I fill you in.

***

"Dad, this the one you want?" Anita's head popped around the door as it creaked open.

Her eyelashes fanned furiously. I had to smile, as I turned around. Her reflection was altogether amusing and heart-warming in equal measure. She'd been up since three, with the hair and make-up artist. The eyelashes, could have been a whole new species, if this was wildlife on one. In her hands, was a red silk tie, embossed with a gold, sparkly, Paisley motif.

"That's the one," I nodded, as I finished buttoning up my shirt. I tucked the tails into my waistband. "Something old," I added as she handed it over. I flicked it over my wrists, around my neck, and under my stiff collar.

"Something new," grinned Anita. She whipped out a blue box from behind her back. "Blue too," she added, flicking open the lid. Sat on a velveteen cushion, were a pair of chrome cufflinks, set with stones that were Birmingham Blue. "Since you didn't do this, the first time around."

Something made my heart flutter as I pulled down my collar. The tie was knotted neatly, all Windsor Fashion. I hugged my first-born close, holding her tightly to kiss the tip of her nose. The only place I could get away with, lest I smudged the war paint.

"Thank you," I replied, removing the cuff-links to set them in place at my wrists. I suddenly became acutely aware of my hands, the nakedness of my left hand in particular. I passed the tip of my thumb across the blank space on my ring finger.

"Oh, that's another thing," Anita's wrists jangled as she rooted around in her pockets.

I had to frown, I couldn't help it; not really. Traditionally, Lenghas don't come with pockets. A lengha, is not like wearing a pair of Levi's. Certainly not stone-washed, that's for sure. Anita, stood there before me, dressed in a mango-coloured bodice, with a matching billowing skirt trimmed with pink. She sparkled as she moved, the embroidery matched the print of my tie.

My daughter revealed yet another box.

"As your Best Man," she beamed broadly; her smile would shame the moon. "I shall keep a safe hold of Mum's ring."

The ruby red of her lipstick accentuated her pearly white teeth and cupid bow mouth. She looked sweet right now. Yet my daughter could kiss me with that mouth having turned the air blue. I remember her first word. It had been the Anglo-Saxon for going forth and procreating.

Her Mum had stepped on Lego. I'd laughed for days. Her grandparents, less so.

"Good," I nodded to let out a hot breath. My stomach also flipped. "Don't you go losing it, not today, Anita. It's important."

"I won't," Anita bit her lip as a tear strayed towards her nose. She wiped it away with finger tipped with shiny, French manicure. "I'll see you in the car. I have bacon butties just need to find a bib."

A bib. I giggled, shook my head as Anita left. There were nine grandchildren. Three of them, under the age of four. One of them, wouldn't mind sharing a bib.

Pulling on my jacket, I looked at the lozenge-shaped, full length mirror that hung on the wall in a wooden frame. Sticky-tacked to the edge, was a photograph.

Me, my wife, and behind us, the statue of James Watt, Matthew Boulton and William Murdoch. All rather dull, and well before it was re-gilded. There was brightness in the image. The fuschia pink of my wife's wedding sari.

Birmingham Registry office, forty years ago. Time really had flown.

Half an hour later, Anita and I were pulling up in a red four by four, outside of Birmingham Botanical Gardens. It had seemed the most fitting place for today's events. The kids, all three of them, had grown up, playing amongst the peacocks.

We sat for a moment, Anita handed me flask of masala chair to settle the nerves. She'd actually dosed it with bourbon; I made no comment. She meant well, it tasted pricey.

I remember bringing my wife here, the first Spring after we'd married. We'd walked amongst the Magnolias. The year after, there'd been a fight. She wanted to drive, to work; to be more than a wife and mother. I was all for it. The senior Patriarchs, less so. I'd hear her pain, but also remembered my vows.

To love, honour and to cherish. To fight and protect. All of which, had meet me here today. Walking toward the bandstand, of all places.

The car park was filling Anita walked me toward the entrance. Our guests were arriving, thick and fast.

"I hope this works," I said quietly, Anita's hand rested between my shoulder blades. "Before it all goes grey." I looked skyward, at fluffy clouds. It wasn't the prospect of rain that bothered me.

"It will, Dad, I know," my daughter smiled me, blew me a kiss before patting my elbow "Today we're making memories. When all is said done, we will still have those."

Memories. This whole day was about memories. Memories, to sustain. To have and to hold.

Before it was all too late.

At the bandstand, seating had been arranged in semi-circles. Chairs, that were candy-coloured and stripy, were being filled. Anita and I walked up the steps. I waved, I smiled. Some of the faces, I knew. Others were fuzzier, greyer.

In the middle of the bandstand, was Anita's own first-born; Arvind. Dressed in a navy suit, tan shoes and with his honey-coloured hair slicked back, he was our newly, internet-ordained, celebrant. I remember the day he was born. All pink, fluffy and bawling his eyes out. He'd been nine pounds and four ounces. No wonder his eyes watered.

Nine pounds four. Of all the things that I remembered.

A whooping sound emanated from the seating.

Then I turned, I saw her. She was wearing the pink sari. Suddenly, it was 1980, I was back in the registry office.

About to marry the woman I love.

About to start a whole new life.

I watched Dipti glide forward, meet me in the middle as Anita and Arvind looked on.

She took my hands into hers. She even tipped me the wink.

"Family and friends," Started Arvind. "On behalf of Nani and Nana, welcome to their vow renewal. Some you remember this from the first time around, all those years ago. They have kids now, grandkids too. There is also a much bigger bar bill."

And so it began. A renewal of our vows. A snapshot, a memory.

In the coming months, I would forget about Anita's eyelashes. Her yellow dress. I would forget about Arvind's Conga through the hot-house full of tropical plants, close to where we had the reception. It would all turn to grey. I would forget the names of my grandkids. My children, theirs too.

At Christmas, I would have forgotten Dipti, her name and smile. I would forget who she was, how much I loved her.

The grey would descent, the mists of a wretched disease.

Renewal, had been to remember.

Room for dessert

Grimacing, Aurelia let the fizzy alcohol bubble over her tongue and down her throat. All she could taste was metal; the wine failed to live up to its sparkling reputation. Tossing the remaining liquid back, she licked the rim of the fluted glass to wipe away lipstick. A badly bruised raspberry bounced passed her tonsils.

The raspberry was the best bit, as Aurelia passed the tip of her tongue over her lips. Raspberries, were okay. Strawberries on the other hand, were a bit like aubergines. Both, were universe's idea of a joke.

Not that she ate food; real food, that was.

Her appetite was altogether other worldly.

She was here however, to play a part. As a waiter glided passed with a salver of canapés, Aurelia stopped him. A genteel tap at his elbow, a silken smile to pick up a salmon and cream cheese belini. He handed her a slate-grey, paper handkerchief before going his way.

Birmingham and business were both booming. All around her, here at the Edwardian Tea room at the BMAG, local business people milled around. She nibbled on the canapé, to scan the contents.

As a local landowner, a woman with her fingers in a variety of pies, Aurelia had more than earned her place here. She'd been earning her right to be here, since the time that tearoom was actually Edwardian. Aurelia had actually taken tea here, back in the day. The teas, the sandwiches back then had been really quite interesting.

Even now, anchovies rather made her stomach turnover.

This was one of the more glamourous events that she had access to. A black tie gala that brought out old money and new.

Absent-mindedly, Aurelia twirled the white-gold band around her wedding finger. Threading it off, she flicked open her aubergine clutch to drop the ring inside. She didn't need it, not tonight. For such a long time, the band had felt like a piece of costume jewellery. From afar, it looked important. Up close, all that glittered, really wasn't so gold.

Another waiter sauntered passed. She offered another smile, to hand over her empty glass. Still, she scanned the room.

Aurelia, was hungry.

"Lady Aurelia, how are you?" A rich, baritone voice echoed with the timbre of The Valleys to cut through the air. It was followed by the owner; all five ten of him, with red hair and a cloud of citrus-noted cologne.

Oranges. Why did half the population of Birmingham always smell of oranges.

Then there was the icy-blue eyes that were deep enough to dive straight into.

"Dai, how lovely to see you," she replied, as an exchange of air kisses took place. "I'm well, thank you. Still chartering narrow boats up and down the country?"

"I am," nodded Dai, passing a palm through his russet locks. A signet ring glinted with the motion. "It's the eighties. Tourists are flocking to Birmingham, the good times are rolling."

"As are you," commented Aurelia, tapping his elbow to fasten a grin to her lips. "With the movers and shakers. Business must be good. Did you fill up on the canapés?" she nodded towards a waitress circling the room. She carried tiny spinach and feta parcels. The sort that you had eat a handful at a time.

"Never," Dai leant in, a wicked smile danced across his face as he looked Aurelia up and down. "I'd rather wait for the main. Besides, I know what I'd quite like for dessert."

Aurelia batted her lashes, coquettishly for the effect. Dessert. Now that was an idea.

Dinner was served shortly thereafter. Aurelia found herself on Dai's table. Something told her, that this was deliberate; that there had been greased palms somewhere in the mechanics of the Birmingham Business machine. One of the documents currently on her desk at home was a business proposal. Something about investing in Dai's next bright idea. Importing data storage devices; whatever that meant.

She'd put bag down next to her, to shuffle a few place cards. She orchestrated it so that Dai was literally her right hand man. It didn't take long for him to sidle up alongside her; ice bucket in the crook of his arm. Aurelia smiled.

"Dom Perignon," she did the batting of lashes thing again; there was even a giggle. "Excellent," Aurelia pulled out his chair, to beam ecstatically. Her teeth flashed white, and she ran her tongue over her canines.

Aurelia really was hungry. As she whipped a napkin across her lap, her stomach grumbled its discontent.

"Steak rare," declared a waiter, plate held aloft.

"Here," replied Aurelia, "Mine," she added, as it was placed delicately before her.

"My, it was only just breathing," Dai blinked to take in the sight.

"Only just," replied Aurelia, picking up her cutlery. "Exactly how I like it." She cut up and devoured each and every morsel. Each mouthful was bloody delight. Each one a necessary defence against Dai's toes running up and down her calves. His hand, occasionally felt into her lamp.

She really was hungry.

Aurelia made it through the main. Made it through the drawn out speeches and awards for paid notoriety. Still Dai's toes travelled. His hands, were hot, sweaty and horribly intrusive.

With dessert, she slid his hands across the table. Knocking over glasses of really very pricey champagne.

"Oh, silly me!" she exclaimed, a palm pressed to her mouth. "I'm sorry," Aurelia had wanted to growl at him. Instead, she was doe-eyed; lashes still a-flutter.

"Quite all right," Dai purred, mopping up a spillage. "Dessert," he pronounced as a stodgy looking vanilla cheesecake appeared with the wait staff.

"Well," Aurelia moved hers away. "I'd much rather take a walk." She narrowed her eyes at Dai, to flash an inviting and not entirely innocent smile.

"I'm staying nearby," Dai leant in close, the scent of oranges was still there. There was more though. A touch of lime. Not to mention lamb, peas and gravy.

Aurelia fought the urge to wrinkle up her nose.

She could smell dinner.

***

An exit from the BMAG, made for a short walk down Broad Street. Aurelia walked in step with Dai. His arm encircled her waist.

"Do you remember the last time?" he asked, his voice a whisper; his breath hot on her neck. "No idea what you did, but you left me for dead. Left by morning, and I didn't get the chance to say goodbye.

Aurelia's eyes momentarily flashed amber as they arrived at The Jury's Inn. She did remember. She remembered every single moment.

"Time to right things," replied Aurelia. She led Dai into a lift. Throwing a glare at an elderly couple who were about to enter, she threw her arm across the door. "We're in a rush," she growled, pulling Dai in, to jab the door shut.

"Are we now?" Dai rubbed his hands together.

"Oh, yes," she flashed her teeth; the proper ones. Canines and all. Aurelia thrust out an arm to push him to the back of the lift. "I never had desert," she said, her tone dripped with menace as she surged towards him. She threw her arms around his very being; her fingers slid into his russet locks.

Dai was distracted, his eyes closed as he headed towards a peak of nirvana. He didn't notice the tip of her tongue across his jugular.

Salt. Aurelia had needed that on her steak. Here it was, intermingled with sweat.

"You really are hungry," whispered Dai, tugging at Aurelia's dress. His fingers pressed against her thigh.

Pressing her lips to his neck, Aurelia played at kisses. Then she let her lips linger, as she took a bit. Canines and all, sunk into warm flesh.

"What are-"Dai couldn't say any more as his legs gave way beneath him.

Aurelia kicked away his ankles, to carry him to the floor. Her lips never moved, She drew in every cell, every string of Dai's fabric. He whimpered with the last drop, as she drew away. She wanted to see it, feel it. See the life leave.

Dai's eye's flickered from blue to grey as Aurelia took one last drink. Wiping a palm across her mouth, she stood the moment she felt full. She really had been hungry. With her feet-clad in patent maroon heels-she tucked in his wayward limbs. On the surface of it all, he simply looked a little worse for wear.

Aurelia scanned the length of the body. It had taste of far more than its dinner. The lift thudded to a stop. She marched out, but felt dazed; she nearly keeled over. Aurelia frowned, to lick her lips.

Chemicals. She could taste chemicals.

This wasn't the first time. It probably wouldn't be the last. They were all the same.

"Disappointing," she said out aloud, whilst shaking her head. "But not surprising."

She got back into a second life, to go back down. Aurelia traipsed down Broad Street to find a taxi. She would head home. Her head hurt, but her stomach was nicely full.

Dai, had got his just desserts.

Bus route

Holding out her palm, Gayatri waggled her fingers. She smiled at the bus driver; he appeared to smile back. The bus in question, was the eponymous Number 50.

Standing outside of Balsall Heath Library, she'd only been waiting for about ten minutes. Gayatri has missed the bus before by a fraction of a second. The wait wasn't exactly a big deal. She might have looked about sixty-eight, but Gayatri was in fact a great deal older. When you've been around since the dawn of time, waiting ten minutes was a bit like the blink of an eye. She remembered the dawn of time; the innocence and the expectation that had come with it. Then Man had appeared, and it had all gone pretty much down-hill from there on in

The Number 50 Bus. It was headed to Birmingham City Centre. You couldn't miss it as it came to a stop. The doors opened as its chassis lowered, to let Gayatri aboard. Dangling from her wrist was a black, rectangular handbag, with a gold clasp. A clasp, crafted in the shape of two crossed snake heads. A millennia ago, she had bumped into a fellow Divine Being. A young man, who went by the name of Hermes. He'd taught her how play cards-of all the things-there'd been a lot of flirting and harmless banter. Hermes had lost a hand, and staked her a wish as Ante.

Gayatri had wished for a handbag. The sort of handbag that would make her look important; in which, she could carry important things. Hermes had conjured up that very bag. He'd also said something about how a Hermes in the fashion world would someday be iconic.

Iconic. She liked the sound of that. It sounded as good, if not better than important.

Rooting around in the pocket of biscuit-coloured coat, Gayatri eventually pulled out her bus pass.

The bus driver was smiling still.

"Morning, Gayatri, nice to see you," As he spoke, his cheeks dimpled. His smile was bright and beautiful, against his teak skin. Such a smile was rare, and mostly always heaven sent. "Town today, eh?"

"Yes, please," Gayatri flashed a smile back. She still had her own teeth, and didn't it necessary to conjure up dentures. "Nice to see you too. Perhaps I'll see you on the way back as well."

"Maybe. Go on in, take a seat," the driver nodded as the doors closed behind her.

Gayatri shuffled along the bus to take a seat. This had become something of a regular jaunt over the last couple of years. Wednesdays, ten thirty. She would take the bus into two. The Number 50, and more recently, with Gerald. Gayatri sat tight. Her Hermes sat on her lap, with her hands curled tightly around the handle. Looking out through the window, she watched the city blur passed as the bus moved.

Three years ago, Gayatri has been passing through Birmingham. She'd been in Handsworth, to be exact. Drawn by the sound of music; the heady beats of Calypso beats and steel pans, she'd ventured into a carnival. There, she had met Gerald. They had talked over fizzy pop, a vegetable biryani and curried goat. He had told her about his children, how he worked on the buses and that every year he would come to the carnival. He said that came here to enjoy the rhythm of the city, to be part of the rich and diverse tapestry that was Birmingham.

"Birmingham is like a rainbow," Gerald had said. "So many different people; so much kindness. We all get along. Especially, when there is food, rhythm, dancing and some glorious sunshine too." He had grinned broadly at her; his smile was full of kindness and light. The sort, that was very rare and difficult to find. She had felt his openness, his goodness too.

Being a Goddess, Gayatri was drawn to goodness, wherever it might be. When she found it, as she did with meeting Gerald, she had a tendency to stick around. She would do her best to keep a hold of it. To protect it, too.

She frowned as the Number 50 paused outside Joseph Chamberlain College. Gayatri shook her head as she remembered. Six months ago, after she and Gerald had met; he had suffered a heart attack. From far away, from way up on high, Gayatri had felt his heart break. There had even been a messenger at her door; Narad himself, had come to tell her. She had wasted no time. She took on mortal form, to visit him at the Queen Elizabeth Hospital. Gerald had been dosed up at the time, all very bleary eyed and out of sync with reality.

She had held his hands in hers, to tell him that he would get better.

On his bedside table, Gayatri had left Gerald a cassette player. The tape inside, was a recording of steel pans in Trinidad. She had pressed play, before departing back to the heavens.

Music, the melody; divine intercession to help the medicine work that bit better.

Ever since then, Gayatri had kept an eye on Gerald. She had decided to be part of his earthly universe. She would appear at ten, at the Gurdwara near the library. Her ethereal essence would float around at that time, interwoven in the words being read from the Guru Granth Sahib. At ten twenty five, she would assume human form to wait at the bus stop for Gerald.

She would sit, silent and unassuming; watching the streets of Birmingham has he drove. Gayatri kept watching as Gerald turned the bus passed a fire station. Before long, the Number 50 trudged towards Camp Hill, to then stop near what used to be a Lotus garage. There, Gayatri was met by a travel companion. She shuffled along on her seat as the bus shook and shuddered. May be in a passed life, Gerald was a mahout herding elephants.

"Fancy seeing you here," the second elderly woman shuffled along the bus in the same way Gayatri had.

"Hello, Laxhmi," Gayatri was all sing song as the two exchanged kisses on dimpled cheeks. "Nice to see you. You okay?"

"Yes, thank you," Laxhmi sank into the seat next to Gayatri. At her wrist, gold bangles jangled. She tugged the corner of a powder blue khameez over her knee.

Gayatri and Laxhmi. They looked altogether ordinary. Two ladies, of a mature vintage, sat on a bus together. You wouldn't have a batted an eyelid as they nattered. Two innocent, innocuous Aunts or Grandmothers. There was nothing about them, to suggest that they were out of place in the City of Birmingham. They were probably going to town to visit the market, to pick up a punnet of lychees.

These two were, however, far from normal. As for being innocuous, that bit was true.

These two, were Goddesses.

"Oh, I like this," Laxhmi clasped her hands over her own handbag. It wasn't as glamorous looking as Gayatri's, but it was serviceable nonetheless. Laxhmi's had a long strap, was Royal Blue in colour and more a purse. "Adventuring around Birmingham. It's busy, but not beastly. It doesn't assault the senses like London, Delhi or New York. There's a lot to be said for second cities."

"La Hacienda," smirked Gayatri, only to start laughing. "Oh, my, those were interesting days in Manchester," she momentarily closed her eyes. "I even floated around into The Cavern once. Those boys, The Beatles. They really well, apparently. That was Liverpool, though. Manchester, that's technically the third city. What would you like to do today?" She let out a deep breath as she opened her handbag and furtled around inside. A few seconds later, Gayatri pulled out a cellophane bag; it was a hoard of black and white sweets.

"Oh, may I?" asked Laxhmi, eyeing them up.

"Here," Gayatri untwisted the corners to open the bag up wide. "Apparently, all grandmothers should be equipped with a handbag and confectionary of some description. The vintage granny, and not a mod and rocker one."

"Noted," said Laxhmi, grabbing a humbug. "Any particular sort, and for future reference."

"Sweets," pronounced Gayatri, shrugging her shoulders. "Candy. Something to placate children, both big and small.

"These are interesting," Laxhmi had thrown one into her mouth, to pull funny faces. She smacked her lips together as her brow furrowed.

"Minty," commented Gayatri. "Rhubarb and Custard is also good." She handed over a few more sweets, in the middle of her palm.

Diligently, obediently, Laxhmi picked up the sweeties, to throw them into her purse. Opening the flap, she let out a beam of blinding light. For a brief second, there was a display of doubloons, sovereigns, drachmas and guineas; other currencies were in there too. Coinage flashed in the distorted fabric of space and time. To any on looking mortal, there would appear to be a hefty stash of pounds and pence.

Crisp notes and shiny coins. All in an elderly lady's handbag.

Gayatri quickly snapped the purse closed.

"Careful," she hissed, albeit in a whisper. "All that money," Gayatri surreptitiously looked around. "You don't want someone walking off with all that. What you doing, carrying that lot around with you?"

"Goddess of wealth," Laxhmi whispered back. "You know that," she pinched her purse closed. "Loose change."

"Loose change," huffed Gayatri. "Honestly, there is so much to teach you. Adventuring, isn't easy, you know."

"It's been a while," shrugged Laxhmi. "New York is pretty much self-sufficient. London sold its soul in the last economic downturn. Delhi, confuses me. Sometimes I'm welcome, sometimes not. For a country that likes to worship us both, their level of gender equality is beyond my divine remit."

"I'll ask again," sighed Gayatri. "What would you like to do today?"

"You know what," Laxhmi grinned. Her eyes flickered amber for a moment, with eagerness and delight. "I've done a lot of things, as a Goddess, and in human form. Yet, I've never been to a pub. You know, where people go; to socialise, have a good time. I've heard that there's alcohol. That folks like to play games, spend this…."she rattled her purse. The contents made for a metallic, rasping sound.

"There is a place," said Gayatri; her eyes narrowed. "I heard about the music there, but also because of Sarasvati too. She goes there regularly."

"The Creativity Goddess?" posed Laxhmi.

"Yeah," nodded Gayatri. "I went along once, to see what the deal was. The Gunmaker's Arms, Bath Street. Supports all sorts of creatives across the region. Fancy it?"

"I do," grinned Laxhmi, her eyes glistened amber again. "I really do."

***

Driven by Gerald, the Number 50 snaked towards the city centre. Eventually it stopped at the St.Martin's in the Bull ring. There, the two Goddesses took in the view of the market.

"I was there the day started," said Laxhmi. "A simple idea. Works a treat most days. There's been the odd debacle about scrapping it. Yet it means too much to Birmingham, to just disappear."

"You gave someone a nudge, to keep it there?" posed Gayatri. She eyed a stack of mangos that seemed really quite enticing. "Every time, a debacle comes around."

"When I have to," replied the Goddess of Wealth. "Birmingham was the workshop of the world Sometimes people forget that. Not to mention, the city of a thousand trades. It's always been a beacon and I hope that will never change."

Bouncing on its suspension, Gerald's Number 50 bus revved to get a move on. Moving passed Selfridges, it eventually terminated its route outside Primark. Gayatri nudged Laxhmi from her seat. Along with the other passengers, they disembarked.

Gayatri paused at the door. "Thank you, Gerald," she said, waving at him as a plastic screen separated them. "Have a good day, don't forget your lunch." She snapped open her Hermes, to put out a yellow and green cereal bar. She plonked it on top of the bus pass scanner.

"Right, we'll need to walk through town," she said, stepping off the bus to nudge Laxhmi again. This was all part of blending in; the pair of them. Two senior citizens. With Gayatri's handbag still open, she tugged out a silken, floral motif scarf. Wrapping it around her head, she knotted it below her chin.

"It's windy," she told Laxhmi.

The fellow goddess look at her, all very confused. "I'm old," commented Laxhmi, "But I'm not that old. Whatever floats your boat. Where are we going, exactly?"

"Up there," Gayatri wafted a hand at the ramp that led to the Bull Ring. "That will get us to the New Street, as we come out near the bull."

Looking altogether unimpressed, Laxhmi clicked her fingers.

"We're supposed to be little old ladies," huffed Gayatri, clicking her fingers and in quick succession. In the blink of an eye, she and Laxhmi were both standing by the Birmingham Bull.

"It's a funny looking thing," commented Laxhmi, holding out a 'phone to take pictures. It looked like the done thing as shoppers milled around, dong the same thing. It really was the done thing. People always stood there, to take pictures of the Bull, and that was where you asked people to meet you. You really couldn't miss the Birmingham Bull.

"C'mon, Laxhmi, we need to get going," chided Gayatri, hoping to chivvy her on. "It's quite a long walk to the Gunmaker's. At our age, we'll being doing it slowly and not in the blink of an eye." She glared to emphasis her point. "We walk amongst mortals. A flash and a dash, is likely to raise both eyebrows and questions. Not everyone on this green earth has the capacity for Divinity."

"Da Vinci did," grumbled Laxhmi. "Just never got rich though; at least, not whilst he was alive. Van Gogh too; he was just as bad. A supremely horrible waste and of such potential. We tried. Me having a go; you and of course, Sarasvati. Michelangelo; well, he was cute."

"Michelangelo," Gayatri sighed. "That chapel, La Pieta too. That soul was a pleasure to inspire. He couldn't sing for toffee, but there was music and melody to his art."

"I'll never get it," Laxhmi pouted, whilst shaking her head. "Nearly all of them make no wealth; they die penniless. And I try; I try to make it all better for them. Sadly, it only works once they have shuffled off the mortal coil. That bit," said Laxhmi "Is never, ever, anything to do with me."

"That's the human condition, my dear," Gayatri put out her hand as they approached the metro line. New Street crossed here, with Corporation Street. "That is the fine line," she said, as the metro slunk passed. "That exists between Divine Beings and Mortals. Heavenly bodies can only do so much."

Ambling down Corporation Street, they headed towards St. Phillip's Cathedral. Standing behind railings and in the middle of Pigeon Park, the cathedral was statuesque. In comparison to St. Martin's, in sprawled out. St. Martin's was really quite compact.

The two Goddesses stopped by the window.

In a moment, the fabric of space and time, pinged and vibrated. Their mortal forms briefly fizzed away. Time froze, the denizens of Birmingham stood still, unaware. In divine glory, resplendent in the colours of the universe clasped their hands to bow their heads.

They paid obeisance to the fellow Spiritus Sanctus that resided in the walls of the cathedral. This was a moment of communion; a moment of shared divinity and being.

Across the skies of Birmingham, the air zinged with deep, resonating sounds of a conch.

Just as quickly as it had started, the moment flickered away. Time resumed. The people of Birmingham once more milled around. Pigeons cooed, to waddle around the flagstones and memorials.

Exiting Pigeon Park, the two women headed down Colmore Row. Next, they encountered Snow hill and eventually The Children's Hospital. Navigating an underpass, they came out by The Gunmaker's Arms, Bath Street Birmingham.

Going through two sets of doors, they entered the bar. Behind the bar was a young man. Gayatri put him about twenty, barely even a twinkle for a supernova. He had bitter chocolate-coloured hair and scooped it backward with a palm.

"Ladies, we've only just opened," he said, folding up a red and white bar towel. "So that's good timing. What can I get for you both?"

"Well," Laxhmi's eyes grew wide. She surveyed the refrigerator behind the bar. It was full of bottles. There was beer, wine; red, white and rose. She held her blue purse close to her chest.

Gayatri on the other hand, picked up two cheese and onion cobs that were sat on black, circular tray.

"Some of those, please," Laxhmi pointed at the 'fridge, at half-bottles of wine. "Four of the white one."

"Four?" the barman scoffed, there was even the raising of a quizzical eyebrow.

"Yes, please," Laxhmi opened her purse, to pull out a sheaf of crisp bank notes. "Tot it up; tot it all up."

Seeing the money, Gayatri made a grab for more sandwiches. "We'll need them, to mop up the booze," she directed her comments at the rather curious barman. She couldn't help but tip him a wink.

Looking at the money, the barman turned to the 'fridge pretty sharpish. Pulling out bottles, he stacked a tray; glasses were found too. He totted it all up as Laxhmi put down her sheaf cash. He was just about to tell her how much.

"That should cover it," she said, not even waiting to hear how much the damage was. "Keep the change; should buy a couple of rounds for the house."

Laxhmi scooped up the tray as Gayatri had armfuls of sandwiches. They traipsed to a round table nearby. As they sat, two dark, very fluffy cats sashayed across the floor.

"That one's Tia," Said Gayatri; she pointed at a fluff ball. "The other, is her sister Maria. They are The Gunmaker's cats. They have the run of the place; this is their territory. If they like you, they might decide to come over and say hello. Otherwise, they sit, they stare; they watch as they size you up."

"All that power," Laxhmi tutted. She unscrewed the lid off a bottle of wine to slosh some of it into a glass. "And given to fur balls on legs."

Tia hissed first, then Maria followed suit. The two cats looked Laxhmi with pure contempt. Laxhmi glared back; her eyes glowing amber.

"Let them be," Gayatri had unwrapped some of the sandwiches. There was a bed of cellophane strewn across the table. "All that wine, Laxhmi. It's of no use to us; not really. We don't get drunk. Sure, it tastes nice, but that's about it. Doesn't really have an effect."

"Taste rather good, actually," Laxhmi had already taken a hefty swig. Then another had to be taken. Her glass needed re-filling. "One of the many upsides of divinity, is this. I'm able to sample pleasure, but without a price. Though technically, I did pay the man." She picked slices of red onion from her sandwich, to then bite into it.

Gayatri poured a glass for herself. She inhaled the scent of melon and papaya. It was a rather intriguing fragrance that had her looking at the label. She was taking an interest in the grape and vintage. Then, unlike Laxhmi, she sipped her wine slowly.

From the corner of her eye, she saw Tia the cat slope over to wander beneath their table. There was the audible sound of Tia purring as she rested upon Gayatri's feet.

"She likes you," commented Laxhmi, as Maria padded over too. The cat dropped her haunches to recline. "And this one wants belly rubs. Guess we won them over." She left her seat to oblige. Maria purred too, doing her best impression of a car engine humming away. For the moment, the felines had been placated.

Gayatri fiddled with her own sandwich. She wasn't too fussed about the onion. What she did take umbrage at, were the slices of tomato. Sliding these out, she dumped them onto the onions that had no offended Laxhmi.

Sated, Maria the Cat gathered herself up to trot away. There were no longer any hostilities to be had between felines and Goddesses.

Laxhmi and Gayatri watched a photographer hang her artworks in the bar. It was really useful exhibition space from time to time.

"Creative?" asked Laxhmi.

"Yes," nodded Gayatri. "Give it half an hour, and you'll see a few more."

In that half an hour, the two Goddesses ate their sandwiches and drank two bottles of wine. They watched a corner get cleared, as the manager of the brewery-Two Towers, it's lovely-made space. He set up a microphone and a PA system. The bar started to throng as people wandered in. Gayatri nodded towards a flyer pinned to the wall. A blue halo formed around it.

"Literature at lunch time," read Laxhmi. She squinted for effect, though Divinity made for perfect vision. "Hear stories from local writers and support creative talent."

"Well, hello there," A shrill, unexpected voice smashed through the otherwise serene atmosphere. "Of all the pubs in Birmingham, you two ended up here. How lovely to see you both."

As their heads span to the door, you could hear a whip crack.

There, stood resplendent in a purple velveteen kaftan, a matching boa and snakeskin boots was Sarasvati.

Sarasvati, the Goddess of Creativity.

Tucked under her arm, as though light as a feather, was a Spanish Guitar. It was covered in festival stickers. It was actually her sitar, but in a not-so-clever disguise. That wasn't the incongruent bit. She like the other two, was a lady of more mature years. Her hair was worn long; it cascaded down her shoulders, twinkling as though a river of moonbeams.

"Laxhmi, Gayatri," she ran towards them, in something of a sprint. Her boots clattered across the carpeted floor.

Spurs. The Goddess of Creativity wore spurs. They helped inspiration get a move on. That was her logic, anyway.

The three Goddesses met each other, to hold one another in a tight embrace. Air kisses were exchanged. They were more than friends, they were family. Once untangled from one another's arms, Sarasvati pulled up a chair. She waved at the barman, to get another glass. Once it had arrived, it was dutifully filled.

Sarasvati softly strummed her guitar.

Soon, literature at lunch was underway.

Three Goddesses had walked into a bar. They planned to enjoy it.

Love letters

Nandini threaded on her glasses. She held the arms, to press the bridge against her nose.

"Jyoti, can you see me?" she asked, clasping her hands in her lap. "Is it working?"

"I see you, Dadima, yes," replied Jyoti. She was fiddling with a camera. It was attached to a tripod which rested squarely on a coffee table. An electrical cable snaked down and across deep purple carpet towards the wall.

"What would you like me to say?" Nandini took in a deep breath. There was a great deal of nervousness in her voice; her words trembled as they tumbled from her lips. She was anxious about what to say and how. "You want me to talk about the wedding, what happened?" Reaching into the pocket of her powder-blue cardigan, Nandini pulled out some folded-up kitchen roll. Her hands returned to her lap; she tugged at the corners of her kameez to cover her knees.

Behind her glasses, Nandini's eyelashes fluttered gently. She gulped a little. There was so much sitting-a bit like a toad-in both her mind and her throat.

"Yes," nodded Jyoti, pressing record. She then sat in an armchair. In her lap, was a spiral bound notebook and a pink biro. "How did you prepare, what did you feel, that sort of thing. How did you feel about the wedding, how you think things have changed. Now that I'm getting married and to Daniel, what would you like to share with us?"

Nandini nodded, she momentarily gnarled at her lip. She even closed her eyes for a couple of seconds.

"You and Daniel," she said quietly. "You two got to know each other. You love each other, you always will; I can tell. A dadima knows such things. My story, Jyoti. Beta, my story is a little different."

Nandini inclined her head. She looked at youngest granddaughter and smiled. She would tell her story. She'd been holding onto it, for such a long time.

***

Nandini had been woken up by the birds. Singing all too delightfully, they had roused her from a somewhat fragmented sleep. Pushing aside her thin duvet and the coarse, brown woollen blanket that covered it, Nandini slid out from below the covers. She pulled on a blue dressing gown to tie it firmly at her narrow waist. Slowly, Nandini ambled towards the window, to nudge apart the curtains. A thin shaft of light streamed into the room; she frowned at the brightness.

Snow was falling; densely, at that.

Nandini had never seen snow before, not in such quantity anyway. Her eyes grew wider, her mouth fell agape. She watched flakes fall; twisting in the air. One after another, flakes fluttered to the floor and into a heap. No wonder she had felt cold. The duvet was entirely useless. Her outfit, a thin nightdress was threadbare. Like the dressing gown, it was borrowed from her cousin, Shakuntala.

Shakuntala and her husband, Ranbir, had helped Nandini come over from The Punjab. It was also them, that had brokered the relationship.

Relationship. *Rishtah.* That was why she here.

Nandini, was here in Birmingham, to be married. She would be marrying Sunil, in six months exactly.

Closing the curtain, Nandini padded back to her bed. Sat next to it, was a night-stand. She tugged open the drawer; just a fraction, mind. Sliding in her fingers, she put the tips to a photograph. Pinching the coolness between her digits, she raised the image up and out of the drawer.

"Sunil," she whispered, running her palm across the surface of the photograph. Across his jaw, towards his shoulder. He was, a bit like a statue, at an angle. There was something of a stifled smile that was captured by the camera.

"Looks human," Nandini told herself. "You were *human*. I didn't have anything to say. You were kind, you asked me my name. Gave me this. Said you'd see when the date was fixed. To think I've only seen you twice."

Nandini held up the black and white, three by three, square photograph.

"You were shy; was all very sweet really," Nandini smiled, but felt her cheeks flush somewhat. "Shakuntala Bahen was right; you will look after me. Perhaps, we can look after one another. Perhaps, we can learn to love, to like and be with one another."

Feeling a ball of sadness form in the pit of her stomach, Nandini slid the image back into the drawer. She tapped the drawer closed with her fingers.

Then she remembered.

The drawer was opened once more.

Wider, this time. Reaching in, Nandini put her hand to a bundle of envelopes. They were reverently taken out, as though a precious gift. In a way, they were. Letters, from Sunil. Crisp white envelops with coloured stamps. They were tied, with a red and white ribbon.

Nandini's cheeks dimpled, as she read her name. Read, each and every stroke that formed the letters. Such a simple thing, to read her name. She could do that; her sister couldn't.

Over a year ago, a decision had been made. She would go to England. Then, Nandini had asked her friend Sharmila, to help her read; to write as well.

Sunil had asked her. When all the talking was happening, when the elders were deciding.

"Do you?" he had asked. So gently, with such innocence. "Nandini, do you know how to read?"

They had both looked at one another. She had said nothing. Yet, he had taken her face into his hands. Kissed her nose.

Kissed her nose. She'd gone read. No one, had done that before.

She was more than a little surprised. To have only met the man twice. A kiss. Had scared her too, and felt altogether scandalous.

The second meeting had been a couple of months ago. That was when he had handed her the photography. He'd asked about the letters.

"You write beautifully," Sunil had sounded so proud. "It helps, to read your words. I feel as though we're getting to know one another."

She had nodded, still very shy. She had also been a little embarrassed. Sunil would write to her weekly; she would send one in return. Nandin plucked at the ribbon.

Love letters. These were love letters.

"You will learn," he had said, carefully. "I will write to you, so that you can practice. Make sure that you do. I'll help. We'll do this together."

***

"Oh, Dadima, how romantic!" Jyoti clapped her hands together. "You learned to read," she all but swooned. "To write as well. I'm so proud of you. Love letters, Dadima. You and Dadaji, wrote each other love letters.

"Go on," Jyoti ushered Nandini on. "Tell me about the embroidery. The buree that you made."

***

"Saint Dunstan's church hall," Nandini read the name out slowly. Sat at the small table in the kitchen, she was looking at a stack of wedding cards. There were only eight weeks left. "Kings Heath, Birmingham."

"It's not far," Ranbir stood back from the sink as he decanted tea from a saucepan, into a stout-looking Thermos. He worked on the track at Longbridge, and did the night-shift. "Do you like them?" he asked, looking at her over his left shoulder. "There are a couple of spelling mistakes, but these things happen."

Nandini frowned to re-read the card. She hadn't even noticed.

"I'll see you later," declared Ranbir, screwing the lid onto the Thermos. "Don't work too hard," he nodded at the pile of fabric that was heaped next to the cards. "It's beautiful though, Chottee Bahen. I hope that he appreciates you; looks after you. He's educated, and works hard. A doctor, Nandini. I wish you both a happy life together. I must go."

"Yes, you should!" Shakuntala shuffled in. She held onto the door, the table too as she moved. Seven months pregnant, she looked flustered but actually glowed as she sat down. "Go earn the baby some money."

Setting aside the cards, Nandini pulled the bundle of fabric towards her. The one packet, was encased in polythene and rustled as it was moved.

Vermillion red. Sparkling and glistening. This, was her wedding sari. Nandini gently teased out the fabric to spread it out over the small table.

"Gently," whispered Shakuntala. She folded up a duvet cover. There was even a pair of housewife pillow cases too. The smell of oil briefly burst into the air. It was from sequins. Each and everyone of them had been stitched painstakingly into place by hand.

"You did well with these," Shakuntala cradled the bed linen across her bump. She looked closely at the yellow and blue embroidery. A floral motif that had been traced from a magazine. "All being well, will make for a fruitful marital bed."

Nandini kept her eyes on the sari. A silent smirk skulked across her face.

The kiss. All she remembered, was the kiss.

"I hope that I can finish this," Nandini pressed a finger into a pile of sequins. With her free hand, she picked up a needle threaded with gold. "My sister was kind, to send the fabric."

"And your mother marked out the design," Shakuntala smiled a little. "Just think. One day, you might have a little girl of your own. The two of you, might sit your own kitchen. Having the same conversation that we are."

Nandini shrugged. Knotting the thread, she used the tip of the needle to pick up a sequin. She worked on the sari for weeks. It was done a week before; one week exactly, before her wedding day. A vermillion sari, there were red bangles to match. Her mother's gold Tikkah too. A beautiful piece of research that had travelled with her from The Punjab. A talisman, to her safe, loved too.

It soon came around. Six weeks. Six weeks, and Nandini married Sunil.

***

"Jyoti?" Nandini knocked on the door. She pushed it open a little, to peer through the gap. Sat at the vanity table, was her granddaughter.

"Dadima, come on in," Jyoti rose from her chair, gathering up her blue dressing gown. "Did you bring it?" she asked, her hands clasped before her.

Nandini nodded as she entered the well-appointed hotel room. "You look beautiful," she beamed, to blow an air kiss. Over her wrist, was a trouser hanger. Attached to it, was a garment in a polythene bag. Nandini caught sight of another garment. Hanging on the wardrobe, it was an ivory coloured gown that was embellished with silver embroidery and a smattering of sequins.

Jyoti looked at the sari. "Vermillion red," she whispered. "It's so sparkly and glittery." Her words came out light, fluffy and filled with awe.

"Oh, beta," Nandini stepped forward, whilst trying to avoid Jyoti's freshly applied make-up. She dabbed a piece of tissue delicately against Jyoti's nose. "It's clean, pressed. All ready for you. Do you really want to wear it?"

"Yes," nodded Jyoti. "Do you have the Tikkah too? For me to wear in church." Jyoti waved at the hairdresser who overing close by. He had been asked to wait for a moment.

Rooting around in the pocket of her pink cardigan, Nandini pulled out a blue, rectangular, velveteen box. She turned it over to the hairdresser.

"I hope it will match," Said Nandini as she also handed over the sari. "It's silver, should match your white dress perfectly." She held her breath as Jyoti sat back at the vanity table. The hair dresser fiddled with Jyoti's hair to place it neatly into her parting.

She saw herself in Jyoti's face. All those years ago, she had been a fresh-faced young woman with the world at her feet.

"Nandini, where are you?" A voice travelled, from outside of the room, down the hall. It broke her daydream, to shatter the memory.

"I will see you later," smiled Nandini, blowing another kiss. "Must got see your grandad. Safety pins!" she squealed loudly. Once more rummaging in her pocket. She pulled out a plastic box. It was full of large safety pins. Some of them, tucked into the box, were even older than Jyoti. She plonked the box onto the table.

One last hand-me-down. One last heirloom.

"Tie it properly," blowing one more kiss as she left. She was fizzing with sheer joy.

***

"Do you remember?" Nandini stood at the door Dangling from her wrist, was a large, baby pink, Hermes handbag. Attached to the handle, was a key ring in the shape of the Birmingham Bull. "We got married here," Nandini looked at the people who milled around St.Dunstan's Church hall.

"It looks tiny now," replied Sunil, holding out his hand. "We only had forty people. Most of them men."

"All of them men," tutted Nandini. "There was me, Shakuntala. Her little boy."

"Talking of which," Sunil waved at the photographer. The baby at their wedding now a strapping adult who now photographed other people's nuptials. The small, church hall was being used as photography studio.

"She looks lovely," sighed Nandini, as Jyoti swooshed into a shot. A clutch of flower girls jostled around her skirts in something of a beautiful train.

"Did you give her your sari?" asked Sunil. "She already has your Tikkah. That was lovely. We did try, my darling sunshine. Two boys. A little girl. It was all too much, and I couldn't bear the thought of losing you."

"Don't," Nandini tutted, to elbow her husband as tears formed. "Not today, my sweet boy."

Darling sunshine. My sweet boy. She was his darling sunshine. He'd always called her that. It always made her smile, to giggle on the inside. His terms of endearment was full of love, honour and always said with respect.

"I remember reading that," Sunil kissed her hand. "In your letters. Made very happy, every time. We've been so happy. Each and every single day."

She had practiced. To write it, to say it. To call him that. He was her sweet boy.

***

Jyoti had asked them to lead. To lead the bridal party into the reception. As they entered, a dhol player dressed in blue heralded their arrival.

"We could do it all again," Sunil whispered as they walked. "Dhol players at the wedding, my darling sunshine. We could have one of those."

Nandini shushed her husband as they made for the head table. Behind them, were Daniel's grandparents. Then the over-joyed parents too.

Last but not least Jyoti and Daniel arrived. The Dhol player had quickened to a crescendo.

Jyoti swooshed in her sari. It was hers now. Vermillion red, shiny and sparkly. All pinned into place, with crisp pleats. As Jyoti moved, it caught the light beautifully.

Tea and Tonic

Letting out a deep breath, Ida closed her rectangular, red hand bag. She rubbed a finger over the gold clasp as she ran the tip of her tongue over her lips. The handbag, the mink coat that wore and the pink lipstick that she wore, were all borrowed. Borrowed from the girl that she shared a room with. The same girl who had sent her here, on a blind date.

"Oh, he's a friend of a friend," Therese had been all very vague. "He's from Derry. A real nice fella. I'm sure he'll be grand on the day. Meet him in The Kerryman. You'll have a whale of time. I'll even lend you my coat. It'll fit you a treat."

Ida had agreed. She had nothing to lose, not really.

"I suppose," he had said, wafting a cigarette out of the window. "It'd be nice to meet new people. And if he's from Derry, it's a good as being neighbours."

Pressing a glass of vodka and tonic to her lips, Ida scanned the bar. A few brickies that she knew from The Irish Centre milled around. She nodded and smiled in all the right places. Yet her heart was still racing ten to the dozen.

The Irish Centre.

She'd been there a few times over the last couple of months. They'd helped her with a few bits and pieces. Ida had needed some advice getting on her feet, having come over from Wicklow.

Grimacing at the Vodka and Tonic, she glugged the rest down quick to land the glass down heavily. It just about landed upon a beer mat.

The Irish centre definitely had better Vodka-Tonics. Shandy too, that stuff was probably better there as well. Ida couldn't have felt more of a fraud. She tugged down the hem of her black and white, checked dress. She held it firm over her knee for a moment, only for it to quickly ping back a little. A little, for it only just not be indecent. As with the rest of her ensemble, the dress was also borrowed. Made of horribly scratchy material, it was uncomfortable on multiple levels.

"I'll wait a little longer," she told herself. Her heart rapidly still, but with a blueness to the beat. The blueness that came from knowing that she'd been stood up.

"Half an hour," she looked at the drained glass on the beer mat. "You never know who might turn up."

Carefully climbing down the steps of the bus, Amit took in a gulp of fresh air. He'd been travelling a while; he'd had a long journey to get here.

He'd started at Delhi, with a layover in Paris. Then he had landed at Gatwick. The bus had the brought him here, to Birmingham.

Standing in something of a motley crue of travellers, Amit waited for his luggage. Rummaging around in canvas bag slung over his shoulder, he pulled out a blue and white copy book. Inside, listed in neat cursive handwriting, were the different stages of his journey. He'd been nervous, about travelling here; travelling to study in a foreign country. Amit had also heard the stories. The good ones, about coming to Britain; how the United Kingdom was opening its doors to the members of The Commonwealth.

How Britain, was the land of milk and honey.

A Brave New World.

A heavy, gunmetal grey attaché case landed with a clunk onto the black tarmac. Clutching at the copy book, Amit scrambled to retrieve it. It was all he had. All that he had been able to bring with him. All of his worldly possessions, so few and far between, had fit into that case.

Dragging it close, Amit hoiked it up into his hand. He looked at the copy book; there was an address inside, that wasn't too far from here. A boarding house, that was happy to accept someone from the Indian

Sub-continent. There weren't many such establishments who expressed that sentiment. There was another place on the list, another address that had he'd been given.

The Kerryman. That sounded interesting.

A public house. Ah, that was the rub.

Amit shuddered a little; there was also a feeling of being abashed. He'd heard about pubs. How people would drink, brawl; they'd waste away their earnings.

He patted his pocket; the contents jangled. There were a few shillings in there. Perhaps he'd get some tea, something to eat. His friend Ashish-who he was meant to be sharing with-was meant to meet him there. Together, they would be enrolling in the local technical college later in the year. The two of them were here to better themselves, so as to be part of this Brave New British World. Dropping the copy book back into his bag, Amit pulled out a map. Unfolding it, he headed out of Digbeth Coach station.

Something made Ida look at the door. Her eyes darted towards it, as it swung open with a groan. For all of three seconds, she felt a zing of excitement. Perhaps he would show after all.

Only, it wasn't him. He was different; very different. Didn't look in the least bit Gaelic, for one. Not that Ida knew what her date actually looked like. This was after all, meant to be a blind date.

The suitcase caught her attention. She'd never seen one like that before. Grey, metal; it looked heavy.

Ida watched as the traveller went to the bar. She heard an accent over the hubbub. Given how she had one too, she liked to listen out for those beyond the broad, Brummie twang that she was still getting used to hearing.

He ordered a drink. His suitcase clattered to the floor.

Two drinks. Perhaps he was here on a date as well?

One, was a lager dash. There was a lot lemonade. The other was a pot of tea. A pot of tea that was plonked onto a tray with a dish of sugar cubes.

As he looked for a seat, Ida caught his eye. Head on, without thinking; for a good minute or so.

She looked away, embarrassed. Biting her lip, Ida pulled a face to focus on her handbag. Mammy had been right. It was rude to stare. She really had stared; right at him. But once more, Ida had a feeling.

"Erm," she looked up, with conviction, and even waved. "Your case." Ida got up; she hobbled to the bar. Her feel really didn't like these heels. These, or any other heels, for that matter. "Don't leave it there. You'll lose it. Come sit with me, if you like."

"Oh, I…" Amit blinked. Words, were suddenly very hard to form. His brows knitted together, to take in the sight of the rather attractive young woman. She had the most beautifully formed eyes, and lips that looked like a rubies. He was more than a little confused. He was also trying to understand what she had said; she spoke with a rhythm. "I'm sorry, what did you…"

He had no idea where that accent came from; it certainly wasn't local. Amit had some ear for English; the basic kind, at least. Vaguely. This, wasn't the same.

Amit watched as his case was dragged away. That worried him a little.

Ida beckoned him over, to sit back down. *'You have nothing to lose,'* she told herself.

"What's the harm?" Amit muttered to himself. He bundled the pint-he'd wanted to try it, see what the fuss was all about-onto to the tray with the tea. He'd also asked for loads of Soda, just in case he had an unwelcome experience of the alcohol. Amit also wondered what Ashish may think, if he came across as being a little worse for wear. Amit and alcohol didn't mix very often, if at all.

"I'm Ida," she held out a hand; a trembling hand. It may have also been a bit hot and greasy with the anxiety of meeting a perfect stranger.

"Amit," he replied, sitting down to also shake her hand. Then he placed his other hand over it. "Nice to meet you," he said whispering. "Ida."

Ida was scared, but the way he held her hand was comforting. She had been taught to stay away from strangers; strange men in particular. Amit, could qualify on both counts. He didn't know her from Eve.

Amit flashed her a smile. It was the only thing that he could do, in not keeling over. He was struck by her friendliness, the sheer warmth and kindness of a perfect stranger. That, and he had no clue as to what he was supposed to. He'd never been accosted by a strange woman before.

"I was waiting for a da-friend," Ida pipped. "Didn't show, so I'm here by myself, alone."

Amit followed, as best he could. The accent, there was music beyond the words. But he also fallen into her eyes. Eyes, that were a beautiful shade of grey-blue. A colour, that Amit had never seen before.

"Not anymore," he shook his head, to pour tea. "Would you like that?" Amit nodded at the lager.

She wasn't alone, not any more. That actually made Ida blush; not so much the words, as the meaning behind them. "Don't you fancy it?" she asked, seriously considering the offer. She didn't fancy another vodka and tonic any time soon.

Amit shook his head. "Not really, it was just an idea," tapped his mug of tea with a finger. "This will do for now. Should probably eat before…"his nose wrinkled as the lager.

"Well," Ida shrugged to pick it up, and took a mouthful. "Oh, dear," she pulled a face to match Amit's. "All that lemonade. There's a better one down the road, and at The Irish Centre. Will do for now, though. You new in town?" she asked, her eyes wide.

Ida was more than a little curious.

Amit nodded; he was still trying to follow her every word. "Yes," he sipped his tea slowly. "Perhaps, Ida, you could show me around."

"Perhaps I could," Ida tipped him a cheeky wink. She had no idea what has possessed her. That, and the way he said her name.

That was just magic; pure, magic.

Shadows

Pulling up the collar of her midnight-blue trench coat, Orca glided into the grounds of the cathedral. She darted her inky-blue eyes from left to right.

This was perfectly ordinary.

Her black, patent heels clicked across the paving slabs that skirted around St.Phillip's. One of the smaller cathedrals in Britain, it was nestled amongst concrete surrounded by a parcel of green. A parcel of green that was home to what felt like hundreds of pigeons.

Pigeon Park. This was it. The cooing, was an incongruent beat across the sound of bustling Birmingham. The birds made the most of their patch; ambling around in a slate of oblivion as rain fell in greasy globules.

Hence, the trench.

That and given her job spec, Orca felt she could blend in and get something of a kick out of it.

She was here to meet somebody

Heading towards a bench by the Chancel window, Orca quickened her pace. The rain continued to beat down hard; her coat was getting heaver by the second. Rifling through her pockets, she pulled out a compact umbrella. Flinging it open, with a flourish, Orca wiped the bench down with a coat sleave to sit.

She took a deep breath in, to focus on the stained-glass window. Designed by Edward Burne-Jones, it was all very bright today as grey clouds cloaked the city. Orca couldn't help but smile, if only for a moment.

It was nice to get out of the office at Waterloo House. Nice to get out, and if only for a few minutes. She was out, for a good reason. Waterloo House, was a centre for Localised Operations for Espionage. Yes, here, and in Birmingham. So far away from Birmingham, the whole thing was all very innocuous. Any would be superpower, of the nefarious kind at least, probably wouldn't come looking. That was the logic, to some part, at least.

Most innocent people wouldn't need to look either. Not here, in Birmingham. The City of a thousand trades.

"I hear Valencia is very nice this time of year."

Lost in her reverie, hadn't registered the hand reaching out towards her mouth. Her reflexes had slowed down of late. Held tightly between the fingers, was a lighter. Her moment of solitude was smashed further by a click and the rise of a yellow flame that billowed in the damp air.

Orca smirked. Once more, she rifled in her pockets. This time, she pulled out a packet of cigarettes. Tearing away the wrapper, she slid one out to hold it between her lips.

Dancing seductively, the flame from the lighter caressed and finally kissed the end of the cigarette. Orca took a drag, before pulling it away with a manicured finger.

"Tarragona, is to die for," she replied; her words tumbling out in a plume of smoke. "Wonderful, at fiesta time." She turned to face the fellow field worker, with whom she was sharing a damp bench. Orca recognised him; his accent was something of a legend amongst the secretaries. Many of whom would draw lots to simply take a message or volunteering to take down a dictation.

"Tabitha Grey is waiting as the dishwasher," his eyes narrowed with intrigue as he spoke. Caledonia tumbled out with each and every word. "Once the crockery is clean, she'll stack it for delivery."

"Very good," Orca took another drag. She was trying not to get distracted by his rhythm and blues idiolect. Hers, in contrast, was all very clipped glass. "She will need to make a dessert. For the Lieutenant. He is headed to Barcelona."

"Noted," Orca's Caledonian colleague nodded as he wrapped his hands around one knee crossed over the other. "A delicate, frothy dessert, or a full-scale Eton Mess."

"Delicate," Orca rolled the word out very slowly. "Eton Mess always leads to questions, and is somewhat difficult to clean up. After dessert, Tabitha should take the long way to Tipperary. That will allow the dust to settle."

"Lilly Beth is returning," Caledonia pouted a little, his lips were pursed all very dramatically. "From her own sojourn to Tipperary. She is curious, about her next piece of cake. What is her next recipe?"

"Tiramisu," replied Orca, tapping away ash. Embers flickered to the floor in the breeze. "And by Lake Como. In Bellagio, she'll find an armoire. It needs to be broken up."

"To be turned into kindling?" Caledonia arched a brow.

"To be turned into as many fragments as possible," she returned. "Which are then thrown away, dispersed through all the colours on the wind. Check, Ciaran, that Lilly Beth, is treated for splinters. The Masala Wine of this Tiramisu has the potential to cause an almighty hangover."

"Orca," Ciaran leant in, his ear touching hers. "You only use my name, when you are trying to protect me. Despite what the secretaries say, you're actually human. One with a soul. Thank you, I love you too."

Closing her eyes, Orca inhaled what remained of her cigarette. Once it was all done with, she the slipped the filter tip into her pocket. She handed over her umbrella.

"The kids miss you, Orca," Ciaran let out a deep breath. "You should check in with them, and soon.

Adelphi goes to Cardiff in the Autumn, His A-levels, Orca, man alive; he got your brain."

"I'll call," she dipped her gaze to the floor. Her palms were planted downwards either side of her knees on the bench. "Poppy?" She asked, focusing on a puddle as the chancel window reflected into it.

"Is looking after our grandchildren." Ciaran rose to his feet, clutching the umbrella. "We have two. The one is three. The other is five. So you know."

Reaching out her hand, Orca took Ciaran's left one into hers. She twirled the thin band on his finger.

"You've lost weight," she all but whispered it; her words were filled with lament. "That used to be wedged on. I remember, as I put it there."

"Blame my wife," Ciaran coughed to tug at his collar. He too wore a trench; only his was bottle green. "I miss her roast dinners. No one, makes a roast leg of lamb, in the same way as the love of my life. Yorkshires are always a bit limp though."

Orca tutted to smack his perfectly-formed backside, to spur him away. It was most definitely one of his better features.

Ciaran walked away as thunder cracked across the sky. Birmingham's usually bright blue sky flashed with lightning.

She left soon after, to return to her desk at Waterloo House. Her secretary put in video call to both Poppy and Adelphi. Then she set the grandchildren toys. Fluffy ones.

Market Day

Eleanor stirred softly. She had slept well, having eaten well. There was little for her to complain about. Her life was filled with comfort, as would have been expected for a lady of her station. Wriggling her toes across bed linen, Eleanor sighed. She had spent yet another night alone.

Another.

It was a month, maybe more, since she had last shared her bed. She kept track, she had to. There were certain expectations and obligations that came in having this particular life. The notion of having once more slept alone, filled her head and her heart with a heavy sadness. Eleanor held her coverlet close as she turned on her side.

Peter's side of the bed was cold. Empty. She had so hoped that he would join her. Gnarling at her lip, she pulled her braid to her bosom. Her heart beat was as hollow and unfulfilled as her sheets.

"You are always so busy," she whispered, twirling the curled ends of her soft brown locks. "Lord of the manor, surveyor of his people. Would it hurt you, put you ill at east, to attend upon your wife once in a while?"

Sliding across, Eleanor removed herself from the marital bed. She exited via Peter's side. Fighting through heavy, damask curtains, her feet landed upon bulrushes strewn across the floor. Pulling a face, as she felt them beneath her naked feet, she kicked a few sheafs aside.

"I would rather have splinters," she muttered, heading towards the nearest encasement. Nudging aside another set of curtains, Eleanor rubbed a finger against the icy, cold pane. Peering out, with one eye closed, she watched a goose waddle across the courtyard. Close behind was a pale pink pig. No doubt both had travelled from a nearby village.

"Thursday," whispered Eleanor. A feint smile danced across her thin, pale pink lips. "Market Day. Thank goodness."

Hurriedly, Eleanor skipped towards a wash-basin. Tapping the thin of layer of ice that had formed, she splashed water across her face. The coldness, was bracing but strangely invigorating.

"Market day," As she repeated the words, she felt her heart beat that bit harder. Then there were the butterflies that did somersaults in her stomach. There was deep joy to be had, and to make her forget an absent husband.

It would be another hour before her lady's maid finished helping her dress. The encasement drapes had been pulled back to let in hazy, but beautiful sunshine. As her wood green-coloured bodice was laced tightly, Eleanor smiled to let the light fall upon her face. With her eyes closed, she savoured the warmth as it enveloped her.

The touch of brightness, lingered on her skin as though a kiss. How she longed, for her lips, to feel such a kiss.

"Lydia," she said, opening her eyes as she clapped her hands together. "Fetch young Geoffrey, his sister, Rose, too. After I have broken my fast, I would like to venture into the court yard. To inspect the wares, being brought in for today's market."

"Right, away, my lady," Lydia bobbed away with a curtesy.

Left alone, Eleanor moved to the small chest under her encasement. Sat in the sun, the dark wood had become warm to the touch. Breathing slowly, she ran a finger over the metal braces that gave the chest a touch of majesty. Contained within it, were a few trinkets, a few jewels. Some ornaments that Eleanor had brough with her as part of her dowry. That had been six years ago.

'*All things precious,*' She thought to herself, as she pulled open the clasp that kept the chest secured closed. Once inside, Eleanor flung around a number of pouches that sat in her way. Eventually, she came upon her quarry.

In her palm, sat a rough, red-coloured parcel. It was the same size, as a freshly harvested apple. The sort that could be found in today's market, having travelled in from Worcester. Unfolding the fabric, she couldn't help but smile as the contents were revealed.

On a black leather cord, hung a medal. It bore the image of blacksmith standing over an anvil.

She had tucked it away; a keepsake. A memento.

A distant memory, of being another woman.

She had been so young, innocent and unworldly. Only for Peter to pass through her father's manor near the Welsh Borders. A few years older, Peter had offered his hand after only one dinner in their home. His suit was snatched up and quickly. Their wedding planned and celebrated in haste, with barely a moment for her to catch her breath.

And here she was; married to His Lordship of the Manor of Birmingham, Eleanor had grown from a slip of a girl to being a lady.

THE Lady.

"Only you took the time," Eleanor neatly folded up the bundle. "To show me that there was a whole world out there. I left one, to be part of another."

Holding onto bundle, Eleanor left her bed chamber. She moved slowly down the stairs to the hall. Last night, she and Peter had dined with company. A band of merchants who had come to scope out today's market. They were hoping to start exporting goods across the seas and to lands afar.

Breaking her fast alone, she nibbled on some hard cheese. There was also a cottage loaf. She ate a little, as her stomach churned to make her feel at unease. She knew why. Why her stomach churned and her pulse raced.

Thursday. Market day.

Washing the food down with small beer, Eleanor summoned Rose and Geoffrey. It was time to visit the court yard.

Eleanor let the children go on ahead. Rose, as a scullery maid, was charged to find a list of items for the kitchen. Geoffrey, as a kitchen hand, would help keep her focused. She, herself, moved from trader to trader. Calls of 'My Lady' every now and again warranted a sweet, interested smile. She would nod her head, perhaps even address those she had met before, by their names. As the wife of the Lord of the Manor, Eleanor knew to take an interest.

Ever since Peter had secured the market charter, the court yard would fill up every week. It would bustle with traders and their wares. Many, came from afar; but there were also locals who were now regulars in the crowd. All around her, there were calls, caws and crowing too. The denizens of Birmingham, were set apart from the chickens and other farmyard creatures ready to be traded.

Eleanor had grown to love Birmingham. To love Peter, too.

She had learned to love the Lord of the Manor. To have loved another, to then love Peter, had been difficult.

Then, on Thursday, she had seen a face. The face of someone familiar. The face of someone, who she couldn't call a stranger. Today, it was Thursday. She looked once more, for that familiar face.

***

"He has a manor in the next county," Eleanor had sobbed. Her every breath hot and pained as it passed through her lips.

"So, he can give you a life," his words been spat out; hurled against the walls of the smithy. "You could never have that with me, a mere blacksmith."

"How I wish that I could!" Eleanor had hurled her words back; to shout, unapologetically. She could do that here. She had then bounded towards him, to hold his hands in hers; before surrendering entirely to his arms. Arms that made her feel safe, loved and above all, wanted. "We could have that; what if we were to run?" Looking up, she had cradled his face, caressed his cheek. Then there was the kiss of longing, of deep-rooted want that she plundered from his pale lips.

"No, we'd be hunted, found in a flash," Pulling away, his face has become ashen. Sadness and frustration pulled his features taut. "I knew that this day would come; that I would lose you. You belong with someone of your station. Someone more fitting and able to give you the life that you were born to lead."

Silence had followed. No formal good, drawn-out goodbye as he heart had torn straight down the middle.

"Here," eventually he turned back to face her. "Take this, and think fondly of me. Perhaps one day, our paths may cross. We part strangers, to meet once more, and become acquaintances."

***

"Those are for the Lord of the Manor. He wanted shoes for the horse. His wife's horse."

Horse shoes clunked aside as an anvil rang. The horse in question wasn't stabled very far. A barbary steed, worthy of well -made shoes. The shoes were to be tinkered with for now, before a farrier was called. The anvil continued to ring and resonate. It was said that the skies of Birmingham rang with the sound of a thousand anvils.

It had seemed a good place to set up the smithy. To move across the border. He'd heard about the charter; the market in the manor.

So, he had travelled, kit and caboodle. His apprenticeship had been served; he was able to forge his own success. He could be his own man.

Part of him had known, part of him had prayed. To have asked, and then to receive.

"Master Blacksmith?"

Bundling up the shoes into coarse, off-white linen, Owen took a deep breath. His eyes had shot up. He knew that voice; the way in which it rang true. The way, in which it made the hairs on the back of his neck stand up.

***

Eleanor had closed the barn door. Owen had all but ran in after.

In a matter of moments, they had swept each other up. They were engulfed in one another's arms. She let loose kisses that had could be barely contained. Pure emotion that had simmered beneath her skin, had soared to the surface.

Emotions, kisses; all that her husband failed to appreciate.

"What if we get caught?" Owen was only just able to utter each word. He stumbled forwards; his feet just about moving as he was led towards a hayloft. Eleanor's headdress hung from his finger-tips. He'd been able to unlace her dress, he'd been thar close to her skin.

***

Braiding her hair, Eleanor made no effort to supress the cat-like grin that had bloomed across her face.

"That was…" Owen shook his head as he carefully laced up Eleanor's dress. "We risk getting caught. You risk everything; your life, your station. As the Lady of the Manor. This…" He span her around his arms; his hazel eyes dipped into hers.

"Has to end," Eleanor snatched away her eyes. She couldn't bare to look into them, having fallen so deep. She longed to stay there, in his arms, with his heart beating close to hers. To so close, and to spend an eternity drowning in his eyes. "And it shall," she whispered. She ruffled her skirts, to hold a ragged bundle in her palm. The bundle from her chest. She held it out, on her palm.

"That was a memory," Owen picked it up with the tips of his fingers. "To be kept, and thought of fondly."

"It was," Eleanor skulked forwards, to kiss the tip of Owen's nose. "But now it is returned, with my undying love and enduring affection."

Owen's face fell once more; the colour ebbed away from his cheeks. One last time, he touched her face. He teased a strand of straw from her hair.

"We are but strangers once more, Owen," She turned away, to climb down from the loft. She paused before she did. "Acquaintances, that will long be forgotten." With those words, she clambered down. Eleanor moved with her eyes closed, lest he saw her tears. But above all, she couldn't bare the sight of his and falling from eyes that she loved so dearly.

Returning to the market, Eleanor found Rose and Geoffrey. They had been looking for her, and feared a stern reprimand in having become lost in the market.

Eleanor shushed them gently. Children were easily placated. They all returned to the Manor house. She looked over her shoulder, at the bustle of the market.

Later, when the market was over, the Lord of the Manor found himself in her bed.

She thought of Owen. Of the gifts given, and the gifts received.

It would be eight and half months later, when the parting gift arrived.

Owen's gift. A neat little bundle, to be looked after. Good times fondly remembered.

Blue is the colour: Allegiance

"I guess I should have been more specific," Gorbind's brow's knitted together. Held aloft in the light of the window in his daughter's room, was her football shirt.

"You said put her name on it," Padmi was kneeling next to Mango's bed, heling the little girl put her shoes on. Shoes, that were dark blue and matched the Birmingham City Football Club shirt.

"Her real name," said Gorbind, shuffling across the room before handing Mango her clothes.

"This beed fine," grinned the little girl. She swept aside locks from dark hair from her face. Placing the shirt across her lap, Mango ran her finger across the lettering. "M-A-N-G-O," she giggled loudly. "No one uses my proper name anyways, Daddy," she pronounced, rolling her shoulders. There was some wisdom in her words, well beyond her six years. "Is okay, not many Mango's in Birmingham." Mango beamed as she pulled on the shirt. "I need a wee," she declared, all too freely. She slid of the bed to leave her room, and her parents alone.

All very wide-eyed, Gorbind watched his baby bounce away. She never ceased to amaze him. Between his wife, his grandmother and Mango, there was also going to be a three-way split on his heart strings.

"You're scared," Padmi had clocked his feelings of whimsy, to wrap her arms around his chest. "You're taking her to a football match: a Blues game. This is a first for you both. It'll be okay," Padmi stood on her tip-toes to splodge a kiss across his cheek. She then licked the tip of her finger, to remove an eyelash that had landed on the bridge of his nose.

"Blow," she said, holding her finger close to his lips.

Pouting, Gorbind made a wish to do what he was told.

"And no one knows," she said softly, threading her hands into the back pockets of Gorbind's jeans. "That you're a Villa fan, wandering into enemy territory."

"You won't tell?" he asked, wariness edged his tone. He was genuinely scared about today.

"Not today," replied Padmi, shaking her head. "Not ever. Let's get down stairs. Suraj will be here soon. He has our tickets."

***

In the lounge, Gorbind helped Mango into her coat. He pulled up her hood, before zipping her in snuggly. He was scared. His baby was going to her first football match.

"Aww, so sweet," Padmi had appeared. With her 'phone in her hands, she'd already taken a picture. "Just like her first day at nursery. Only you cried; you both did. I remember the piles of soggy tissues all over the place." She waved her 'phone at him, to flash the image.

"That was scary too," he said, taking a quick glance. Then he caught sight of what she was wearing. She too had a football shirt. Padmi was buxom, beautiful and in Birmingham City Blue.

She turned, waggled her backside, and flexed two thumbs at the name on the back.

Names, rather and hyphenated.

Dharam-Phalla.

"C'mon then, folks, we should get going." At the door, Suraj clapped his hands together. "Let's get on the road. St.Andrew's awaits." He held out a hand towards the little girl, and waggled his fingers. "Your car seat awaits, missy."

Obediently, Mango clasped the offered hand and followed. Her trainers flashed as she moved. The soles, as they were new, squeaked as though excited.

"Buy him a pint later," Padmi clambered into her own coat, to then take Gorbind by the hand. "C'mon, don't be dragging your claret and blue feet."

Gorbind had no choice to follow and fall into step with his wide. His heart raced so hard, his chest ached. Ached, for his baby going to her first match; for him, being a Villa fan in the middle of the Birmingham Blue sea. It also ached, at the prospect of being in a stadium full of thousands of people.

As he and Padmi climbed into Suraj's car, Gorbind did his best to ground himself. At least he wasn't driving today. That was one less thing to worry about.

"This should be fun," Suraj smiled, to look at Mango in the rear view mirror. "You okay there, Mango."

Mango nodded, grinned, and then gave him two thumbs up.

"Win, lose or draw," muttered Gorbind, buckling up. "Thank you, and in advance, Suraj."

"Don't mention it," Suraj chimed, pressing the start button to fire up the engine. "Family day trip and to the The Blues; it's a pleasure."

Family. Gorbind looked briefly at Padmi. Suraj was her sixth, seventh, eighth cousin, twice removed or something to that effect on her mother's side.

He also happened to have Blues tickets. Suraj was lovely, despite having a brimming passion as a Blue nose. Gorbind got on well with him; perfectly well, in fact. So when Suraj told Padmi that he had tickets for a ding dong Derby, Gorbind didn't have a leg to stand on. He did have a soft spot for the kid. His parents were no longer around. All Suraj had left was his elderly grandmother. Days like today, were about family. As such, being eighth cousin twice removed didn't really matter.

Padmi doted on the boy; she'd been close to his mother. For the pair of the, football was more than the beautiful game. It was a shared, familial connection. Gorbind was yet to reconcile himself with his wife's footballing allegiance. He loved her dearly, but her choice in football teams was something he was yet to fully understand.

Fortunately, it didn't take long to get to the stadium; nearby at least. Suraj parked up close enough not to get tangled in parking dramas and also to spare the strain on Mango's legs.

He and Mango walked on ahead, leaving Padmi and Gorbind to bring up the rear.

"Do you think we'll have another?" asked Padmi.

"I was going to table that motion," Gorbind replied, swinging their interwoven fingers in the space between them. "With words to that effect. We could."

"Really?" she squealed, albeit quietly, as she pulled shoulder closer.

"We'd have fun trying," Gorbind's brow momentarily arched. "That bit wasn't bad the first time 'round. Could do that again, no problem."

"Dirty nappies," commented Padmi. She stopped walking, to pull his hands into hers, "Sleepless nights, the colic and the cravings."

"We've done it before," he kissed both of her hands. "One request though, for now."

Padmi's eyes narrowed, her lips puckered into a pout.

"Next one is a Villa fan," A smirk danced across Gorbind's face. "Or not remotely interested. Whatever comes first?"

"I should second the motion, shouldn't I?" Padmi mirrored the smirk, but bit her lip.

"Technically, you're the one who'll carry it," giggled Gorbind, swinging her hand again. "He, she or them."

Catching up with Suraj and Mango, the family followed the crowds that snaked into St.Andrew's.

***

On the touchline, two opposing managers jumped around. Both gesticulated wildly whilst shouting and screaming at their respective players.

The one, with a shock of red hair, was going positively beetroot with passion. The colour clashed against his Birmingham Blue jacket.

"Unco Sooj, he said a bad word," she patted Suraj on the elbow, and then looked at her father.

"Don't say it, Mango," Gorbind shook his head. "It's a very naughty word. I'd much rather you used something like wet haddock instead. You having fun?"

Mango nodded, having been placated to return to the action. A few moments later, she got to her feet to join in with a chant. There was a bit of blue in the air as she did; causing Suraj to clamp his hands over her ears a few times.

Half-time would eventually come. It didn't come quick enough as tempers frayed and tackles flew.

***

Suraj sat with Mango during half-time. He watched as she munched on a hot dog covered in ketchup. He wondered whether she would make it to her fries.

Mango then caught his curious expression, and gave him a rather spontaneous hug.

She was by far, one of his favourite members of the family. The way that she called him Unco Sooj made him feel loved.

Suraj remembered being the same age when Padmi and her dad had brought him here. They'd brought him to his very first game. As he grew older, he'd keep coming back. The one year, on his eleventh birthday to be exact, he'd even been a mascot. Suraj still had the match day pennant. It hung, in pride of place, on his bedroom wall. To be here with Mango, with her mum and dad; this was a rite of passage. Something, that in ideal world, every six year old should experience.

After the re-start, Suraj and Mango both got to their feet.

A heavy boot had the ball jet across the pitch. It landed in the 18-yard box. Blue shirts crowded out the opposition. Opposition that tussled, as blues crept closer. A dummy, followed by a nutmeg ended with a volley aimed on target.

With the keeper having butter fingers, the ball wasn't parried away. Blues had scored, to send euphoria coursing around the stands. That didn't happen often, so was something to be savoured.

Mango held her arms aloft. Padmi whistled loudly. Suraj, was doing some form of weird moon-walk on the spot.

The Villa fan remained in his seat.

Unaffected, outflanked and out of his comfort zone.

Starship Birmingham

Sat in the chair, she tried to catch her breath. She tried to focus, to understand the full gravity of the situation.

Alex Anand curled her hands around the arm rests.

This was it. And it was down to her, to get the job done. Counsellors generally weren't first in line when it came to handing out a command. They were usually the one's bracing for impact, to make sure the ripples of would-be disasters could be contained or ridden out.

As such, counsellors were ninth, tenth, fifty-first in line, when a star ship needed someone in charge. Fluke, firepower and a glitch in the transport protocols had shoved straight to the front.

Sat in the Captain's office, Alex turned off the computer that sat squarely in front of her.

Her orders were crystal clear.

Once more unto the breach.

Forward.

That was the last thing that she had read. One final missive from Head Office.

"The Captain has gone," she had said, in speaking with the Quadrant Commander. "He was eviscerated whilst travelling in a Mosquito; zapped in cold blood. The Executive Officer; she got scrambled in a sabotaged transport cycle. I'm all that's left of the command team. The XO, she left me in charge."

Quadrant Commander Tracey had looked at her in despair. The agony of potential defeat was etched across his face. He glanced over his shoulder for a moment; at the yellow-gold Wolverhampton Wanderers pennant that hung on the wall.

There was the sound of skirmishes off-screen.

"You are the last line of defence, Acting Captain Anand," his eyes glistened; but a fierce intensity remained in his piercing blue eyes. Captain Benson picked you to be the Counsellor as he valued your integrity. Commander Blenkinsop trusted your humanity. The vessel that you are on is named after a gloriously resilient city. It is named after your hometown. She is solid, strong and built to fight whatever the universe throws at her. She is made, of stern stuff.

Alex had nodded, whilst gulping down unadulterated fear.

"You, Alex," he had said, his bottom lip trembling, "Are made of stern stuff. Stand by, for your final order. So long, and farewell, Alex Anand. Tracey, signing off."

With that, Quadrant Commander had disappeared.

Then, in an instant, her final orders had arrived.

As Alex looked at the door, the walls shook. Overhead, the lights flickered and frazzled; klaxons bruised the increasingly tense atmosphere. A hefty, violent motion had Alex being thrown from the chair.

She was already wounded, so winced as she landed with a thud onto the floor. Prior to the call, Alex had been in Engineering helping to reinforce Birmingham's bruised and barely beating heart. The engine was near breaking point. There wasn't much more that the ship, or her crew, could take.

Alex got to her hands and knees to get moving.

As Birmingham bounced on her interstellar axles, the vessel endured being buffered by barrage. She was under attack by armed to the teeth insurgents. An enemy force, that didn't take too kindly to those with a more peaceful remit.

Alex crawled to the door. She had chemical fuel burns all the way down her left side. There were also two, maybe three broken ribs as she had also been bundled around Engineering. Alex had been hurled by an explosion towards a bulkhead.

If anyone was to ask, the Bulkhead picked a fight with her and she won.

She had to get to get to get to the door. Alex had to get to the bridge.

"Once more," she uttered, climbing up the door to get to her feet. "Unto the breech. We are Birmingham," Alex winced as her chest vibrated. "Forward."

The door the bridge opened. Alex smoothed down her Birmingham Blue Uniform. She took her time to get to the middle of the bridge.

Birmingham Blue. A colour that was meant to signal Peace, Industry and above all, Solidarity.

Solidarity in this case, was the Navigator, the Chief of Ship Wide Infra-structure an ensign from Defence.

"Arm everything," Alex told the Chief of Infrastructure. "You," she nodded towards the Navigator. "Get us into the melee, and then back out again. I have a Fiancé to marry, and children to produce."

Darren nodded back, before lowering a pair of orange-tinted shooting glasses across his eyes.

"Eyes down," Alex let out a deep breath. "Billy, you need to show me the wood for the trees. Okay?"

"Ma'am," Billy flicked a few switches. "Eyes down, ears open. Full System Communications Relay, ready to play ball."

"Forward, Birmingham!" yelled Alex. "Forward!"

***

"And again, another!" A tumbler thudded to the shiny, wooden bar. The sound was heavy and discordant across the sound of a football crowd.

Koby wiped a hand across this mouth. His jacket sleeve was then dragged over his snotty nose. In his other hand, he held a credit-card sized device. The screen was filled with noise, horror and the undisguised brutality of war.

For days, he had refused to watch it; Koby had been cold-cocked into shock. He'd been nothing but numb. Three days ago, when Quadrant Commander Tracey had rocked up at his flat, to talk about a funeral, he'd then decided to watch the footage.

Funeral. That was why Koby was here, propping up the bar at the Gunmaker's Arms. A newly filled tumbled appeared on the bar.

Next to it, was an urn.

Etched across it, in copper place script was a name. Alexandra Shaanti Anand.

That was all that was left. That was all that Billy and Darren had brought back of Alex. All that remained of the woman, who in three weeks, he had been scheduled to marry. Alex, whose very middle name meant peace. She had fought for it, until the bitter end.

This morning, at Sarehole Mill, there had been a final goodbye. Alex had wished to be brought home, regardless of where she might have fallen. Her ashes were to be scattered between the two oaks near the Mill. She'd played there as a child; Koby had proposed there. He'd scaled one of the Oaks, and then blurted out his question. It was a place of joy and love undefined.

Koby slung back more bourbon.

"One more," he leant against the bar, dropping the device, "In fact, keep the damned stuff coming." The device rumbled on.

***

Alex held onto the sparking remnants of the communication array. Her visage filled the broken scream. Her voice crackled, missing earthly notes.

"We held our line," she said. She snorted away blood; fear scribbled across her face. "But it wasn't enough. If you think of us, think of the stars. Think of all that good. Think, of The Birmingham. Alexandra Anand, signing off."

In Custody

"Will be one of those days again, Fred," I glanced over to him, as I leant against the counter. "Never gets any easier, eh?" I couldn't help but shake my head.

With is his lips pursed, Fred cast his slate-grey eyes across the motley cruet that littered the custody suite. He too, shook his head, before crossing his burly arms across his black, woollen uniform.

"All right, James Watt," Called the custody sergeant at Steelhouse Lane Police Station. "Do you want to come on up?"

James Watt sidled up to the counter. He stood right in front of me. I moved out the way, to give the boy some space.

I couldn't help but look him up and down. He was altogether scrappy young thing. Dressed in a rusty-red shirt, tatty blue jeans and a pair of white runners, James looked all a bit forlorn. He was very young, I figured, as he swept back a plume of red-blonde hair that had scruffily flopped across his face.

There was an innocent about the action that brought a smile to my face. He looked like an angel with a very dirty face.

"Don't be taken in, Young Bill," Fred had appeared next to me, having escaped the other side of the desk. For a man of some girth, he was incredibly light on his feet. Fred twirled his auburn whiskers. "Caught in possession of illegal substances," he said, reeling off the charge. "Never had them in my day. A bit of laudanum, opium, what have you; gin. Gin would always make folks a bit raucous. But this…" Slinking his hands into his jacket pockets, Fred rocked on his heels.

"It's early yet," I looked at the circular clock that hung above the counter. "Only just gone eight. The night is still young."

I glanced at the information that James had given the desk sergeant. I wondered how someone who was so young, could end up with such a long charge sheet. Young James Watt had something of a colourful history. The computer screen made my head and heart hurt; they weren't my favourite things in this universe.

This was Birmingham. Yet at times, it felt as though this was the movies. As though someone had picked up the Bronx, to dump it here; here, in the middle of England.

"Refreshments, Young Bill," Fred put his hand to my shoulder. He's always called me that. Ever since we had first met, all those years ago.

I'd been one side of the counter; Fred on the other. It was strange at first. The noise, the people. They all looked a bit different; smaller, more distant and harder to get a hold of. Fred had taken me under his wing. He knew Steelhouse lane like the back of his hand.

There were sixty years between Fred and I. Didn't feel like it though. Plus, we both had the same look of weariness that came with the job that we did.

At ten, with our refreshments taken, we ventured back. This is our lot, as Policemen. We walk the corridors, watching justice being doled out. Sometimes, sadly, it's not. A wholly infuriating notion: this reminds me that there are times when Lady Justice should remove her blindfold.

Fred and I, we watch recompense, retribution and reparation in all its forms. The job never gets old, and here at Steelhouse Lane.

"They don't look like harlots," Fred frowned, as he held a mug of tea. "I remember them looking a bit more…. showy."

"We don't use that word anymore," I replied, and through a shiny grin. I watched a young woman totter up to the desk. She'd lost the one heel. Her cobalt blue fish nets were as torn and wear as she looked. "A more acceptable term; I saw it on the computer, is Sex Worker."

Fred looked at me as though he'd sucked half a lemon. He did the same, when I inadvertently swore from time to time.

"In your day, there was class," I said, laughing a little. "I know. You'd never had said something to vulgar, so common."

"Oldest profession though, Young Bill," Fred waved his mug in the direction of the blue tights.

She blinked, cocked her head; as though she'd seen something. We were however, easy to miss.

"A girl still got to eat," Fred continued. "I mean, she means no harm. It is, after the way of this world and every world. Here are, here come the drunk and disorderlies. Those who really can't hold their liquor. Must be that time of the evening already."

I stood out the way as rabble of inebriated revellers caroused into the suite. A few were sporting bloodied bruises. One, was half-naked.

A fairly straight-forward evening, here at Steelhouse Lane.

Not the way that I remembered it being though. The one night, had been especially quiet.

***

I watched Young Bill for some time. I'd watched them, behind the counter. Each one was very different; with a unique way of dealing with the delinquents and reprobates that would tumble into Steelhouse Lane. There was something of a turnover. There is, with any job. Every five years, there would be another fresh face behind the desk. Young whippersnappers had a tendency to develop ambition. All so very different, compared to when I was behind the desk.

I was there a while. I did my duty for nigh on ten years; I loved every minute of it. Every minute, until the final one.

The one day that I came out from behind my desk; to intervene.

A brawl had broken out between a common cut purse and one of the ladies from Cheapside. The one was drunk, the other chancing his luck. What I never saw coming, was the blade.

He'd already slashed around; he was the gangly sort. Not having control of his limbs at the best of times, would've posed a challenge.

I got in the way. He'd thrown his arms around; to strike and slash. It was all over very quickly. According to the coroner, the blade had made short work of arteries in my stomach and my neck. I soon bled out and became a puddle on the floor.

To most, that was par for the course at Steelhouse Lane.

I stayed. Even after the funeral, where the guard of honour had made my Bessie howl into her handkerchief. I couldn't bring myself to leave. Other than my black-eyed Bessie, Steelhouse Lane was the other love of my life. My poor children, would be third and fourth respectively.

I couldn't leave, not really. I want to make sure that the desk was looked after. That Steelhouse Lane was in a safe pair of hands. That someone decent, would be at the helm.

When Young Bill turned up, he seemed to know what he was doing. He seemed to know the job, inside and out.

***

I'd heard about Fred Bannock.

The desk sergeant killed in the line of duty. The legend had it, that he'd thrown his frame-substantial as it was-across a rather inebriated lady of the night. Some hot-head had tried it on, pulled out a blade. Our man Fred, had been caught in the middle, trying to wrestle the doughnut to the floor.

Another legend, was that on Halloween, Fred would haunt the station demanding justice. He was said to demand revenge as all the blood that he'd lost was magically appear in the custody suite. It would appear, and then disappear in the blink of an eye.

Complete and utter poppycock; but an interesting piece of the Steelhouse Lane history.

Standing there on Halloween, behind the desk, I didn't think. I didn't think that Fred would actually appear, that the blood would either. Given everything that I had heard about him; he was a gentle soul. Married to job, as well his wife Bessie; there was nothing to suggest that Fred, in death, could be so malevolent.

I thought nothing of it.

Nothing really happens at Halloween. We don't even get slightly stoned trick or treaters. Just the odd spanner, who whilst drunk, breaks and enters an abandoned warehouse. Last year, whilst under the influence, a doofus had tried to scale the council house.

The deep joy, I tell you.

I wasn't feeling too clever, to be honest. But I wasn't going to call in sick. It was only a headache, a bit of nausea that came and went. I'd pulled a few double shifts over the last month odd so. I wouldn't say I was more tired, or had done too much. I didn't think much of it, not really.

Sat there, I was waiting for whatever the night shift would bring in. I only closed my eyes for a second. Didn't feel a thing; there was no pain whatsoever.

The next thing I knew, I was on the floor.

Face to face, with Fred Bannock.

The man was supposed to be dead. But no. Here he was, looking straight at me. I didn't believe it at first. The man in question, was a ghost.

The Ghost, of Fred Bannock.

***

I took Young Bill under my wing. I did my best to reassure him, to help him understand. He was all very confused at first; it took time for him to understand. To, what was it the youngsters say?-Process it.

It's been nearly ten years and we've been having fun. Especially with Halloween. I know my own legend.

I'm Fred Bannock. He's Young Bill.

We're the desk sergeants that were, of Steelhouse
Lane.

Friends of the Floozy

"Don't forget her strap!" Holding onto her bright pink beret, Jaya yelled across the wind. Autumn was ready to take flight as September ebbed away. Birmingham had seemed positively balmy of late.

"I'm trying not to fall over," yelled a man, who dressed in overalls and work boots. "Don't really want to break anything, and least of all, because of the Birmingham Floozy. His rosy cheeks pulled taut into smile as he laughed at the nickname.

"She's not a real Floozy," trilled Jaya, she too was smiling. "Just looks like one."

Shaking his head, Dylan Jeffried edged around the reclining figure who sat in the middle of what was one a very watery pool.

"Just looks like one," commented Dylan, as he negotiated a route around the assortment of flora and fauna that replaced the water. He tugged at a rather large, very broad, glittering bra strap.

"Up a bit," directed Jaya; her smile had bloomed and blossomed in a full scale grin. "A nice bit of support never hurt anyone."

Catching her eye, Dylan pulled out his tongue to be altogether childish. A crowd had gathered now, outside the council house. A few of them waved, nodded at him. A couple of kids mingled around amongst the handful of adults.

Most of the crowd were wearing something pink. There was a definite theme.

"Go on, Dylan, but don't be falling into the flowers," Maureen O'Breen yelled loudly as she waved.

"He'll probably sneeze first," that was Kat, her daughter. "What with the pollen."

Both of them were survivors; both of them had a story to tell.

From the corner of his eye, Dylan saw Jaya go meet the crowd. She clutched at her beret still. It was barely anchored down onto dark brown hair that snaked down between her shoulder blades. There were ringlets that bounced as she moved.

Yet it wasn't real. The hair wasn't hers.

Dylan carried on; carried on adjusting the bra. Yes. The Birmingham Floozy was wearing a bright, fuchsia-pink bra; it was decorated with glitter and sparkles. For once, the Floozy was wearing clothes. Albeit not many. Her underwear was on display, for a very good reason.

He listened in to the conversations had by the rowed. He knew most of those that had gathered. There were also some newer faces.

"This would've made Archie giggle," Dana Arbroath wiped away a tear. "He'd always go a bit pink anyway, what with her always being bare breasted. All for a good cause."

"Fancier than mine," Avni rolled her eyes before wrinkling them up in good humour. "A reminder though, that we should all check our bits; regularly."

"Agreed," nodded Jaya as Avni pulled her close. The two women linked their arms. "Maybe one day we won't have to. One day, maybe the c-word will be consigned to history. Then, we wouldn't have to do this, to help get rid of it."

"Until then, we keep going," Maureen was all very matter of fact in her tone. She pulled her coat closer. The wind really was on one today; it whistled through the streets of Birmingham in a rather bracing fashion.

"We're in this together, Jaya," Maureen pressed two fingers to her lips, to blow a kiss. "We've all survived, and we've got a story to tell. How's Dylan doing?" she flicked her eyes towards him.

"He has his good days," sighed Jaya, catching sight of Dylan, just as he bent over. "And his bad days.

Misses his mum terribly. That's why he helps. To feel connected. Have her close, one last time."

Dylan righted himself to look at the sign that he'd placed earlier. A sign that told Birmingham that October was Breast Cancer Awareness Month.

That was why. Why, for once, The Floozy wore a bra.

Picking his way through the foliage, Dylan stepped out of the garden. He made his way towards the crowd. Kat Fielden, another survivor, handed him a coffee in a polystyrene cup. It was gratefully received as he took a swig and warmed up a little.

Stood there, with family, friends and fellow survivors, Jaya kept her cool. These were all important people. People, who in her darkest hours, had kept her safe. Kept her buoyant and on her feet, when she just wanted to crawl away. People, who had fished her out, of the darkest of depths.

As Dylan put a hand to hers, she let herself be pulled into his arms. Arms that were protective as she felt them around her waist. It was because of this group, that Dylan had come into her life. Being part of a support group had become a big part of their healing journey.

"Are you okay?" he asked, leaning in a little. "Only you look as white as sheet."

"I'm fine," whispered Jaya, patting his hand, but taking a deep breath. "Just enjoying the look of a full cup," she said, nodding towards the Floozy.

"Nervous?" Dylan was tentative, with the one word. "It's okay to be nervous. Surgery is a big deal. An I know, that it's easy for me to say; the whole full cup thing. That you're beautiful, and for you, you always will be to me. You're my fighter, my Jaya Chopra."

"Don't," Jaya bit back tears to cradle his face. She couldn't keep her composure as she snatched a kiss from his lips. She took some comfort in the kiss; but there was also the control in wanting to silence him. Jaya could feel her knees go week. "No one else knows," she said, looking around furtively. "About the reconstruction. And I know, how you feel. Thank you. Without you, Dylan, I'd be even more wobblier."

"Wobble all you want," Dylan kissed the tip of her nose, before tugging her beret into a jaunty angle. "I'm here to catch you."

She'd hold him to that. To catch her, if and when she wobbled.

Just after Christmas, Jaya had a wobble.

Dylan stood next to her. The pair of them were near the top of the escalators, outside of Victoria's Secrets in The Bull Ring.

"Some notes here, please," Dylan wrapped an arm around Jaya's waist. "What would you like me to do?" his anxiety had him absentmindedly rubbing her elbow.

"Walk with me," Jaya replied; her words spoken just as softly as his. "I just want to look. To figure out...."

"Babe, you're one of the bravest and strongest women on the face of this planet," Dylan clutched at her arm that bit tighter. "This, is entirely up to you, and

I'm right here. A hot-blooded, willing male, more than happy to walk with you in a ladies knicker shop. No many would, you know, agree to do so; but I want to. I want to, because I love you and do anything for you."

Slowly, Jaya moved toward the shop front. She held on Dylan's arm, to catch a glimpse of the diamond solitaire that he had proposed with during Christmas dinner.

"And if I wobble," She asked, stopping at the threshold. Jaya gulped, her chest rose and fell in feeling horribly tight.

"I will catch you," Dylan took her hand into his. "You're shaking," He encased her fingers with his, as he moved closer. "I'll walk with you. I'll hold onto every bra, every pair of knickers-apple catchers or not- that you want to take a look at. I will be there, for every second, every moment that you'll have me."

"The boobs…"Jayaa was all very plaintive as her eyes widened in anxiety. Eyelashes batted with every breath.

"Are brand spanking new," Dylan spoke with a devilish laugh that he couldn't prevent from escaping. "And pretty damned lovely, to be perfectly honest. I can't complain, I never have done. And don't pretend," Dylan wiped away tears that sat upon Jaya's left cheek. "You spend as much time as I do, if not more, looking at them."

"Oi, cheeky!" Jaya gasped to poke Dylan anywhere that she could reach. All a bit difficult given the heavy duffle coat that was draped over his wiry frame. "I'm trying to get used them, that's all. Thought that this might help with that. Be bit a giggle."

"And," Dylan leant in, his nose clipped hers. "They have post-Christmas sales on. Could make the most if now, and save up for Valentine's."

"For the wedding lingerie too," Jaya smiled, but sniffled too to wipe her nose across a claret-coloured sleeve.

"Wedding lingerie, eh?" Dylan's grin grew that bit wider. He even blushed a little. "I can follow that bit of your logic. Perhaps help pick out a few things, by way of careful suggestion."

"I don't want to be careful," Jaya sighed out aloud, dragging Dylan across the threshold. Dragging him across, with reckless abandon.

THE BATTLE OF GRAVELLY HILL INTERCHANGE

One

This didn't start with a cough, a cold or a sneeze. Not this time.

This wasn't about feeling under the weather, to shake of a winter bug. This was something far beyond anything that the world had seen before.

There had been pandemics. Two, that changed the face of the world. Changed the way in which folks spoke about what they thought was normal. Normal, was something of a distant memory. The new normal, would linger long enough to be unchallenged. Unquestioned, the fabric of the everyday universe became warped and somewhat other worldly.

This, was the wind of change.

There were no butterflies flapping their wings to cause a tornado. It wasn't that far-fetched, of even that simple.

You see, the universe, the world as we know it; the planets, the entire solar system. It's a pretty big place.

Yet all it takes is a speck of dust, a few atoms or spots of ash to get caught in a flare. These are then carried; pushed, pulled across a sea of gravitational tides. Tides that cause them to float as though jetsam through the vast expanse that is space.

Space dust. If you believe the fiction; worse still, if you watch the movies. Such a thing is never innocuous.

It never ends well.

Space dust. That is where our story starts. Well, it actually starts with a weird crash landing in the middle of the ocean. A capsule landed with a plop, in the biggest, wettest puddle known to man, woman and carrier pigeon. The crew, the three of them, were all fished out. Feted, celebrated for having gone to space and back. Celebrated, for having survived such an adventure.

It was all one big shindig. It truly was.

The celebrations, the interviews and photo shoots, these lasted for a few months. Our party of three went back to their jobs; the proper jobs, that didn't involve being splashed across the glossies.

Member number one, went back to Montana. They decided to go find a cabin in the wood; to write science-fiction, of all things, in secluded desolation. Her mind, her soul had seen the colours of the wind from upon high. She would still work on her astrophysics too, without having anyone destroy her peace.

Member number two, decided to go to Italy. There were deals to be done with the European Space Agency. He would also ply his trade by travelling to schools, encouraging the next generation of star gazers. He wanted to share the pure joy that came from having walked amongst the stars.

Member number three.

Hers, was a slightly different story. Not so romantic, not so cute.

She decided to travel the globe. Her feet were to stay grounded upon terra firma. Her plan was to globe trot and mostly with reckless abandon.

(Yes, space dust; I'm coming to it.)

Simple really.

Whilst on board the space station, she'd been amazed and in awe, of the grit and grime that amassed in space. No one up there, ever thought about giving the whole cosmos a bit of a damp wipe. It probably wouldn't have killed someone to pass a vacuum around the rings of Saturn from time to time.

So, when she wiped down her suit; her helmet with a standard issue handkerchief, she wasn't best pleased. Not really.

She came back, handkerchief and all.

The globe-trotting; it started in Mexico. She headed to The Unites States of America later.

All that time, she kept a hold of that handkerchief. It lived, neatly fold up, in the bottom of her hand bag.

Just in case, she coughed, sneezed or needed to wipe away bogey.

And she did. She coughed, sneezed and there was bogey. That handkerchief was then, never far away.

Passing through Birmingham, she visited The Red Brick, Aston University too. She developed hay fever. Grass pollen rose with the onset of spring.

That handkerchief, had already had an effect. That space dust was already in there, in system. It had started to do what it was supposed to.

(You're probably wondering if the hanky was washed. At this point, probably; having served it's initial purpose. No one, wants a grotty hanky; I mean, really.)

By the time she had got to Italy; there was a dalliance with her former colleague. A dalliance; that's all it was, a flying visit. It's true, what they say. In space, no one can hear you scream.

No one in space can hear you both arrive screaming at the synchronised point of passion.

On earth, everyone could-they did-and it felt woefully ordinary.

She and the colleague had laughed about it, whilst in space. Of all the places to join The Mile High Club, that was fairly unique.

She left Italy feeling groggy, to venture towards the Far East.

She got to Tokyo, before things got a little hairy. Her hay fever didn't seem to abate. There were prescriptions to be filled; a boat load of anti-histamines that didn't really touch the sides. Her chest felt tight, her nose was sore. Collapsing in the park during her morning run, she quickly abandoned the idea that this was run of the mill, garden variety hay fever.

Hospitalised, she grew weaker. Her body, started to shut down. It was giving up the ghost.

For, for her globe-trotting and more, it was Goodnight Vienna.

At a quarter to ten, on a Friday night; the body really did give up the ghost. She fell asleep, her eyes slowly closed. Her earthly adventures were over, as she shuffled off the mortal coil.

She was left alone, having quietly slipped away. Medics kicked themselves. Policies and procedures had been somewhat neglected. The orderlies went about finding next of kin. They would see to repatriating her; where ever she had come from. She deserved to go home.

When the orderlies came back, they were somewhat aghast. The body. Hers.

Shona.

She was gone.

Two

Then there were reports. Reports of a ghost, a ghoul; wandering around the streets of Tokyo. Not the one, who by tradition, demolished buildings, but one that looked like death itself.

A spectre; so pained that it screamed and wailed. It preyed on you. When it was hungry or enraged, it would take you into its arms.

It would give you a kiss, so tender and sweet; before devouring you. It would devour you, and then others.

All in the blink of an eye.

The reports kept rolling in. A police force so adept at keeping the crime and disorder in check was quickly befuddled.

People were being attacked, usually at dusk. Just as the light dimmed and earth kicked off its shoes to take a sundowner. Once attacked, infected or in close contact, the casualties would end up in the Emergency Room. Their wounds would be tended to. But more often than not, something would appear; a strange group of cells in the blood work. Tissue that appeared to be mutated and on a cellular level.

There was an elevation in both red and white blood cells. Your average leucocyte and phagocyte had become something else. Leukaemia and septicaemia were no longer labels that made sense.

Chaos and confused reigned.

Immune systems were compromised. With the body at war with itself, multi-organ failure wasn't far behind and happened at the drop of a hat. Organs failed, death checked-in, quick smart. There were bodies all over. Make shift morgues and mortuaries appeared, often over-night and in a flash.

Nightingales too. Field hospitals, managed by the military.

Bodies would arrive.

Only to disappear.

Disappear at dusk and into the dead of night.

Stories started to be told. The kiss of death, the devouring and it's cold embrace. This wasn't just an urban myth that was on the rise, or a legend being born. There were no wandering minstrels, for a start. Stories started to travel across the globe. A trend was starting to develop; the WHO felt it's radar ping as patterns were spotted.

From Mexico, Latin America via Italy. Britain too and into the Far East.

There was a twisting trail, that made El Nino look like a tabby cat.

Shona had made many friends as her hay fever had risen to an almighty crescendo. Some friends were closer than others. A kiss, a caress, there was a simple handshake or two; an otherwise innocent hug, that probably didn't mean a thing. Human beings were social creatures.

Who knew that being friendly, might cause such a ruckus?

With every infection came an onward surge. Transmission. That space dust kept on travelling; it kept on moving. It didn't have the wherewithal to stop. Each and every interaction, had a target in the cross-hairs. Each and every infection, was an unsuspecting victim. A victim, plundered for all they were worth.

With every turn, the story that carried was the same. You could be out walking; to see something amongst the undergrowth. To hear a sinister rustling in the undergrowth. You needn't blink, to be caught in the cold embrace. To be kissed and caressed by death. Each and every inch of you would be devoured; to then be left to rot.

Your bones were gnawed upon; your soul stripped away from your marrow.

The bodies, they would disappear into the night. They grouped together, they convened.

They formed an uprising, to become a superpower. Society was scared; it looked to its defences. Defences, that in battling an unknown enemy, crumbled. This was uncharted territory. Solace could no longer be found in myth or magic.

Faith, was about to be sorely tested.

On the space dust pathway and beyond, cities found themselves under siege. Hierarchies, law and order; all that had been trained to bear, were over run. The world changed; it moved from order to ramshackle, barely contained chaos.

A world away from Tokyo, Birmingham was no different. The city of a thousand trades changed too. The kiss of death, the cold embrace descended there as well. It didn't discriminate.

Birmingham too, was under siege.

Birmingham too, would have to fight.

Fight, the kiss of death that dared to devour it whole.

Birmingham could fall, and to her knees.

Three

"And that was all six years ago," Anand let out a deep breath, as he closed the red and black exercise book. He held it tightly, as it rested upon his lap. He hated telling the story; it was sad beyond measure. But he chose to, it had to be heard. People had to know why things were the way that they were.

Sat in the bar of The Gunmakers Arms, Anand was surrounded by a dozen or so young children. Their parents too. Survivors, all of them; like him.

"She'd ingested something," said Anand, steepling his hands on the exercise book. His nails, he noticed, were in need of clipping. "That handkerchief. They found it after she had…changed," Anand bit his lip to utter the word. "They couldn't identify the strain; it was so complex. The authorities, they investigated. Reports were starting to come in, from around the world. They did their best, to work backwards; from Italy, the boyfriend. Turns out, he was infected too."

A few of the children 'oohed', all very wide-eyed, as they elbowed each other.

Infected.

Anand knew, that there would never again be such a loaded word and in any earthly language.

"When they started to work backwards," Anand took in a deep breath. "They started to realise how far she had travelled…she…." Anand frowned, as his stomach flipped over.

She had a name; he knew that name. He knew it very well.

"Shona," he said letting the name tumble from his lips. "Shona travelled across Europe. She had even come here, to Birmingham. To our city."

A few of the parents murmured quietly amongst themselves.

"Because of her…." Anand's words had descended to be being a whisper. A memory flashed across his mind.

Of him, of Shona. They'd walked from the Uni in the middle of town. They'd made slow and steady progress along the canals. Dinner, at The Malt Shovel.

"I knew her," he coughed, to clear his throat. He even had to blink a few times, as tears formed. He wiped away a few, with his left hand, as these travelled down his cheek. "So, when I tell this story, it's painful. It makes me feel really quite sad. Telling it, is important; to you, to your parents." He did his best, to conjure up something of a luke warm smile.

"Because we survived, Anand." Josie, a precocious seven-year-old, with icy-blue eyes and beautiful red hair, looked directly at him. In her arms, she carried a stuffed dragon.

"Because we survived, Josie," nodded Anand. "Now, it's dinner time," he said, rising from a rickety bar stool. "Then bed time, for you all. Off you go, story time is over."

The children filed out; not neatly, but in a rag tag fashion that looked as though someone was herding cats. They jostled towards the lounge, where all the meals for the Gunmakers Gang were shared.

Anand half-smiled as they bounced away, along with the adults. They were important, each and every one of them. Crossing his arms, he hugged his exercise book close.

"Never gets any easier for you, does it?"

Anand turned in the direction of the voice; towards the shadows. The Gunmaker's Arms was a far cry from it's glory days as a thriving pub in the middle of Birmingham. Dark, with its doors and windows battened down; the main bar was illuminated by smoky candles, grimy lamps and lanterns.

"Enough with the lurking, Gorbind," sighed Anand. "You're far too cute, to be at ease in the shadows. You don't belong on the darker side. You are, after all, something of a White Knight."

Flashing a bright grin, Gorbind edged out of the fragmented light. In his hands, he held a crumpled paper bag.

"Some supplies, Anand," Gorbind planted the bag down, onto a stout, rectangular table. "Basic medical. Some odds and ends, by way of fruit that came in the barge from Worcester." He rummaged around in the bag, to pull out a satsuma. He tossed it into the air, towards Anand.

Anand caught it with one hand, whilst hanging onto his exercise book.

"Josie will be pleased. Sujal too." Anand pressed the satsuma to his nose. To inhale the strong, citrus scent. "It's important, that the kids have the occasional drop of sunshine. There's more though, yes?" he flicked his gaze towards Gorbind. "You didn't just pop by, to hand over fruit and veg, to ward off scurvy."

"Just passing through." Replied Gorbind, slinking his hands into his pockets. His dark blue, woollen overcoat was something of a constant. A costume, in playing a role. His role, was incredibly important, if only to himself. "And…" he let out a hot, deeply constrained breath. "Advising you to secure your walls. Waves of infection have been seen, forming in Digbeth. Rumour has it, that the Necromancer is up to no good. He's building some form of army. Then there is the Hag."

The Hag. Anand bristled a moment. The satsuma slipped between his fingers, to be clumsily re-caught.

"Digbeth," Anand passed the tip of his tongue, over dry, chapped lips. "That would be the Hag, all right. Thought the Necromancer held Small Heath."

"He does," nodded Gorbind. "For now. City Watch....is keeping an eye on things. But for you, the danger, is closest to home. The danger, is Felicity at The Rotunda."

Anand scoffed, to toss the satsuma up and down. As though it were a cricket ball. Not that he liked cricket. He'd driven passed Edgbaston Cricket ground, way back when. But much preferred a game of five-aside instead.

"Don't underestimate her," Sounded Gorbind, terseness edged his words. "No one saw her coming, to take siege of The Rotunda. No one, figured that she'd roll up, with her mad, bad, band of merry men to get so close to St.Martin's. You have eight hours. In two, Arjun will come by, to take the kids to safety. He'll take them all."

Anand snatched the satsuma as it rolled mid-air.

"She wouldn't dare," he said, glaring at Gorbind. "This is a family, a sanctuary."

"Right, so she does, and will," Gorbind rooted around in the paper bag. He pulled out a small bottle of bourbon. "She doesn't need a sanctuary on her pathway to destruction. She's coming for you. For this place. Since you and Shona…" He unscrewed the lid of the bottle.

Anand closed his eyes.

"But you won't be alone," Gorbind pressed the mouth of the bottle to his lips. "There are crews from Sandwell and Solihull on their way. Sparkbrook and

Selly Oak too. They will be forming ring of steel around this place, and a corridor to carry the kids away."

"Those aren't crews, Gorbind," Anand held out a hand for the bottle; his digits waggled in anticipation.

"No," Gorbind shook his head, but handed over the bottle. "It's an army, Anand. My army, and you're going to need it. Get the kids ready. They need to leave, ASAP."

Slugging the bourbon, Anand winced as it hit home. He had no choice, and a matter of hours. Doing as he was told, he rounded up the kids as Gorbind watched on.

As the de facto leader of the city, Gorbind stood apart from the shadows. A reminder of the law, as it had been, before the infection. Law, that now worked a bit differently. It had to maintain a delicate balance, that would otherwise see Birmingham swallowed up whole.

In two hours, the children were prepared.

Arjun, Gorbind's brother, was due to arrive. He was to escort the children to St.Martin's. The crews thar Gorbind selected, would travel with them. An escort for a precious convoy, not to be taken lightly and only then, on pain of death.

Four

As the last of the children departed from The Gunmakers, Gorbind pulled the saloon doors closed. His plan had been to disappear once the crews had set up shop. To use the back alleys to return to the nerve centre of the City Watch. However, he'd spoken with Anand, and something told him to stick around. To lurk, in the shadows.

"I should be pissed with you," Anand loaded up a magazine, before setting the firearm onto the bar. "To come here as though the Angel of Death, heralding potential destruction. To think that you were going to disappear for dust before it all kicked off."

"Normal response," nodded Gorbind; the corners of his mouth had turned downward. "I'd be worried if you're not pissed. Be pissed all you want. Stay pissed, to use that feeling to save this place." He waggled a finger towards the gun.

"What is your guidance," ventured Anand. He was all too aware, of how Gorbind ran the city. A pseudo overlord, who had identified and designated feudal responsibilities to him, amongst others. Others like him, who were every day Brummies, and had a patch of Birmingham to call their own.

Brummies, who in a panic, had pledged their allegiance to someone who had almost superhero status. Someone who never gave orders but gave only advice and made requests. It was then up to the underling, whether or not take it. There were only a handful or so, who had ever dared not to. Those that did, found themselves being caught by the kiss to be devoured fairly quick.

When that happened, Gorbind would call on the crews. They would ride out and clear up the mess. Anand had been there. He'd been part of the Gunmakers Gang contingent that had trekked out to Great Barr. The infected had put up a formidable fight; held their ground for sixteen hours straight. Anand had taken his flame-thrower. The weapon made sure that the final throes were quick, easy and left nothing behind.

His degree from Aston University had never felt more useful.

"Contain her minions," answered Gorbind. "Disarm, disable; send them packing if they become walking wounded. Most of them at the Rotunda do have a brain, if they were to use. Felicity would rather they didn't, and is very misguiding."

"And what about her, Felicity?" Anand poured two shots of bourbon. He handed one to Gorbind.

"Negotiate, in the first instance," Gorbind slung back the alcohol; to then pour another. "Make nice, offer her sanctuary. Same terms as everyone else."

"And when that fails?" Anand winced to savour his one shot. "If she doesn't go kaput in the heat of battle."

Gorbind licked his lips before exhaling. In his mind, there was only one option. An option, that he didn't take lightly. He flicked his brown eyes toward the door.

"Let dusk fall," he said quietly. "Disorientate her; get her giggling and blind drunk, if you have to. Then set her on the kerbside by St.Chad's. Let her be kissed…."

"To be devoured…." Tutted Anand.

"She made her choice, Anand," Gorbind sunk the second shot, to plop the glass upside down onto the bar. "It was only ever going to end one way. Given her lifestyle, and who she chooses to associate with. I'll go check in with the loft." He clamped a hand to Anand's shoulder. "You've got this, all right? That, is my advice."

Anand watched as Gorbind walked away and up a staircase. There were gunners in the loft. Of all the people, to walk into this place. Anand poured himself another shot.

"You've got this," he told himself. He heard it. He just had to believe it.

***

"We should go, it's a long walk." Mango put her hand to Arjun's shoulder. Other than her father, her Uncle Arjun was one of the few men in this world that she trusted. "You okay to take the front, if I take the rear?" she swung a rifle over her shoulder as she turned to leave.

"Yes," nodded Arjun, a watery smile bloomed briefly across his face. "Keep an eye out; but stay within the column," he flicked a finger at the rag-tag crew that were assembled either side of the children's unit. There were twenty-four of them, drawn from assorted crews.

In any other universe, this was a military unit escorting civilian out of a war zone.

Children. They were escorting children.

Arjun looked at his niece, as she took up her place at the back of the convoy. He remembered when Mango was a splodge on a scan. He'd been there, when she had taken her first step. He was there, when the first boy to try and take advantage of her, had suffered a broken nose. Arjun had laughed, as she begged him not to tell Gorbind. She wasn't worried about the jackass trying it on, but the fact that she deviated his septum.

Of course, he'd told his brother. Gorbind had been impressed in some part. But he'd also asked Arjun to accompany him as they both had a chat with the reprobate. Mango may not have been a princess, but her father knew what it was to exert the Majesty of a would-be King.

The last anyone knew or heard, a fella with a deviated septum had shipped himself north.

Arjun had been smelt the scent of burned carpet for months after.

"FALL IN!" roared Arjun. Heading up the column as all around him obeyed. The children all paired up. Each one, wore a helmet and vest.

Across the equipment there was a mark.

Gorbind's sigil.

Chalked on, and made very prominent, was a dove.

All right, it was Birmingham Blue and could therein have been a bluebird.

But it was a marker.

These kids, this moving column, were under Gorbind's protection. Woe betide anyone who might want to get in the way.

Boots thudded across cracked paving stones. A rhythm formed as the column started to move. It would traverse the city centre as an eerie silence hung in the air.

It would take twenty minutes to trek to New Street. They were to pass The Rotunda and get to St.Martin's.

"Rotunda," grimaced Arjun, tugging down his helmet. "Damn you, Felicity Dalton. Damn you, to hell."

Under some interesting terms of engagement, the children were granted free passage passed The Rotunda.

Their progress to a sanctuary wouldn't be impeded. Yet, the column stopped right outside.

The children had made a request. It had made Arjun and Mango laugh a little.

Arjun cranked up a battered, wind-up boom box. It really had seen better days. It had a hard drive, full of music from well before the kiss had arrived. He set it down near the column of kids.

Music crackled out; random songs shuffled, the sound was tinny and stretched. The children decided to dance; they formed a really quite riotous flash mob that bounced around to assorted beats. The last of which, had them all living on a prayer of some description. The crews with the column stood sentry as curtains twitched at not-so-broken windows. A few opened, to join in with the songs.

The Rotunda was a shadow of its former self. Part burned out, its top floors were charred, damp and dark as scar tissue from the early days of the kiss. The once shiny, pristine exterior was now caked in paint, emblems of identity, defiance and destruction. The Rotunda wore a coat of many different colours. A once celebrated icon had fallen from grace.

Housed within, were The Rotunda Rebellion Crew. Felicity, at the head, oversaw a unit of shadow dregs that had also failed to pledge allegiance to Gorbind. Dregs, who for whatever reason, had also fallen foul of the assorted city Crews. Anyone who didn't fit in, or didn't want to quite frankly, landed here.

The Rotunda Rebellion were right under Gorbind's nose, in the beating heart of Birmingham. That was the first thing. Second, in standing with The Bull Ring Sanctuary Accords, he couldn't do anything about it. Anything within a thousand feet of The Bull was within a zone of No Offence. That was a passageway of peace. As such, if anyone wanted to make trouble, and for Gorbind, they had to go beyond that a thousand feet.

As the stadium rock faded, Arjun picked up the boom box. He waved at Felicity. She had appeared at a doorway, and glowered at him with her black-eyes. He turned the other way as Mango flashed an obscene gesture. A gesture that a couple of children then took great delight in mimicking. The column trudged on.

Forward. Towards St. Martin's.

Rolling her eyes, Felicity waved the children on their merry way. She had no problem with kids. It was their adults with whom she had little or no patience with. Felicity pulled a face as Mango disappeared down the hill. She and Mango were of the same age. Their paths had crossed as children. They'd been in the same year group at school, only to lose touch as they headed to college and university. It was only when the kiss arrived, that their paths crossed once more.

Felicity couldn't remember now, how Mango's Dad had become Lord of the Manor of Birmingham. Only that refused to be a vassal lord and pledge allegiance to his regime. In Felicity's mind, Gorbind was akin to the mafia. A racketeer, who promised to look after you in one breath whilst pulling the rug from beneath you in the second.

The fact, that once upon a time, whilst a copper, Gorbind had clocked her for possession with intent to supply, as well as TWOC-ing her Dad's car, was neither here nor there.

Felicity Dalton, refused to recognise his authority. Whilst she stood there, with The Rotunda as her turf. Whilst she lived and breathed, she would continue to do so.

Whilst she lived and breathed.

As Felicity saw the last of the column disappear, she remembered her maths. St. Martin's fell all very deliberately into the thousand feet boundary. There was nothing that she could do about that. The Gunmaker's didn't. That distance was in miles anyway.

She skulked back in doors.

There was an assault to plan.

Five

Outside of St.Martin's the crews fell away to disband the column. Under the Bull Ring Sanctuary Accords, they were barred from entering the church. No armed unit, militia or not, was permitted from entering a place a worship.

A place of sanctuary.

Instead, the crews formed a series of semi-circles as the children were led in. They were to stay, until dismissed by the Rector At Large.

That, was Oban Telford.

He swung open the doors of St.Martin's, to be faced by Arjun, Mango and the children of The Gunmaker's Gang. As the doors moved, Mango and Arjun handed their firearms to members of the crews who stood nearby. This happened with something of a sombre, almost ceremonial reverence. In their pairs, the children entered; Arjun and Mango followed.

Their guns were then placed by the door, in the formation of a cross.

"Farewell," Oban waved his hand at waiting crews. "Tell Detective Inspector Phalla, that I shall take it from here. Peace be with you all."

Boots thumped across concrete once more, as the crews turned and left. They would head back to the Gunmakers. They had another job to do.

As the children ran into the church; Mango, Oban and Arjun hung back at little by the font. A shaft of light fell through a stained window to bathe them all in colours kaleidoscopic.

"I've got some letters for you," Mango opened up a mahogany-coloured, rather weather-beaten, courier bag. "Bits and pieces from the parents. I think there are some last wills and testaments too, Oban. Folks wanted you, to do what you have to." She bit her lip, to hold out the bundle with both hands.

Oban nodded, to take the bundle and hug it close with both arms.

"This will not end well," he said, all too sadly, whilst shaking his head. "Felicity, thinking that she is the law unto herself. Anand; he means her no harm. He means no harm, to anyone. The Gunmaker's is a family, a sanctuary that is second only to St.Martin's."

"He's one of our own," Arjun tutted loudly. "Anand and Gorbind, they look after one another. And let's face it. Gorbind and Felicity, aren't exactly best buddies. She chose not to fall in, be part of the Phalla Family."

Mango scoffed, to give a throaty laugh. "And people think *HE's* the Birmingham Mafia," the young woman kissed her lips. "He just likes rules, order, a sense of stability as the world goes to Hell in a hand-basket."

"Felicity never did like rules," Stated Oban. There was the smallest hint of tenderness and warmth in his words. The sort that only came in being a man of the cloth. "Least of all, falling in, as you put it, Arjun. She had no plans to ever fall in, with those who might try to protect and defend. I shall be thinking of you, of everyone. As things come to pass. Peace be with you both."

Mango and Arjun looked at one another.

"Thank you, Oban," Mango moved forwards, to throw her arms around him. "Keep them safe, each and every one of them. You may be their last hope." Peeling away, Mango headed out of th broken revolving door that preceded the wooden, vaulted one.

Arjun went to follow, but stopped. He looked at Oban over his shoulder.

"He wants her gone," Arjun tittered a moment. "There's no peace with her around. He paces all the time. If and when he stops. Send him your peace. He'll need it."

Oban gave Arjun as curt nod as he followed Mango go. He himself, shuffled to the East window, to kneel and pray. He knew that the Gunmaker's Gang were now precariously vulnerable. That with their children here, with him. They were potentially all that would be left.

Behind him, children were scattered around the knave. A common area, for anyone seeking sanctuary here at St.Martin's. Safety, against the ravages outside.

Oban set Mango's bundle down next to him. He steepled his hands, to balance his elbows on his knees. No part of him, had ever thought that his vocation would bring him to this. Six years ago, he had arrived here, all bright-eyed and bushy tailed. The parish of St.Martin's in the Bull Ring had sounded all very romantic. A church, in the beating heart of England's second city.

Then the kiss of death had arrived. The cold embrace.

In a matter of days, he'd officiated at six funerals, two memorials and consoled a fair few bereaved families. All of whom, wanted someone to lead them through their grief. To help them reconcile themselves with what was happening in the world.

What with all the romance, Oban had been shocked. Shocked at how soon, how quickly. Birmingham had fallen. The largest local authority in England buckled; caved completely as though a house of cards.

There had been complete lawlessness; a breakdown that created a power vacuum. He couldn't remember now, how Gorbind had risen so high. So high, as to be the de facto Lord of the Manor of Birmingham.

What he did remember, was being hauled out of a burning shop. Being thrown across a wooden table at the Gunmaker's, where Gorbind, his wife and brother had tended to his wounds. He remembered Gorbind being sat close by, crying as he prayed, to watch over him during the night. Gorbind never left his side.

It made no bones, that the City Watch believed in a different path to the divine. It mattered to Oban, that Gorbind had believed. Believed in Oban, that he would live. Live, to tend to his flock here at St.Martin's.

Oban had asked Gorbind to write the Bull Ring Sanctuary Accords. For all the hell that ravaged Birmingham, the heart of the city had to be a sanctuary. St.Phillips had been lost in the very early days. Gurudwaras and Mandirs had suffered a similar fate as time went on.

St. Martin's would hold on. It had to.

Peace, had to have a stronghold.

Without peace, there was no sanctuary.

Six

Checking out with the divine, Oban picked up the letters to sit them upon his lap. Behind him, children continued to mill around. The children from the Gunmaker's had started to mingle, and soon settle in properly.

Oban stood from the pew, to survey the knave. This may have been a sanctuary, but it was also his kingdom. Gorbind had made sure of that. Made sure, that St. Martin's sat on the right side of the law. As such, if the sanctuary was ever vulnerable, he knew that the City crews would be here in a heartbeat.

"Felicity." Oban shook his head to think of her. "I shall pray for you too," he muttered. "However, the cookie might crumble." Moving from the pews, he headed towards the enclave below the tower. An enclave where candles could be lit; there could be moments of quiet, personal reflection.

Anyone could light a candle. The front door was always open.

He saw that it was ajar. A shadow hovered at the threshold. Oban retreated into the enclave, to pick up a yellow-tinged candle. The product of bartering, these candles had come down the canals from Manchester.

"He will have a plan, you know," Oban touched the wick of the candle to one that was already alight. The flame danced in the quiet. "I know he does. I know that it's not pretty either; especially not for you."

Felicity picked up a candle, just the one.

"Did he come looking for forgiveness?" she asked, lighting it from Oban's. "Seeking permission, as well?" She shook her head, with something of a snort. "Copper of old, turned into the local sheriff. His gold star is made of nothing more than brass tacks and paper clips."

Oban plugged his candle into hole.

"All very useful," he commented. "If ever we run out of stapled and such like. Fastening things together, is always such a challenge."

Felicity narrowed her eyes, before poking out her tongue.

"And you're here because?" Asked Oban, both curious and concerned. "Not that I'm unhappy to see you, Felicity. It's actually always something of a pleasure. When you come by, I remember…"

"How human I can be?" Felicity dropped her gaze to the floor. "Yes, I know, Oban. We have this conversation every time. The one where I repent, return to the straight and narrow. Well, Gorbind has his plan. I have mine."

Oban held up a finger, to momentarily silence her. He shuffled to the doors to the tower.

He had feeling that Felicity need space and his confidence.

***

"Is that what you want to do?" Oban steadied his breathing; his heart rate on the other hand, wasn't so easily calmed. "This, is how you see it all ending?"

"I'm tired," coughed Felicity. "Of fighting, of having to live moment to moment. And here I am."

"Counting moments," Oban took her hand into his. "And The Rotunda Rebellion, they know of this plan?" He felt his chest tighten with wariness. What he had heard, unsettled him and then some.

"Only the select few," Felicity sniffed to wipe her nose across a grotty orange sleeve. "Once it's all over, bar the shouting, everyone can do for themselves. Your advice, Oban; for once, I need your advice on how to make this work."

Oban's dark features crumpled with concern. He wiped a tear from Felicity's pale cheek. He knew, exactly what Gorbind had planned. What Gorbind had encouraged the Gunmaker's to do.

"You're walking into a bar, Felicity," he leant forward, to gently kiss her forehead. "Drink it dry, if only for Dutch Courage. I wish you my peace. Now, and here after. I hope, I pray. That you finally find it."

"Do that," nodding, Felicity pulled away in a fit of sniffs and snorts. She continued to wipe the tears away with her orange sleeve. "Pray for me."

Closing his eyes, Oban didn't see her leave.

He would pray. He would pray for them all.

Seven

The Rotunda Rebellion took three vehicles, but also had foot soldiers. For all it's brazenness, the crew numbered less than fifty.

Thirty, went to the Gunmaker's.

Felicity led them on foot. Through the streets of Birmingham City Centre. They were armed to the teeth, but whooped and hollered as they went. Then there was the singing. The hash, discordant sound, a cacophony by definition, of songs that were coarse and seriously out of tune.

Everyone had to hear; everyone had to know.

Be aware, that The Rotunda Rebellion were headed to the Gunmaker's.

To take it by any means. To take it, by force.

They snaked down New Street. They trundled through the wrecked ruins of St.Phillips, to churn up the lawn of Pigeon Park. As the crew caroused, Felicity felt her stomach flip over. More than once, she tried to lock gaze with her lieutenant. Wondering every time, if this was reality, or someone else's nightmare.

Her lieutenant, Owen, with his hazel eyes and voice of the valleys, refused to look at her dead on. He turned away; his eyes focused on the route ahead. He had heard her plan; he just didn't like it. Yet, he felt compelled; he owed it to Felicity to see this through. Six years ago, when this had all started. She had taken him in. She had offered him safety, of a sort.

Then, a little later on. Felicity had offered him her bed. That was stopped him. Stopped him for pulling her aside; shaking her, to beg her to stop this madness.

What he felt for her; what she felt for him, was worth more than this. Worth more, than being holed up in The Rotunda as though vermin. Especially now. Living like vermin, couldn't make things better anymore.

It couldn't make their moments together, their madness for one another, last forever. They had asked, asked each and every Medic that they had sought out.

Every moment now, was a moment to be lived. Every moment, was a lifetime to be taken by the scruff of the neck.

Every moment, had to count.

Owen let his gaze settle on her for a moment. She looked so lost; he knew that she felt it too.

"We are The Rotunda Rebellion," she said, wrapped up in his arms. They watched the sun come up over Birmingham. "We do this, just this once. You and me;

we've come this far. This is all, that I ask of you. One last moment. One last rebellion."

"Because I love you." Owen had given an automatic response, in being a post-coital daze.

"Because you love me. Because you love the idea of me," Felicity had kissed him, his heart had felt full to the brim.

The idea of her. That was all that he had; all that would eventually remain.

Rotunda Rebellions vehicles arrived first. To pull up, outside a very sorry looking Gunmaker's Arms. All boarded up, it looked like a shell rather than readied for battle. Those that arrived on foot were somewhat perplexed. There didn't seem to be anyone about.

"This is too easy," Owen stepped towards front doors, to nudge them open.

With the flick of her wrist, Felicity signalled the rest of the crew to follow. Each and every one of them followed.

In the darkness, there was screaming. What ensued next was a disorientation and destruction.

The Gunmaker's Gunners had descended from the attic. The rat-a-tat-tat of heavy machinery soon crushed and quelled the incoming rebellion. From behind the bar, Anand watched faces contort and bodies crumble.

He watched as Owen and Felicity dropped to the floor; they rolled away into a corner.

"AND DOWN!" yelled Anand, letting smoke and grime settle. He appraised the bodies that now littered the bar room floor. There was more noise as more of the Gunmaker's gang poured in from corners and crevices.

"Drag' em out," Anand vaulted over the bar. "The pair of them."

Owen and Felicity were scrambled for.

"The bodies," said Anand, nudging a corpse with a boot. "Can be either left for scrap at dusk, or sent back to the Rotunda. Those that look alive, Gorbind wants to keep."

"All right, all right, I'll come quietly," Felicity squawked, whilst swinging a right hook. "No need to get heavy."

"You speak for yourself," Owen swung hard at those who approached. He headed towards Anand, armed with a homemade shank.

What followed was a fist-fight, that tumbled over bodies and puddles of blood. With no Rotunda Rebellion left to intervene, The Gunmaker's gang quickly stepped in to quell the brawl. As Owen was tumbled onto a table, the front door creaked open. Felicity was hauled into a chair.

Bodies were moved out, being placed into the vehicles that Rotunda Rebellion had brought with them. Not that there was anyone to drive the damned things back.

"What we can't send back," said Anand, "We'll take to the Malvern's for scrap." He shook his head, before rubbing his face with his palms. "It's all flaming carrion now."

Gorbind walked across the bar, to pull up a chair. His coat billowed out behind him, akin to a superhero's cape.

"Kamikaze," he said quietly, addressing Felicity and Owen. "All or nothing. That's one way to do it."

Felicity sneered, to lob a spit ball at him.

"Oh, grow up," huffed Gorbind, wiping away the gunk. "Spoiled a perfectly good hanky," he said waving it; it was red with blue spot today. "And don't be so childish, not now. Not now, Felicity, when your time is running out."

Felicity's face fell. The snarl of defiance ebbed away, to be replaced by fear. Something wasn't right.

"I know, Felicity," Gorbind folded up his handkerchief to tuck it into a coat pocket. "That you have weeks, if not days. Days, Felicity. I run this city, I run the crews. Their medics too. People talk, and to me. I listen, I hear everything; I listen to it all. Did you really think, that I would miss a beat? Anand…." He waved at the booze behind the bar.

"Oban said," Felicity puckered her lips as she spoke. "That you had a plan. That I should drink; drink the bar dry. If only for Dutch Courage."

Gorbind nodded, to look at the Welshman. He'd heard of Owen; of how close he was to Felicity. How this lost soul, had somehow ended up with Rotunda Rebellion. There was something about Owen, that screamed redemption. Something that told Gorbind, that all was not lost.

"Owen," Gorbind kept his tone level; this needed to be calm and measured. "My son Captain's the Selly Oak Crew. He needs a Lieutenant, to be a rudder. To keep things plain sailing."

Owen had scrambled off the table, like a naughty school boy. He stood by Felicity, his hand on her shoulder. "And if I refuse," he posed. "Say I went back to Rotunda Rebellion?"

"You'd be wasting your time," replied Gorbind. "Those that stayed, didn't want to come here. They didn't think that this would work. Those that came, were here to give up; albeit in a slightly different way."

The unmistakable sound of guns cocking thudded against the walls.

"If you run," continued Gorbind, "And to The Rotunda. They will knee cap you, before your out of the door. Walk, and to Selly Oak. Your decision, Owen Belden."

Felicity shrugged her shoulder, to dislodge Owen's palm.

Owen recoiled, as though scalded.

"He has rum runners," Gorbind sat back in his chair to cross his legs. He cupped his palms around a knee. "From here to Ayrshire. Sometimes, he haggles, trades all sorts of unmentionables. Not the sort, that you'd want your law-enforcing Old Man to know about. He can make it worth your while. Walk, Owen. Whilst you still can."

Felicity moved her seat, away from Owen. Her eyes were rivetted by floor.

The front door creaked; a beam of light fell across the floor. Owen's flight path was lit for him. He saw the beam appear, and followed it out. He didn't look back; he simply couldn't.

Gorbind was handed a bottle by Anand. Dark rum; the good stuff that hustlers only ever dreamt of. He poured the booze into a stout tumbler. Some for him. But more her.

"Drink," he said, as Felicity looked back at him. "You have but a moment, and no damned tomorrow."

Eight

Anand pressed two fingers against the jugular. "It's slow, but it's there," he was all very matter of act. His own heart was thudding that hard, he feared being sick. "The gaps are getting bigger though." Anand looked at Gorbind's reflection in the rear-view mirror. The beams of the car's headlights lit the way as darkness enveloped Birmingham. "She's not far off, not really. Won't be long, I guess."

Gorbind looked briefly into the mirror; for traffic, for Anand. Felicity was slumped across Anand's shoulder.

"I didn't think she'd take the pills too," Anand blinked, to stretch his eyes wide. "What with all the booze she out away. Pills too," he shook his head, to puff out his cheeks. "Enough to bring a small Rhino to its knees."

Focused on the road, Gorbind was driving to the Malvern's. The moon had risen high, and was a floaty, spectral being from up on high.

"She didn't want more pain," he said quietly. "Just wanted it over. Funny this, so did I."

Twenty minutes later, Gorbind had parked up. He and Anand hauled Felicity out. The two of them, were all very furtive as they laid her out on the crest of a hill.

"I don't like this," Anand hugged his arms around his chest; The wind had started to pick up, the air was crisp. "To be out here, when they….."

"It's what we discussed, what we agreed," Gorbind used a blue and white checked blanket to tuck Felicity in. "She won't feel a thing."

In the undergrowth, something moved. Something rustled in the foliage.

Gorbind and Anand scarpered to the car. Gorbind, put his foot down. He drove like the devil, back to Birmingham. Back to safety; to the city that should be a sanctuary.

First, there was one. Then, there were two.

Felicity put up no resistance. She didn't feel the kiss, or the embrace either.

They devoured her. They devoured her, whole.

Nine

Walking passed Digbeth Coach station; Delia sipped her coffee. She paused at the entrance; travel mug clutched between both hands. Dawn had just broken. The sun was rising through murky grey clouds that swaddled the city of Birmingham. She blew into her coffee, and the scent filled her nose. A perfectly formed nosed, given what people called her.

Delia Entwhistle, might have been her official, all very neutral, as harmless as chocolate name. Yet, she had another. A name, that rather made her smile, but based upon the emotional baggage of others.

She slurped her coffee to watch two red and orange buses pull in. Slowly, and in something of a daze, travellers alighted to disembark. Delia looked at the routes.

Swansea and Manchester.

The latest batch of cannon fodder had arrived. Over the last few months, the population of Birmingham-the uninfected, never been kissed-portion, had started to swell. It was a slowly building tide, that could easily become a tsunami.

From the corner of her eye, she espied Phalla Junior; Delia gave him a polite nod. He was all very smartly dressed. Dark blue combat fatigues. His father's sigil was pinned to his left breast. She could see by mere presence, his energy. It was altogether hard to miss. The vibration and feel, it was golden. Delia decided to wave too. She remembered when he was knee-high to a grasshopper. Rather than his father's sigil, the crest of Aston Villa Football Club had been pride of place. In the time that it had taken for him to shoot up, go through his adolescence and mature into a Pseudo Warrior, Birmingham had changed.

The world had changed; completely, and beyond recognition.

Delia had been confused at first. Her card readings had been mixed; runes bounced around wildly. The earthly elements had become altogether erratic with their patterns and presence. Even the constellations had buzzed with what she best described as static; white noise that gave her headache.

Her coven had broken off in the directions of the four winds. Scattered and cast askew by something ineffable.

Hell, was about to break loose.

So, she chose to stay. Stay here in Birmingham. In the Custard Factory, to be exact.

She and Gorbind had been quick to form an alliance. Her life, her work; it was all about natural order. Ensuring that some form of homeostasis could be maintained here, in England's second city. Gorbind had added law into the mix. She saw a kindness and also a power within him.

The same power in the earthly elements. The same power in the constellations.

Delia had read his heart, his mind and his soul too; the latter for good measure. With a simple handshake, she had felt the pulsating. The energy, vivacity that ran through his synapses had sent her flying across the room.

"I'm not magic," he had set, thundering across the room to bundle Delia back to her feet.

"A man," she had said, "On a mission, to save the city and all the souls within its limits. I will help," Delia had told him. "You'll need that help; all the help that you can get. No White Knight, should right out alone."

Leaving the bus station, Delia headed home. She had preparations to make.

Preparations for a change of events. Events that required reinforcements to travel from Swansea and Manchester. Events that would change the face of Birmingham. Delia glowered at a seagull that crossed her path. Even now, despite being land-locked, the birds still managed to land in Birmingham.

The reinforcements were here to make a difference. A battle was coming.

Across the city, the infection, the kiss of death had coalesced to form an army. Those that had been claimed and devoured, had grouped together. Clumped together, under the leadership of someone really quite diabolical and macabre.

Arriving at the Custard Factory, Delia muttered curses under her breath.

The leader, the commander-in-chief, of the infected army, had once seemed altogether innocent. Too good to be true, and here it was. The evidence of being bad to the bone.

Delia had known him as Eli Benedict. A relatively minor league would-be wizard, who had skill, peppered with baroque flourishes. He had charm enough; he would often leave covens giggling and broken in his wake.

Something, however, had changed.

When Birmingham had fallen, Eli rose.

Unsuspected, he became a force in the city. Rumours were abound as the infection soared, the number of kisses bloomed.

Eli, had some part in it.

The man that Delia knew, the low-level contender, had become an unfettered power. A power, that whilst deliciously dark, was seduction by magics that were best left alone. The sort of magics, that could tear an unsuspecting soul into a thousand pieces.

Eli Benedict was now the Nefarious Necromancer of Small Heath.

A name, that almost matched the one that people called her. It had started out as a joke. Gorbind had started it; his son pounced upon it in child-like glee, in wanting to know what it meant.

She ran with it. It made her laugh, but also made feel important.

Delia Entwhistle shook her head to enter the Custard factory.

Her name?

The Mad, Bad and Dangerous Hag of Digbeth.

Cross her, at your peril.

Ten

Standing at the ravaged balcony, Eli looked out across the stadium. Once home of Birmingham City Football Club, it was now something altogether unsavoury. In the stands, across the pitch; an army slept.

Not just an army. His army.

St.Andrew's only contained half of it. The rest, was at Villa Park.

Two halves, of a whole. Soon, this would all come together.

Eli had a plan.

A plan to completely and utterly decimate Birmingham. His plan had been to do it year ago, when the infection had first arrived. That was when he had realised. Realised that his innate ability to manipulate bodies, bones and blood beyond the boundaries of medicine.

Beyond something that the Hippocratic Oath really didn't cover.

He would have wiped out Birmingham. It was only ever his adoptive home. He'd come here to study, to eventually practice when he qualified. He'd spent ten years at the QE, healing ills and rebuilding lives by day.

By night, he conjured malevolence and macabre. Usually in the morgue, and usually without being found out.

Then, when the infection had arrived, the kiss of death with its embrace; Eli had a thought.

He could preserve life, all day, every day.

This kiss of death, it's embrace was different.

His work meant that he could, in part, conquer death.

What if, death could be commanded?

Having found The Order of Rag and Bone, he had learned to develop his talent for the malevolent and macabre. The inner embers that had first bloomed and blossomed during adolescence burned brighter.

Ever since he had first resurrected dead animals on his Uncle's Farm, he'd known that he had something. That he had power that no earthly explanation could cover.

The Order of Rag and Bone, had invited him in. It had fostered the darkness within.

Medicine had tempered it somewhat; it allowed containment.

With the infection, the QE changed. As did he.

Eli had dabbled; he'd sailed a little to close the wind. The Order found out, and even asked a couple of local covens to help.

They had tried, and failed, to fetter him.

Even Delia-the darling-Entwhistle.

At first glance, she seemed ordinary and innocuous. Straight forward at best. She'd tried to hold him; she'd been the only one able to conjure up the force to enter his soul. Delia had tried to cleanse his mind, change his direction. In effect, she had tried to neuter him, as though he were a local alley cat.

He'd had the last laugh though.

He'd robbed her of her earthly sight. She now walked around with milky eyes, covered with a pair of horn-rimmed sunglasses. Rumour has it, that her powers were getting stronger by way of compensation. She was a blind as a bat, but could read energies a mile off.

Energies.

Eli smirked to himself.

The sort that this army didn't have; couldn't have, on account of not being living.

If ever he met Hades, the legendary Lord of the Underworld. They might have an interesting conversation.

Delia wasn't the only one on his pathway, to offer resistance. Gorbind Phalla, the would-be Lord of the Manor of Birmingham, was another irritant. Protector, Policeman and a peace-loving pain in Eli's backside.

Gorbind and Delia, were getting in his way. So, it was time to shake things up, before settling things once and for all. He had the power, the army. The intention, to change the face of Birmingham forever. Eli rubbed his jaw as he studied the sleeping corpses.

The power, the potential. All waiting to be tapped.

Such was the privilege of being the Nefarious Necromancer of Small Heath.

Eleven

"DAD, SIX O'CLOCK!" Junior yelled, whilst throwing an axe. He, himself, landed heavily onto concrete. His face wore a pained expression as he felt the impact in already having bruised and battered limbs.

"Anna, I'm sorry," Gorbind swung his shotgun across his chest to fill the animated corpse with several rounds of lead.

They'd been hunting this nest for days. Little did he realise, that one of them, was a dear friend. He'd aimed between the eyes, then the sternum; Anna was also knee-capped. She had been the last one. The rest had been picked off fairly easily. The infection took away brains as well as anything that might resemble a soul. Anna's had been beautiful; the sort that was like sunshine on a rainy day.

Crumpled in a heap, the Anna Maria that was, lay agog. There was torn flesh, sinew; she really was a bloody mess. Gorbind used a boot to roll her over. Stuck in her back, was the axe that his son had hurled.

The younger man hobbled up close, to wrench out the blade. "Shall I chop her up for you?" he asked, wiping the blade across his thigh.

"Yes, please," Gorbind snapped the shot gun in half, to confirm that Anna had got both barrels. "Chop her properly. Throw her into the canal; tell her goodbye properly, Armaan. Eli was never going to get her. Not our Anna Maria."

Armaan nodded as he dragged Anna away by her arms. He winced as he managed to dislocate the both.

"Oh, Aunty Anna," snorted Armaan, "This was for your own good. You're not the sort for the Nefarious Necromancer. Not if we could help it."

Gorbind watched Armaan dismember the body. The boy did it very neatly, working with all the joints. Eventually, the bits and pieces were thrown into the canal. After, father and son headed back to Birmingham Central Library. Once a beautiful repository, it was now the nerve centre for all of Gorbind's operations.

Sat in what was still the Shakespeare Room, Anand and Oban were talking over cups of tea. They were deep in conversation as Padmi and Mango left them.

Padmi shepherded Mango into an office; she closed the door behind them. Her facial expression was somewhat grave.

"Mum, you're scaring me," Mango pushed herself onto a desk, to cross her arms.

"I'm scared too," Padmi took a deep breath, to lean against the door. "Mango, I need you to come back. You, in one piece. From the Melee."

"Why wouldn't I?" Mango unfurled her arms; her head was tilted to one side. "Of course, I'll be back. Armaan and Dad too. This'll all be okay."

Sliding forward, Padmi engulfed her first-born into her arms. She showered her daughter with kisses.

"And what if it isn't, Chandni?" Padmi kissed her daughter's nose. "There is no knowing, not really, of what will happen at Spaghetti. Your Dad, he has all these plans. Generally, they do work. Yet, there is always a what if. I despair, at the what if, Chandni."

Chandni wrapped her arms around her mother. She gave Padmi the biggest hug that she could muster. It wasn't often that anyone used her real name. So when she was addressed by it, something was afoot, big time.

"Promise me, Chandni," Padmi cradled her daughters face in her palms. "That when all is said and done; that you, Chandni Kaur Dharam-Phalla, will come back to me. You need to come back, to tell the world your father's story. Armaan's too."

"EXCUSE ME!" A loud cough at the door broke the moment. "I plan to do that myself actually. I'm coming back too, Mum." Armaan pulled a face as he stepped in, his father followed. Armaan landed himself next to his sister on the desk.

He the put his wrist across her knee, as he rooted around in pocket. He pulled out a piece of Birmingham Blue knotted thread.

A rakhi. A thread to bond them, and protect them. A sacred thread, tied to keep them safe.

Come what may.

Gorbind slid his hand into Padmi's.

"You're a doughnut," tutted Chandni. Her eyes were glossy as she took the thread to tie it around Armaan's wrist. She tied it carefully, with a series of double knots.

"Your favourite doughnut," Armaan pulled out a second thread; he tied it around her wrist.

"Chandni," Gorbind blew out his cheeks. He felt physically sick. "You take the left wing. Armaan, you'll be on the right. Anand and Oban, will be the storm surge in the middle, riding with the crews."

Gorbind felt Padmi's fingers tighten around his. His children nodded to slide off the table, to lead their parents to it. Husband and wife stood toe to toe, holding each other in one another's arms.

"This is what we do…." Gorbind started, but he couldn't finish. He couldn't get the words out.

"Don't," Padmi clamped her arms around Gorbind, that bit tighter. "Just walk through the storm, Gorbind. Be the fire, unleash hell, but please come back."

Gorbind kissed his wife, one last time. It wasn't long enough, not really.

Padmi poked the love of her life in his stomach, to step aside. She bowed her head, closed her eyes.

He left quickly, quietly. The door closing silently behind him.

Twelve

Spaghetti junction had seen better days. This would not be one of them.

This would be, by far, one of the worst.

Armaan Singh Dharam-Phalla stood with this sister in front of the crews. They were all a captive audience.

Gorbind Singh Phalla stood on top of a maroon-coloured four by far, and he was delivering a battle address. He had no need, for a bull horn.

"We are what's left," he shouted; with courage and conviction. "We are what's left of Birmingham. The second city; the city of a thousand trades. The city, that once upon a time, was the workshop of the world. We, were the centre. We, stand firm. We, endure."

The crews caroused with bravado. Rifles and body armour rattled. Boots thumped across concrete. Then, the mass parted. Out of the centred, from within the crowd, came Delia.

She nodded to Gorbind. It was time.

Armaan and Chandni saw the signal. With one last hug, they parted company.

Gorbind climbed into the vehicle. The stereo crackled.

An eerie calm descended across Gravelly Hill Interchange. The soundtrack, the instrumental version of a song about a king on his throne; his hair about to be cut. Love, as the subject of the verse, was not a victimless art. It made for a surreal anthem of war.

One army had converged on the one side of Spaghetti; it now rolled towards its fate.

On the other side, there was a second. An army of the undead, of the infected. Those who had been kissed by death, to be enveloped in its cold embrace.

With the river Thame behind him, Eli let his lips twist into a knowing smile. He raised his arms aloft, to feel the elements surge through him. Every bit of him felt electric.

"Go ahead, Gorbind," he cackled. "Take your best shot."

In the four by four, Gorbind looked at the rear-view mirror. He saw Delia with her milky white eyes as she absorbed the power of the universe. The power of all that was good, the power that came from love, life and laughter.

It was pure, unadulterated and beyond simple human comprehension.

Delia flashed Gorbind a grin.

He turned back to the road ahead. All around him the storm surge of crews swelled the interchange.

The skies over Birmingham rumbled and flashed. The clouds became gun-metal grey. Lightning cracked as boots thumped across the ground. Rifles fired, flares were thrown.

Two armies converged. The Battle of Gravelly Hill Interchange rumbled, ravaged and roared.

Birmingham would never be the same again. It was torn apart.

It suffered the kiss; it didn't take long.

Birmingham fell. Into the cold embrace.

ACKNOWLEDGMENTS

First and foremost, a huge thank you to Annie Lindwurm and Fi Hewkin for their support and encouragement in writing this book. They are beyond a doubt, the biggest cheerleaders of the characters assembled within. Without that, I wouldn't have thought about putting this all together in such a cornucopia of different stories.

My Brother-In-Law, Ketan, also had a major role to play. In gifting me a James Bond notebook for my birthday, I had a canvas to fill with the contents of my imagination. The notebook was destined to be filled with something special and look what happened.

A massive nod to Helen Blenkinsop, Martin Tracey and Lee Benson, who as fellow authors from Birmingham have inspired, motivated and encouraged me to grasp the nettle; to have fun whilst writing and to share it with the world.

Helen, introduced to me the Gunmaker's Arms, and now, that is history.

Last but not least, Howard Coates. His artistic genius, makes for a fabulous cover. As ever, his unwavering support for all things book-related is immensely appreciated. It is in his honour, that Gorbind and Hades are both Villa fans.

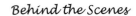

ABOUT THE AUTHOR

Punam Farmah is a teacher of Counselling, Psychology and Social Sciences with horticultural tendencies, a qualified counsellor, and lives in Birmingham, England. She is very appreciative of the help from the rest of her family and acknowledges that without them, this book would be devoid of any words, motivation or happy thoughts. When not teaching or experimenting with the plot, she rather likes Star Trek, Shakespeare, the Whedon-verse as well as seeing what can be made with the preserving pan.

Playing with Plant Pots: Tales from the Allotment

Chillies and tomatoes, you can grow your own and look at the food you eat in an entirely different way.. Be it on your kitchen window sill or in your garden. Growing your own fruit and vegetables need not be scary or complicated.

This book contains learning experiences of a novice allotmenteer, Ideas as to what worked, what didn't and what to do with too many courgettes. From first having an allotment, and not knowing what to do, to growing chillies that are some of the hottest in the world. Anecdotal evidence of success, failure and ideas to help make growing your own fruit and vegetables a little simpler. All of the details are real, that means influenced by rain, shine, slugs and snails. The details are honest, and aim to inform readers of how allotments are worth the hard work put in and will yield fruit that makes it all worthwhile.

Sow Grow and Eat: From Plot to Kitchen

If you ever wondered how to sow and grow chillies, or what might be useful to know when growing tomatoes and what happens when radishes go wrong, then you will need to have a look inside! Building on the experiences of 'Playing with Plant Pots: Tales from the allotment' there is more to be learned from the fruit and vegetable plot. With a few allotment plot staples revisited and others that you might not ordinarily think about, this second book also contains further recipes to be tried using plot fruit and vegetables. Growing your own fruit and vegetables is still uncomplicated and still an opportunity to create edible experiments. Within these pages there are jams, jellies, chutneys and infusions all just waiting for you to read about them and to create them in the comfort of your own kitchen

Fragments

Life starts and life ends. In between we form relationships and friendships. We have husbands, wives, sons, daughters and we mustn't forget pets. Memories form that shape who we are and what we do. Only for death to cast it all askew. What we know becomes nothing by fragments, torn up and thrown to the winds. The Anands lose a wife and mother, Matthew is lost without his grandmother, Daniel loses the man he loved, Michael wonders about having children and Maya is a mother bereaved. Within are six inter-related stories explore what happens when the universe as we know it implodes and entirely. Grief is a journey to be travelled by them with emotions to be experienced as their lives are changed. Whilst they feel alone they are all connected and these are their stories. Family, friends and even our pets cannot escape when it comes to the footprint that is left by death

Kangana

There is no such thing as a straight forward romance.

Sometimes when you think you are falling for one person, you are really falling in love with everyone else around them too.

Gorbind's family are his whole world, even if they are far from normal. His kid brother needs looking after and his Grandmother just wants him to find happiness.

His whole world changes when he meets Padmi. Life gets more interesting as she changes Gorbind's universe completely. Romance with Padmi is anything but straightforward.

Retreating to Peace: A Peace Series Novella

Devan Coultrie was at a loss. His world had been shaken, his heart fractured and emptied by death. In search of a way to heal and shake of the damage, Devan sticks a pin a map with the intention of going wherever it lands. Leaving the shores of the United Kingdom, he ends up Stateside, deep in the heart of Montana. With all of his worldly possessions, Devan drives into Peace and onto a plot to land to start life over.

Like him, the farm and its acreage is downbeat, derelict and defeated. When Aditi Rao arrives in Peace, Devan's plans for himself and his home are disrupted. He has history with Aditi and she'd quite like to write another chapter. Can he show Aditi that his retreat to Peace is more than just a plot of land and on a different continent? Can he find a way to share his home, his heart and a new beginning?

Postcards From Peace: A Peace Series Collection

In Retreating to Peace, Devan Coultrie moved kit and caboodle to Montana. Before long, he was joined by Aditi Rao. Their history laid the foundations for a rosy future together. Devan now calls Peace home and his life has become eventful.

This collection of short stories sees his family visit, his romance with Aditi develop further and his dreams in Peace blossom.

Devan Coultrie's life in Peace is a picture postcard with more to it than meets the eye.

Peace Betrayed: A Peace Series Novella

Devan Coultrie has found his Peace. He has a home, a business; his relationship with Aditi is ready to move to the next stage. They have plans to start a family, their life together could finally settle down properly.

Retreating to Peace was the first stage. The next was to make it all a picture perfect postcard.

Only Devan and Aditi's relationship isn't that straight forward. Its strength is about to be sorely tested.

Devan Coultrie has a decision to make.

He could keep and enjoy his 'Happily Ever After' in Peace, Montana.

Or will he betray it and lose everything that he has ever wanted?

Printed in Great Britain
by Amazon